Asda Tickled Pink

45p from the sale of this book will be donated to Tickled Pink.

Asda Tickled Pink wants to ensure all breast cancer is diagnosed early and help improve people's many different experiences of the disease. Working with our charity partners, Breast Cancer Now and CoppaFeel!, we're on a mission to make checking your boobs, pecs and chests, whoever you are, as normal as your Asda shop. And with your help, we're raising funds for new treatments, vital education and life-changing support, for anyone who needs it. Together, we're putting breast cancer awareness on everyone's list.

Since the partnership began in 1996, Asda Tickled Pink has raised over £82 million for its charity partners. Through the campaign, Asda has been committed to raising funds and breast-check awareness via in-store fundraising, disruptive awareness campaigns, and products turning pink to support the campaign. The funds have been vital for Breast Cancer Now's world-class research and life-changing support services, such as their Helpline, there for anyone affected by breast cancer to cope with the emotional impact of the disease. Asda Tickled Pink's educational and outreach work with CoppaFeel! aims to empower 1 million 18 - 24 year olds to adopt a regular boob-checking behaviour by 2025. Together we will continue to make a tangible difference to breast cancer in the UK.

Asda Tickled Pink and the Penguin Random House have teamed up to bring you Tickled Pink Books. By buying this book and supporting the partnership, you ensure that 45p goes directly to the Breast Cancer Now and CoppaFeel!

Breast Cancer is the most common cancer in women in the UK, with one in seven women facing it in their lifetime.

Around 55,000 women and 370 men are diagnosed with breast cancer every year in the UK and nearly 1,000 people still lose their life to the disease each month. This is one person every 45 minutes and this is why your support and the support from Asda Tickled Pink is so important.

A new Tickled Pink Book will go on sale in Asda stores every two weeks – we aim to bring you the best stories of friendship, love, heartbreak and laughter.

To find out more about the Tickled Pink partnership visit www.asda.com/tickled-pink

Penguin Random House UK

STAY BREAST AWARE AND CHECK YOURSELF REGULARLY

One in seven women in the UK will be diagnosed with breast cancer in their lifetime

'TOUCH, LOOK, KNOW YOUR NORMAL, REPEAT REGULARLY'

Make sure you stay breast aware
- Get to know what's normal for you
- Look and feel to notice any unusual changes early
- The earlier breast cancer is diagnosed, the better the chance of successful treatment
- Check your boobs regularly and see a GP if you notice a change

PENGUIN BOOKS

Write Me For You

Tillie Cole hails from a small town in the northeast of England. She grew up on a farm with her English mother, Scottish father, older sister, and a multitude of rescue animals. As soon as she could, Tillie left her rural roots for the bright lights of the big city. After graduating from Newcastle University with a BA Hons in religious studies, Tillie followed her professional rugby player husband around the world for a decade, becoming a teacher in between, and thoroughly enjoyed teaching high school students social studies before putting pen to paper and finishing her first novel.

After several years living in Italy, Canada, and the USA, Tillie has now settled back in her hometown in England with her husband and two children. Tillie is both an independent and traditionally published author and writes many genres, including contemporary romance, dark romance, YA, and NA. When she is not writing, Tillie enjoys nothing more than spending time with her little family, curling up on her couch watching movies, drinking far too much coffee, and convincing herself that she really doesn't need that last square of chocolate.

Also By Tillie Cole

A Thousand Boy Kisses
A Thousand Broken Pieces
A Wish for Us

write me for you

Tillie Cole

PENGUIN BOOKS

PENGUIN BOOKS

UK | USA | Canada | Ireland | Australia
India | New Zealand | South Africa

Penguin Books is part of the Penguin Random House group of companies
whose addresses can be found at global.penguinrandomhouse.com

Penguin Random House UK,
One Embassy Gardens, 8 Viaduct Gardens, London SW11 7BW

penguin.co.uk

Penguin Random House UK

First published in the United States of America by Sourcebooks 2025
First published in Great Britain by Penguin Books 2025

001

Copyright © Tillie Cole, 2025

Internal images © lekcej/Getty Images, simonkr/Getty Images, Wavebreakmedia/Getty Images, Prasit photo/Getty Images, Bohdan Bevz/Getty Images, Retrovizor/Getty Images, Xiuxia Huang/Getty Images

The moral right of the author has been asserted

Penguin Random House values and supports copyright.
Copyright fuels creativity, encourages diverse voices, promotes freedom
of expression and supports a vibrant culture. Thank you for purchasing
an authorized edition of this book and for respecting intellectual property
laws by not reproducing, scanning or distributing any part of it by any
means without permission. You are supporting authors and enabling
Penguin Random House to continue to publish books for everyone.
No part of this book may be used or reproduced in any manner for the
purpose of training artificial intelligence technologies or systems. In accordance
with Article 4(3) of the DSM Directive 2019/790, Penguin Random House
expressly reserves this work from the text and data mining exception.

Printed and bound in Great Britain by Clays Ltd, Elcograf S.p.A.

The authorized representative in the EEA is Penguin Random House Ireland,
Morrison Chambers, 32 Nassau Street, Dublin D02 YH68

A CIP catalogue record for this book is available from the British Library

ISBN: 978-1-405-96470-8

Penguin Random House is committed to a sustainable future
for our business, our readers and our planet. This book is made from
Forest Stewardship Council® certified paper.

MIX
Paper | Supporting
responsible forestry
FSC® C018179

*To the dreamers and romantics who always
find light in the darkness.*

playlist

Two Hearts—Dermot Kennedy
Next Thing You Know—Jordan Davis
A Lot More Free—Max McNown
Your Bones—Chelsea Butler
Medication—David Wimbish & The Collection
Behind—Myles Smith
Save You a Seat—Alex Warren
Betting on Us—Myles Smith
My Greatest Fear—Benson Boone
Just Us—James Arthur
Live More & Love More—Cat Burns
Like Real People Do—Hozier
Belong Together—Mark Ambor
Dreams (feat. Judah & The Lion)—NEEDTOBREATHE, Judah & the Lion
Carry Me (feat. Switchfoot)—NEEDTOBREATHE, Switchfoot
Carry You On—Amos Lee
Heaven Is a Place on Earth—The Mayries
Fields of Gold—Kina Grannis
Moon River—Kina Grannis
Face My Fears—Mree
Now We Are Free—Hans Zimmer, Klaus Badelt, Lisa Gerrard, Gavin Greenaway, The Lyndhurst Orchestra
Story of My Life—One Direction

Sweet Ever After (feat. NEEDTOBREATHE)—Ellie Holcomb, Bear Rinehart, NEEDTOBREATHE
A.M.—One Direction
Stardust—ZAYN
Soon You'll Get Better (feat. The Chicks)—Taylor Swift, The Chicks
Magical—Ed Sheeran
Full of Life—Christine and the Queens
Sink—Noah Kahan
Quite Miss Home—James Arthur
Never Be Alone—Shawn Mendes
Put A Little Love On Me—Niall Horan
Miracle—Labrinth
The Story Never Ends—Lauv
Feels Like This—Maisie Peters
Free—Elina
Repeat Until Death—Novo Amor
BE HERE LONG—NEEDTOBREATHE
West Texas Wind—NEEDTOBREATHE
You Feel Like Home—Hills x Hills
Young Blood—Noah Kahan
Save Me—Noah Kahan
Beautiful Things—Benson Boone
Death Wish Love—Benson Boone
Tears For Fun—Griff
Pink Skies—Zach Bryan
Holy Smokes—Bailey Zimmerman
Next To You—Little Big Town
Forever Young—Alphaville
Carry You—Novo Amor
Little Life—Cordelia
Roses—Jenna Raine
Carry You Home—Alex Warren
Already Home—Hills x Hills
River Flows in You—Yiruma
Forever and a Day—Benson Boone

prologue

June

Texas
Age ten

I scribbled down the "The End" and a huge smile broke out on my face. The stars twinkled outside my window, and my heart felt so full that I wasn't sure my chest could contain it.

I closed the notebook that now held my first-ever story. I ran my hand over the title—"Her Prince." It was twenty *whole* pages about a prince and a fairy princess and their treacherous journey to save their lands. And on the way, they fell in love.

Of course they did.

They loved each other deeply, like my mama and daddy. It was because of them that I wanted to write about love. Mama would tell me about seeing Daddy when she was eighteen. She said, just by looking at him, she knew he was the love of her life—the boy she was going to marry. Daddy said the same for him, love at first sight. I wanted that for me so badly. I wanted to meet a boy who was kind but brave, like Daddy, strong but always showed his love for me on his sleeve.

Sighing, I squeezed my eyes shut and tried to imagine the boy who I would meet, the one who would hold my heart in his hand. I tried to think of the color of his hair, his eyes; tried to guess his name... Nothing came to me—just a blurry outline of who he *could* be—but I could imagine the butterflies that would swoop in my stomach when I would see him.

A smile pulled on my lips, and when I opened my eyes, I gazed out of my bedroom window at the full moon outside. In this part of rural Texas—a small, country town, home to only two thousand people—the thought of my future love seemed so far away, so big and out of reach. But when I ran my hand over my notebook with my finished story inside, that dream didn't seem so unattainable anymore.

"Love," my mama said, "is the most powerful thing in the world. It can heal and it can grow in the most unlikely of places. When all is lost, love blooms."

Lying back on my bed, I stared at the bright moon, its glow lighting up the neighboring ranch, and whispered, "I want a love like my mama and daddy. Please, Moon, when I'm old enough, send me someone to love."

chapter one
June

Texas
Age seventeen

"I'm so sorry...but there's nothing more we can do."

The words hit my ears in pieces, like scattered drops of rain. Numbness spread along my limbs until it rendered me immobile. Dr. Long's sorrow-filled face blurred before me as my eyes seemed to lose focus and every inch of my body froze.

I'm so sorry...

Dr. Long's voice repeated in my head like it was caught in a wind tunnel, circling and echoing, trying to reach my shocked heart. I was trapped in some kind of cocoon. A distant, loud wail could be heard outside of it, but I couldn't move to see where it came from. I caught a flash of movement in my periphery but couldn't shift my eyes to see what it was. I heard crashing, then a deep, sorrowful cry filling the room, like it had been ripped from the depths of that person's soul.

...but there's nothing more we can do.

My heart began to pound, Dr. Long's words still trying to break through, along with the outside cries and wails clattering at my impenetrable walls.

I shook my head, tried to think, tried to get my bearings, but it was no use. My breathing came quickly, and I distantly felt wetness falling down my cheeks. A hand wrapped around mine, clutching it tight like they would never let it go. I blinked and blinked again, trying to focus, trying to find my way back from this frozen, shadowed state. Then the comforting feel of my mama's arms wrapping around my neck hurtled me back into the present, until the doctor's office slammed back into twenty-twenty view. Until the raw rasp of my daddy's broken cries whipped around me and my mama's shaking arms seemed to ground me. I gasped and allowed the cool air from the air conditioning to inflate my lungs.

Dr. Long still sat before me, and I stared at his sorrowful face. *I'm so sorry...but there's nothing more we can do.*

I waited for the heavy weight of reality to push down upon me, for the cries and screams to rip from my mouth, for the anxiety that I'd been fighting for so long to take me in its unyielding grasp. But none of it came. My mama cried into my neck, my daddy dropped to his knees before where we sat and encased both Mama and me in his strong arms, but I was completely still. There was no shaking. No cries or screams. Just...stillness.

I was going to die.

I was seventeen, and I was going to die.

After all the fighting over the past couple of years—the chemo, the drugs, the panic attacks, all the pain—it was coming to an end. I was surprised to find that there was a morsel of relief to that. No more pain, no more medication, no more needles, just the realization that it was time to let go.

"June," my mama whispered, lifting her head from the crook of my neck.

As I stared at her, my lips began to tremble. Not for me but for *her*...for my daddy.

Daddy lifted his head, his eyes filled with so much pain, raw and acute.

"It's okay," I managed to say, my voice barely audible. "I'm...I'm okay."

"Baby..." my mama said, placing her hands on my cheeks. She searched my face like she was seeing me for the very last time.

Dr. Long rose from his seat. I followed his movements. My parents looked up at him as if he were going to tell them he'd gotten it all wrong. That he'd read the chart incorrectly. That, actually, the results said there was a chance. Hope...

But there wasn't.

Dr. Long pressed his lips together and said, "Take as long as you need in this room. I'll be in touch in the next few days with a plan for palliative treatment." He paused, and I watched his Adam's apple bob in his throat as if he was fighting back his own emotions too. Then he nodded and left, shutting the door behind him.

The silence his exit brought was stifling. Mama and Daddy reared their heads back, bloodshot eyes watching me to see if I would break. But the numbness remained. "Can we go home?" I asked. I didn't want to stay in this hospital any longer than I had to. My parents glanced to one another, having some silent conversation I didn't understand.

"Of course," my mama said, and took hold of my hand.

I stared down at our entwined fingers. It didn't feel like my hand she was holding. It felt as if I were suddenly watching the world from a detached standpoint. Like I was no longer in control of my body. I wasn't in the driver's seat. Rather I was in the back, watching all of this unfold from a distance I couldn't close.

I kept my eyes straight ahead as we left the room and walked through the Pediatric Oncology unit. The rhythm of my mama's heels on the linoleum floor accompanied us until we were outside in the warm Texan air—four hundred and twenty-two steps.

My mama held on to me tightly until we reached our car. Daddy opened the door and helped me inside. I buckled myself in, all on autopilot. I tried to feel something, to let my conscious mind fight back the peculiar detachment, but there was nothing.

Daddy started the car, and we drove in silence all the way home. I caught the worried glances my parents shared in my periphery. Saw their heads frequently turn back to me, waiting for me to break, to speak, to do *anything*. But I focused only on the views outside the car window, staying within the cocoon of safety I had found within myself.

The trees swayed in the afternoon breeze. Birds sang and launched themselves into the sky, swooping and soaring. The sun blazed in a crystal-blue sky. The world remained the same.

But I was going to die.

I inhaled a deep breath, feeling a slight catch in my chest as I did. I waited for the panic, the pain, the absolute gutting fear that must come with being told your days on this earth were finite—but the numbness held strong. I stared down at my hand; it still didn't feel like mine.

In what felt like no time at all, we arrived at home. I glanced up at our small house. Everything looked the same. There was comfort in that, that when life turned on its head, some things remained the same.

My door opened and Daddy reached in to help me out of the car. I took his hand and let him lead me into the house. But once inside, the silence that swallowed us began to chase away the numbness. Prick by prick, needlelike piercings of anxiety began to press against my chest.

"June?" Mama said. Her sad eyes searched my face. I didn't know how to react. How were you supposed to act when you were told you were dying? I didn't know the protocol.

"I need some fresh air," I said, and made my way to the backyard. I heard my parents following. I stopped and, without turning, said, "Please...let me just go out there by myself. I need to be alone."

I didn't look to them. I couldn't bear to see the sadness on their faces anymore. I wasn't pushing them away—I just needed to *breathe*. I needed to find my way back to myself.

The sun coming in the windows made spears of rainbows on the kitchen counters, and the distant smell of the bread my mama baked this morning clung to the air. I let it all wash over me, then stepped out onto the back porch. The wooden deck creaked beneath my feet. I walked to the railing and leaned against it. I looked down at my hands again, curling my fingers. My nails were short and brittle but otherwise looked okay. I breathed in deeply, the air filling my lungs. My legs and my arm joints ached.

But I was *okay*. I didn't feel like I was done on this earth.

My body might have been failing, but my soul felt *alive*. I couldn't reconcile the two. A bird sang from a treetop in the woods to the side of our home, and I found myself looking up. The breeze kissed my cheeks, and I watched the bird, perched on a branch. As if it felt my attention, it looked my way.

Seconds later, it took flight.

I wished I could do that right now—take to the skies and lose myself in clouds.

I'm so sorry...

I'd been fighting for so long. I supposed, in my naiveté, I hadn't believed I *wouldn't* be healed. Yes, many treatments had failed for me, but I always thought there would be something that took, that one of the treatments would work. It was just a question of which.

My heart increased in rhythm. I curled my hands into fists, but that detached feeling was still in place, like my true self had been sequestered somewhere inside of my mind.

I moved to the porch swing and sat down.

The door opened behind me, and I turned to see my parents walking through. For the first time in a couple of hours, I smiled. "How did I know you wouldn't be able to stay away?"

Mama smiled, but that smile quickly turned to sorrow as tears began spilling from her eyes. Mama and Daddy flanked me on the swing's bench seat. They each took hold of my hands, and for a moment, they felt like mine again.

"Darlin'," Daddy said. I turned to him. "How are you feeling?"

"I don't know," I said, then shook my head. "No, I'm numb." I gave a self-deprecating laugh. "I think I'm in shock." My mama wiped her eyes. I turned away to lay my head on her shoulder, looking out onto the fields behind our house, and the wood that sat to the side. I adored this view. "I just never thought we'd get here."

"Neither did we," Daddy said, and my mama wrapped her arms around me. "Neither did we." Nothing else was said. What was there to say? So we sat out on the porch until the sun set and stayed awhile longer, as the moon became visible in the sky, reminding us that another of my now-limited days was done.

I had no idea what would happen from here on out, so for now, I'd drink in the world, while I sat beside my two favorite people, and just breathe.

Two days later, we were back in Dr. Long's office. We had no idea why we were here, and despite how much I had warned my heart not to get too excited, I couldn't help but feel a flicker of hope.

My daddy and mama were sitting close to me. In the past two days, they had barely let me go. The last forty-eight hours had brought with it myriad emotions. But the detachment stayed. I found myself catching my reflection and not recognizing the girl before me though that had happened many times over the course of my treatment. Month by month, I felt I had turned into someone else, looked like someone completely different. Only one thing had remained the same.

My love of writing.

A flash of pain cut through me again. Despite the pain I knew was coming, the weakness, the slowly dying day by day, the one thought that felled me most was that I wouldn't become a writer like I'd planned. My dreams, my plans…all of them would turn to vapor.

My heart almost stuttered to a halt when I realized I would never fall in love. I was seventeen and had never been in love. I hadn't ever been kissed. No boy had held my hand. I'd never gotten my happily ever after.

And now I never would.

The door clicked open behind us. Dr. Long gave us a smile as he made his way to his desk chair. "Hello, thank y'all for coming in."

"Is everything okay?" my daddy asked.

My heart seemed to jump into my throat as I waited for Dr. Long to speak.

Mama and Daddy each took hold of my hands, squeezing them tightly. Dr. Long held some papers in his hands, and I realized his expression was different than it had been two days ago. It held what appeared to be a hint of…hope?

My heart beat faster still.

"I'm so sorry to call you back in so quickly, but I've literally just gotten some news that I'm eager to share with you and it's extremely time sensitive."

"Yes?" my daddy asked.

"There's a clinical trial that's being carried out just outside of Austin," Dr. Long said, getting straight to it. "Several weeks ago, when I suspected the treatments for June weren't working as they should, I put her name down as a possible candidate should her results come back as I feared."

A clinical trial? I hadn't even entertained the idea of being nominated for one.

Dr. Long turned his computer screen toward us and brought up an email. He pointed to the screen, but I kept my eyes firmly on his. "There's a drug company that is developing a new treatment for teenage patients with acute myeloid leukemia." I stilled. The disease I had been fighting for over a year now. "There are eight places available at a private hospital on a ranch just under an hour from Marble Falls, which is near Austin." He pushed a brochure nearer us, across his desk. "Initially, June was rejected, as she still showed some signs of improvement. But when I spoke to them a few days ago about how your treatment had stopped working, they said there might be a spot opening back up."

Dr. Long paused, a flicker of sadness in his demeanor. Then it hit me—the spot had become free because someone else hadn't made it. A teen with AML, like me, had lost their life.

A strangled sob came from my mama, but I was too gripped by what Dr. Long was saying. "June," he addressed me directly. "This trial..." He shook his head. "I'm not gonna lie, it'll be tough, but this is our last chance." He then addressed my parents. "It's residential, of course. There are family quarters. I don't know how it'll work with your jobs, but this is a real chance of remission for June." Dr. Long tapped the brochure. "Take a few hours to look through this, but we must give them a decision by the end of the day. It'll be a total life upheaval...but it's a *chance*. Our final chance."

I glanced to my parents beside me. They were completely wrecked. The past couple of days had been too much for them to cope with. "I want to do it," I said, voice strong.

My mama nodded. She glanced at my daddy.

"We'll make it work no matter what," Daddy said. A flicker of a smile touched his lips. He turned to me and kissed my forehead. "Baby girl, we are going to give you this chance and we are going to make sure it works." His voice broke. "I can't lose you." He shook his head, tears falling to the linoleum floor. "I won't."

Only then did tears spill from my eyes. For the first time since being told I was stage four, I broke down. I nodded at my daddy, unable to speak.

When I looked down at my hands again, I exhaled a shaky breath. They felt like mine again. I glanced out of the window—I felt like I was *me* again.

"We'll do it," Daddy said to Dr. Long, taking me from my thoughts. "When do we leave?"

The sound of Dr. Long and my parents making plans turned to white noise as I stared out the window at the bright Texas sun. I could almost feel its healing rays kissing my face.

Hope.

I was feeling a flicker of hope.

And I was going to hold on to it as tightly as I could.

chapter two

June

Harmony Ranch, Texas
Three days later...

THE BUTTERFLIES OF ANXIETY IN MY STOMACH MORPHED INTO ones of awe as I drank in the view of the hospital that would be my home for the next few months. It was like no other hospital I'd ever been in. The pamphlet about the trial explained how it was once a working ranch, until it was repurposed and was approved as a hospital many years ago. The drive up to the ranch on its own had seemed utopian. The driveway was neatly graveled, and trees lined the side of the road. I smiled when I saw in the fields that made up the property and the horses grazing in the grass paddocks.

I adored horses. Before my illness, I was a rider. When the pain in my bones and limbs became too much, I'd had to pull back. It broke my heart. I hadn't visited the stables since. It was too painful to visit the place that had once provided so much peace and solitude for me. It was a slice of happiness that had been taken from me. But I couldn't help the smile that etched itself on my face as a chestnut gelding lifted his head at our car passing by.

My mama looked back at me, clearly seeing him too, and our eyes met. Her expression mirrored mine. The sun was high in the sky, and the Texas warmth wrapped around me as I opened my window and inhaled the close, humid air. It kissed my face, tiny droplets of heat penetrating my skin. My nerves abated and a serene feeling embraced me.

I saw picnic benches and comfortable sitting areas, stables and barbeque areas. Lights wrapped around the trees that I knew would look magical as dusk fell and the burnt-orange Texan sunset enrobed the sky.

This place was utterly beautiful.

We rounded the corner, and the building came into view. "Incredible," I whispered. It was hard to believe that this place was a hospital. It was like something from a movie—a sprawling wooden ranch house, with brown window frames and a brown tin roof. The front entrance boasted large, rustic, wooden pillars and a wide wraparound porch. Rocking chairs were placed along it, which would allow me to do one of my very favorite things: rocking in a porch chair as the sun rose and fell. We had them at home, and a pang of homesickness washed through me, a sudden bout of fear following when I wondered if I would ever see it again.

I thought of our small, white home with its own porch and thick crop of trees to the side of it. The sound of the crickets at night, the water tower that could be seen just over the treetops, the stars that reigned above us like a million diamonds scattered in the sky.

I closed my eyes to fight away the fear. I tried my hardest to not let it in, but this was *it*. This ranch—as majestic as it was—was all that stood between me and death. It was a surreal state to exist within, one foot in the afterlife and one still firmly rooted to this earth. Living with a terminal disease so far had felt like I would wake up one morning and thank the Lord that it was all just a bad dream. But every day I did wake, I remembered that it wasn't a dream.

This was my life.

This was my fight. I was still in it. And I intended to win.

"Darlin'." My daddy's voice broke through my racing thoughts. I opened my eyes to see we had stopped in front of the ranch. It appeared even more imposing up close. Daddy opened the car door for me, and I stepped outside. I reached for my notebook that I always kept with me, for when inspiration struck.

I heard water bubbling and wondered if there was a pool. Probably. This place was incredible. There was a building off to the right side. "I think that's where the parents stay," Daddy said. I nodded, feeling relieved. I needed my parents close. I couldn't do this without them.

Mama stood next to me and wrapped her arm around my shoulders just as the large doors to the ranch opened. A middle-aged woman with a riot of curls; stunning, deep-brown skin; and a bright-pink suit came walking toward us. Her smile was wide, and kindness radiated from her every movement. "Hey, y'all!" she greeted, then began to shake our hands. "Y'all must be the Scotts, and you must be June."

"Yes, ma'am," I replied.

She held my hand in both of hers. "I'm Neenee, the ranch's director. And we are so happy to have you with us."

"Thank you," I said, as she gestured for us to follow her inside.

"Y'all are the last to arrive. So I'll show June to her room, then give you a tour. Then, Mom and Dad, I'm gonna need to steal you away to the office for some paperwork."

"No problem," Mama said, placing her arm around me once more. I knew my parents were nervous too, but we were all optimistic. We had reviewed the findings of this new drug, and it was working for so many. More were cured than not. And for the first time in weeks, I had seen light shining in my mama's eyes and my daddy standing just that little bit taller.

Neenee led us into the foyer, and I came to a dead stop. The walls were a deep mahogany, varnished and shining. The floors were too, with vintage-looking carpet and rugs adding a sense of comfort. A vast staircase was at the end of the hallway, sweeping and ornate. It broke into two at the top.

Stairs had become a little difficult for me. My illness had left me with an obvious limp in my right leg. Clearly seeing this on my face, Neenee said, "All of the bedroom suites are on the ground floor. Upstairs is reserved for the offices and the staff." I smiled at her and reached up to make sure my headscarf was still in place. Today's color was sage green, to match the dress I wore, over which was an oversized, cream-colored cardigan that kept away the chill. I felt the cold a lot these days, even when the Texas heat soared.

"Harmony Ranch is set on over one hundred acres, and the main property is just a fraction over twelve thousand square feet." She stopped at an oil painting of an older man dressed in a suit. "The man who built it, Mr. Owens, lost his teen daughter to cancer, and after his death, he wished for this place to become a place of hope for teens with cancer to keep fighting. It took years to get the ranch approved as a hospital, but it has become a beacon of light to those who come to heal here since."

A burst of warmth filled my veins followed by sorrow for the man who had lost his child. I discreetly looked to my mama and daddy and saw sadness on their faces. I knew losing me was their biggest fear.

"If you'll come this way," Neenee said, and took us toward the room I'd be staying in. I followed along and marveled at the decor—the intricate cornices, the artwork, the ornaments making the vast ranch house feel so homey. Despite the size, there was a coziness to the place. It wasn't sterile and clinical, like all the other hospitals and treatments centers I'd been in. This truly was a harmonious sanctuary. Nothing about it screamed "medical."

We turned down three long hallways and stopped at a door where the room read *Dove*. "This is your suite, June," Neenee said. She opened the door, and we followed her inside.

I gasped at its beauty. Rich, green-paneled walls brought a sense of peace to the room. It was large but not so much that I felt lost within it. There was a plush couch, a substantial TV-and-living space to one side, and a double bed at the other. The linens were floral in the most elegant way. On closer inspection, I realized that the bed was a clinical one. It had the call buttons and the controls to move it to sitting position, for the harder days, when staying bed was the only choice. There were large chairs to the side of the bed, clearly for visitors. IV stands were collected in the corner, and a medical cabinet disguised as a tall dresser was beside the bed. They had tried their absolute best to tone down why we were here and make it a place of rest and comfort.

I went through the closed door at the end of the room and was greeted with a bathroom. The walls were paneled and dusky pink, with a claw-foot bathtub and roomy cubicle shower, with subtle handrails and stools. There was an emergency pull and anything else I could need when I didn't feel so strong, like a shower stool, a walker and long handled brushes to name a few.

When I came back into the main space, I noticed the wardrobe that rivaled the one to Narnia along the far wall. "It's beautiful," I said, feeling completely overwhelmed.

I could heal here, I thought. *I could make it a home while I complete the treatment.*

"You like it, honey?" my mama asked.

"I do," I said, nodding. "I really do."

"Some place, huh?" Daddy said and dropped a kiss on my head. "This'll be a nice place to stay for a while," he said just as a knock on the door sounded.

A young man carried in my luggage.

"Thank you, Bailey," Neenee said as he placed them by the wardrobe.

Bailey smiled at us. "Nice to meet y'all," he greeted, then left the room.

"June, will you be okay here to settle in while I steal away your parents for a while?" Neenee asked.

"Of course." I smiled at them as they left, then held my notebook to my chest and turned a full 360, taking it all in. I waited for the fear, the nerves about what lay before me, but they didn't come. A heady peace settled over me, and a flicker of excitement sprouted in my stomach too. Something about this place felt special somehow. I *knew* deep down that it was going to help me. Change my life. Something about my being here just felt right...destined.

I sat on the end of the bed, noting it's softness, but then turned to the French doors that led outside. I looked beyond them, and a happy laugh spilled from my lips when I saw that same chestnut gelding from the paddock had moved to the part of the field my room faced.

A loud laugh came through the door from somewhere else in the house. Deciding to explore some, I was leaving my room when I heard the laugh again. I turned left and, with my notebook still clutched to my chest, tried to track down what sounded like a group of people talking. A smattering of nerves did rush through me this time. In all the time I had fought my leukemia, I hadn't made many friends in the same position as me. We had to travel to big cities for my many treatments and all the back-and-forth traveling hadn't afforded me many people to take into my confidence.

The truth was, making friends had *never* come easy to me. I had many acquaintances, but no one I would consider a best friend. I had always hoped those relationships would come later in high school, but then I was diagnosed with cancer at fifteen, and I watched those dreams slip away like sand in an hourglass.

I wasn't lonely. I adored my parents, and I always had my characters in my books to keep me company. But I couldn't deny that I longed to know what a true, close friendship felt like. Someone to completely confide in.

I made a right, then a left, marveling at the living spaces that were filled with board games and couches, a vast kitchen, and even a movie room. The glass doors to the outside showed a large swimming pool and a firepit ringed with Adirondack chairs. There were other outbuildings, no doubt filled with exciting things.

But as I turned right again, I realized that I was completely lost. The laughter from someone in the house had faded away, and I could no longer follow the intriguing sound to navigate through the many corridors.

I turned left, hoping it would help me circle back to something familiar, when I came to a sudden stop just before I barreled into someone turning my way. "Oh, I'm so sorry," I said as I stepped back.

When I looked up, it was to see a tall boy in a blue shirt with the sleeves cut off, faded blue jeans, an orange baseball cap on his head—worn backwards—a football in his hands, and the most striking green eyes I'd ever seen. My breath lodged in my throat as I took in his whole face.

He was, simply put, the most handsome boy I'd ever laid eyes on.

"Wow," he said, country-boy Texan accent thick as he stared down at me too. "You're beautiful."

I felt heat instantly flood my cheeks, and a small smirk pulled onto his mouth. An unfamiliar sensation trickled down my spine. A boy had never called me beautiful before, never even looked my way—especially not one that looked like him. Disbelief quickly followed. Because when I looked in the mirror these days, I felt far from beautiful.

But despite my fluster, I couldn't pull myself away from this boy. He quickly wiped his hand on his shirt and held it out. "I'm Jesse."

I forced one hand to release the notebook clutched to my chest, placing it in his, and said, "June." There was shyness to my voice, but when I saw a tint of redness kiss his cheeks too, I knew I wasn't the only one experiencing this strange feeling.

One look at the lack of hair under his baseball cap told me he was obviously one of the patients here too. I swallowed, heart flipping as Jesse smiled and dimples popped in his cheeks. He was tall and, despite his illness, broad in frame with slightly muscled arms. He held on to his football, and I held on to my notebook—and I realized we were still holding hands...

I quickly pulled mine back, and Jesse shook his head. "Sorry about that, June." His voice was as graveled as the driveway outside.

"That's okay," I said. I tried to walk away, but my legs wouldn't move. There was something about this boy that kept me close. And the same peace that had washed over me in my room flowed over me again—as did the same flicker of excitement and the feeling that I was meant to be here.

Destined.

chapter three

Jesse

BROWN EYES, SLIGHTLY TANNED SKIN, AND A SPRAY OF FRECKLES over her cute nose. Maybe five foot five, with a blush to her smooth cheeks. I cleared my throat when I realized I was staring at her.

June.

By the headscarf, I knew she must have been the eighth patient in the trial who we had heard would be arriving today—but I hadn't expected *her*. She was…stunning…beautiful. I couldn't really find the words to do her justice.

I clenched my hand that had shaken hers, a heat stamp imprinted within it. June held a notebook of some kind to her chest like it was a shield. Her eyes flickered everywhere but on me, only for a fresh blush to burst onto her cheeks when they were finally drawn back to my stare.

The color green of her headscarf and dress made her deep-brown eyes shine like glazed dark chocolate. I cleared my throat, realizing I had to speak. "So, June, are you here for the trial?" I wanted to slap myself. Considering she was as follicularly challenged as I was, that was obvious.

What a dumbass question.

"Yeah," she said, her soft voice hitting my chest with the force of a bullet. She looked down at her feet, then shyly met my eyes, gesturing around us with her hand. "I was trying to explore some while my folks are in with Neenee and got myself lost."

I grinned. She was breathtaking. I hadn't expected to come to this trial and meet a walking dream. "This place is huge," I said. "I arrived two days ago and I'm still figuring things out."

The smile June gave me in return nearly knocked me to the floor. Pulling myself together, I pointed my thumb behind me. "You want to meet everyone else?"

June took a deep breath, like she was nervous, but nodded. I was outgoing and a bit too loud at times, but it seemed June was the total opposite. I gestured with a flick of my head for her to follow. Like I always did, I began passing the football between my hands. I couldn't remember a time in my life when I didn't have one with me.

"So," I said, "where are you from?"

"North Texas, small town," she said, following me down the long hallways. She flicked her nervous eyes up at me. "You?"

"A rinky-dink town called McIntyre in West Texas. But I love it. It's my home and I already miss it." I looked back at June and realized she walked slightly slower than most. I clocked the slight limp in her right leg and made sure not to get too far ahead.

"Sorry," she said as she caught up. "My leg isn't as good as before."

I knew what she meant. I rolled the shoulder of my throwing arm. "It's my arm for me."

June nodded in understanding and smiled, and I felt my stomach flip. Well, this was new. I wasn't used to butterflies and all that shit, but I guessed there was a first time for everything. We turned right, and I heard the others chatting in the main rec room. June didn't say anything in response, and I guessed it was going to take her a while to come out of her shell.

We reached the door, and I glanced down at her. "You ready to meet the AML gang?"

A small laugh slipped from her mouth. "I am." The sound of her laugh… Jesus. I was screwed. I opened the door, and the other six members of the trial came into view. Chris, who I had grown closest to in the past couple days, got off one of the couches. An athlete like me—but a baseball player, instead of football—he came straight over.

"Who's this?" he asked.

I turned to June. "Junebug, this is Chris. Chris, this is June."

Chris's eyes met mine and he gave me a subtle eyebrow raise. "Junebug?"

"*June*," June said, cheeks flushed clearly from the nickname. "June."

"Well, *June*, welcome to the trial." Chris announced that like we were on some kind of messed-up reality show, and June laughed that soft laugh that was my new favorite sound.

The others in the room laughed too. It was the best thing I'd found about coming here: the laughter. I had worried I'd be walking into the most depressing place on earth, but everyone was excited to have been chosen for the trial. In a way, we'd won the life lottery—a final chance at survival. How could anyone not be happy about that?

"Hi, I'm Emma." Emma's arrival broke through my wayward thoughts as she came to meet June. Emma was taller than June by a few inches, and having gotten to know Emma over the past two days, she seemed to be more outgoing. She was real sweet too.

"Hi," June said, and Emma pointed to me and Chris.

"I see you met the troublesome twosome." June smiled wide. Emma pointed to June's headscarf. "Love the color." She pointed her own red headscarf. "Girl after my own heart. Wigs itch too much."

"Exactly my thoughts!" June said, eyes sparkling.

The rest of the group came over and introduced themselves—Silas, Toby, Kate, and Cherry. They had all arrived on the same day and had formed their own group of sorts. I'd meshed most with Chris and Emma; hopefully, June could join us to make a foursome.

When everyone had met June, I spread my arms wide and said, "Well, June, welcome to the Last-Chance Ranch!"

Emma groaned and tipped her head back in exasperation.

"What?" June said incredulously but laughing lightly.

I moved beside her. Her big, brown eyes met mine and reeled me in. "It's what we've called this place. Yeah, Harmony Ranch is nice, but we prefer Last-Chance Ranch."

"*He* prefers it," Chris said, elbowing me in my side. "Literally, no one else has been calling it that."

"Bro, watch the ribs. My bones are fragile," I said, rubbing my side. I was only half joking. I felt as breakable as glass lately. I was counting on this new miracle treatment to give me both my strength and health back, so I could get back on the football field and do what I did best.

"*All* of our bones are fragile, dick," Chris said.

I gave him my middle finger in response.

June took in the room, ignoring us two idiots. I traced what she was seeing—couches, a widescreen TV, and vending machines (but only stocked with appropriate nutritional food, of course) that were in the corner. "This has become the main room we hang out in," I said.

June nodded.

"Obviously, we start treatment in a couple of days, so I don't know what happens from there. We're all just clutching on to freedom while we have it."

June released a shaky sigh, but Emma sidled next to her, distracting her. "Want a drink?"

"Yeah, thanks," June said and took off toward the vending machines.

"Dude," Chris said, arm sliding over my shoulders. "Could you be more obvious?" He shook his head, laughing at me.

I didn't care. I couldn't take my eyes off June. I had nothing to hide. She was gorgeous. I'd never really been a subtle person, but getting told you wouldn't live to your eighteenth birthday kind of made you hasty about telling people how you felt—or showing it.

I saw June take a bottle of water off Emma, keeping that notebook clutched to her chest with her other hand.

"She's perfect, man," I said to Chris, and he groaned. I ignored him. "Have you ever just looked at a girl and thought, *damn*? Because that is me today." I shrugged. "Never happened before, but I'm not going to ignore it now."

"Oh, jeez, man, down already?" Chris said. "We just got here! You're meant to be my partner in crime."

"Chill, my dude," I said. "I'm just saying, seeing June has kind of knocked me on my ass." Then June turned my way, and as our gazes caught again, I felt something in my chest explode. She cast me a small, shy smile, and I exhaled a long, calming breath.

Gorgeous.

Emma and June seemed to be hitting it off well, but when June came back over to me and Chris, she said, "I've really enjoyed meeting y'all, but I'd better go and find my suite again. I wasn't meant to leave it. My parents will be finished with Neenee and wondering where I am."

"Which is your suite?" I asked.

"Dove."

Chris slapped my shoulder and groaned dramatically. I laughed at my friend.

"Emma! Join me on the couch," Chris said.

"Why?" she questioned.

"I gotta tell you something." Chris waggled his eyebrows at me.

I rolled my eyes. No doubt Emma would know about my little crush on June in no time.

"I'm so confused," Emma said but followed him anyway, turning back to June to say, "Why are boys so damn weird? Thank God you're here, girl. I'll need you for my sanity."

June's responding smile was blinding. She turned to me. "Why did Chris groan like that? What's he telling Emma?"

I tapped my head. "He's totally weird. Pretty sure too many baseballs have hit his head." An empty water bottle hit the back of mine.

"I heard that!" Chris said, the obvious culprit of the bottle throw.

I decided to ignore him again. "Come on, Junebug," I said and opened the rec room door, gesturing for her to join me. "I'll walk you back to your suite."

"You know where it is?" she asked.

"I do." A shiver ran down my back as we walked down the maze of hallways, just the two of us. It felt like a sudden flash of nerves.

Strange.

I threw my football between my hands to settle myself as June asked, "Are your parents staying in the guest house too?"

Homesickness immediately surged through my veins, but I shook my head. "Nah. It's just me, my mom, and two little sisters—no dad in the picture—and they can't come."

"Oh, I'm sorry. I-I didn't mean to assume…" June stuttered.

Like it always did, my gut twisted to the point of pain when someone asked about my family situation. I rubbed the back of my neck like I was casually shrugging off the comment. "No problem, Junebug," I said, pasting on my well-practiced smile. Then added, "Mom can't come here with me. Her work is back home, and she couldn't get leave. Plus, my little sisters are at school, and I didn't want to uproot them. I'm here alone. I speak to them every day, several times a day, and they'll visit some on the weekends while I'm here." I shrugged, hoping I sounded as cool about it as I wanted to present. I'd gotten real good at hiding my feelings throughout the years.

I understood that my family couldn't be here with me, I did. My mom was a single parent, had a low-income job, and had my two little sisters to take care of. She was already completely in debt due to my chemotherapy and treatments over the past few months. A good chunk of this new treatment was paid for by the drug company alongside of my insurance, taking away some of the financial burden from my mom. It was too much of an opportunity to miss out on.

Not having them here felt like a stab in my chest, yet I had no choice but to cope with it. It wasn't like my wayward dad was coming back into the picture to help. Nah, that would be far too much to expect of him.

I took a quiet, deep breath, so June didn't notice my inner turmoil. I was seventeen. I could do this alone. I *had* to. Plus, I had my fellow patients to lean on, and they were all pretty cool. It all didn't seem so bad now that I was here.

I can do this...

June's silence made me turn my attention to her. She clearly felt the heaviness of my gaze as she met my eyes. "I'm so sorry they couldn't come." She sounded heartbroken for me. My chest squeezed at that. I wasn't used to people caring for me outside of my little family. It was...nice. Unfamiliar but nice all the same. I didn't really know how to process that.

"It's okay," I said nonchalantly. "I intend to go back to them fully healed and ready to live the rest of my life in perfect health." I meant every word of it.

June's responding smile was blinding. "I believe you will," she said. I smiled back as we rounded the corner to her suite. "Ah, thank you!" she said, humor in her soft voice. "I would never have found my way here. I'd have been calling out an SOS." We stopped at her door. She faced me. "You've really sussed this place out in the couple of days you've been here, huh?"

"Eh, not really." I dramatically stepped backwards a few steps until I stood before the next suite's door. "This is me," I said, tapping on the door's nameplate. "Stag."

"You're room's next door to mine?" June said, kind of breathless.

"Looks that way."

"Ah, there you are!" A man's voice came from behind June right before he came into view. He was middle-aged and looked kind of like June. Her dad, I assumed. He was followed by who had to be June's mom. Neenee brought up the rear.

"Jesse," Neenee said, spotting me by my door. "I see you've met June."

I looked to June and winked. "I have."

She blushed.

"I'm Greg Scott, June's dad," the man said, and I shook his hand.

"Nice to meet you, sir. I'm Jesse Taylor."

Mr. Scott looked to my baseball cap for a few moments, then said, "Jesse Taylor who is set to join the Longhorns next year? Jesse Taylor, offensive player of the year, QB?"

"Yes, sir," I said, and just like happened with most people I met, his gaze turned sympathetic. I tossed the ball between my hands faster—it was part of me at this point, and it helped calm me. "Just got to kick this cancer's butt first," I said, trying to keep things light. I *needed* to keep things positive. I couldn't entertain anything but a full recovery here at the ranch, so I was making no room for the alternative. I had dreams to fulfill and goals to achieve, and I only had a small window for that to happen.

"You managed to still play football sick?" June asked, shocked, and that twist was back in my gut. The truth was, we hadn't *known*.

"We didn't pick up on the signs, Jesse. I'm so sorry. We thought they were injury related, not this," the team doc said, his hand on my shoulder. *"I don't know how you managed to push through each game, son, through practice. You're nothing if not tenacious. If anyone can beat this, it's you."*

The flashback to a few months ago made every fiber in my body strain.

I rubbed the back of my neck again. When I felt that pit in my stomach begin, I didn't want anyone else to notice it. I was outgoing Jesse. MVP QB Jesse. Would beat this cancer and get to UT next year Jesse.

I wasn't weak.

Mr. Scott cleared his throat, and when I looked to him, I panicked that he could see through me, could see the cracks in who I tried to be. "I wish you nothing but the best, son," he said. "Truly. I saw highlights of you on our local football channel. You've got a great talent that I hope to see on the Longhorn field someday soon."

"Thank you, sir," I said, meaning it. I could see June's brows pulled down in confusion, but she didn't ask anything else—thankfully. "Are you a UT alumnus?"

"I am," he said, then put his hand on his wife's arm, a proud expression on his face. "We both are. It's where we met, freshman year." He then put his arm around June. "June is set to go there too." His demeanor shifted. "After—"

"After she also kicks cancer's butt," I interrupted, and watched as June's anxious face morphed into one of amusement.

"That she will," Mr. Scott said. "Oh, how rude of me! This is my wife, Claire."

I shook Mrs. Scott's hand. It was like seeing June in the future. "Nice to meet y'all," I said, then looked to June. "I guess I'll be seeing you soon, Junebug." I nodded at them all as I turned to leave.

I headed back in the direction of the rec room while June finished up with settling in, only to hear, "Goodbye, Jesse." I looked over my shoulder. June's parents and Neenee had gone inside her suite, but she remained there, alone, green scarf on her head, brown eyes beautifully locked on me as she still clutched that notebook to her chest.

"First rule of the Last-Chance Ranch, Junebug: we *never* say goodbye, only good night."

June laughed.

"*Good night*, Junebug," I stressed.

June smiled, then said, "Sleep tight, Jesse." She ducked inside her room, her cheeks flushing. My heart was racing, and shivers had broken out along my skin.

June Scott…what a revelation. Suddenly my time here didn't look so bleak.

chapter four

June

I stared at the girl in the mirror before me. I ran my fingers over cheeks that were slightly swollen due to the many months of taking steroids. I rubbed together lips slathered in the lip balm I constantly wore to stop them from cracking.

Next, I ran my fingers over my chest where my chemo port had been. Even after two years, it still felt foreign to me. No matter how much I stared at my reflection, it still took me a while to recognize the girl before me.

"Hello, June," I whispered, finally running my hands over my bald head and bare brow. It was something I did each day: reacquainted myself with "Cancer June." And as much as I struggled to believe this girl was me, this sort of imposter, I couldn't help but love her for how well she had fought for us.

Was *still* fighting.

It was a heady feeling.

A knock sounded on my door just as I tied a long, pale-pink scarf around my head, securing it at the back. I glanced in the mirror one more time. I wore a plain white T-shirt and comfortable, well-worn jeans, a pink sweater tied around my waist for when I inevitably felt the chill.

I opened the door only to find Jesse Taylor casually leaning against the frame. "Mornin', Junebug," he said, and my heart skipped a beat. He was so handsome. I felt like I could get lost in his forest-green eyes that reminded me of the trees behind my home. He was wearing a Longhorns T-shirt and jeans, with the same orange, Longhorns baseball cap he had on yesterday—worn backwards, of course.

A true country boy.

"Morning, Jesse," I said, nerves accosting me. I'd tried to sleep last night. While the start of treatment in a couple days' time should have been the reason why I hadn't, it was because of this boy who had catapulted into my life in the most unlikely of circumstances. The boy I knew was sleeping just on the other side of my bedroom wall.

I wasn't vain. I had never seen myself as anything but normal—not pretty but not plain. Just somewhere in between. Pleasantly average. But since meeting Jesse yesterday, I had been rocked. He'd called me beautiful. *Me.* This superstar QB who was destined for greatness—who I just knew was popular at school—had called me beautiful.

I couldn't see the beauty on my face that Jesse seemed so taken by.

I was so confused.

"Chris, Emma, and I are going for a walk, to explore the grounds and just hang out. We wanna do it before treatment starts and we're all puking for Texas. You coming?" he asked, wearing a playful smirk on his plush lips. Jesse Taylor had charm in abundance. But he wasn't arrogant. He was innocently cocky and cheeky. Frankly, he was magnetic, and so far, when I was near him, I felt like I was being pulled into his orbit.

I laughed at his joke, but my stomach swirled with butterflies at the invite. Here he was again, showing interest. "Sure," I said, and followed him out of my door. "Ah, wait!" I ducked back into my room to grab my notebook.

When I came back outside, Jesse pointed at my notebook. "You're gonna have to tell me what's with the notebook at some point, Junebug."

I shrugged. "Maybe I will tell you sometime…if you're lucky."

Jesse turned to face me, walking backwards a few steps. "Junebug Scott! Are you flirting with me?" he asked, opening his mouth in mock shock.

I came to a dead stop, sudden nerves swallowing me down. "I-I-I—" I stuttered. Had I been? I wasn't sure I knew what it was to flirt, never mind intentionally doing it.

"Don't worry," he said, falling back in step with me just a fraction closer than before. "I liked it."

I looked at him and exhaled out my embarrassment in one long breath, shaking my head in admonishment. "You're trouble."

Jesse's hand landed on his chest, as though he was offended. "Junebug. How could you say that? I'm a nice, respectable mama's boy." I rolled my eyes at him. "Okay," he said, and pinched his forefinger and thumb together. "Maybe I'm a little trouble. But only in the best possible way."

And as much as we were joking around, I believed him. This boy lit up any room he walked into, as though he operated off his own grid—I could tell that by knowing him a grand total of a day. I couldn't imagine what it would be like to be around him in a few months' time. Though yesterday, when I had asked him about football, there had been something else that flickered in his eyes, a crack in his armor that made me pull back on the questions. And last night, when I'd been unable to sleep, I'd wondered if Jesse was quite as carefree as he led people to believe.

Jesse began tossing the ball between his hands again, and I noticed what looked like a rather large pencil or charcoal smudge on the side of his left hand. "Do you draw?" I asked, and Jesse paused in throwing the ball, as if my question caught him off guard.

He tipped his hand to the side, inspecting the smudge himself, then looked at me. "What? You think jocks can't be talented artists too?"

I couldn't stop the loud laugh that escaped me. "Do you ever give a straight answer to anything?"

Jesse moved before me; I was now mere inches from him. "I said you were beautiful, didn't I? I've never been more serious about anything in my life."

Time stretched before us, my breathing quickening and growing louder in my ears. The cover of my notebook creaked under my hands with how tightly I had gripped it. My heart began to flutter, and when Jesse smirked, I knew the blush on my cheeks was scarlet red.

Jesse stepped closer again, so close I could smell a musky scent that must have been from a subtle spray of cologne. It reminded me of summer nights on the porch back home—slightly woody and earthy with a warming fireside note.

"June," he said, raising his hand toward my cheek.

I held my breath, anticipating the move, and then—

"Jesse? June? Is that you two I hear?" The familiar sound of Chris's voice sailed to where we stood in the hallway. Jesse gave me a playful roll of his eyes, then dropped his hand and stepped back just as Chris rounded the corner, but Chris's eyes still went wide seeing us standing so close together. "Errrr..." He awkwardly hitched his thumb over his shoulder. "Me and Em were done waiting for your slow asses, and I volunteered to come looking for you." His attention ping-ponged between us. "Are we going to hang or what?"

I nervously played with the tail of my headscarf that hung over my shoulder, then ducked around Jesse, avoiding his heavy stare. I cast Chris a tight smile in greeting as I passed, then rushed down the hallway until I saw Emma near the exit.

Emma waved, smiling, but her smile dropped when she saw my face. "You okay?"

I nodded just as Chris and Jesse walked up behind us. I knew my cheeks were blazing. I could feel the heat on my skin. I didn't look behind me. I couldn't face Jesse right now.

What even *was* that?

My skin itched so badly I wanted to crawl out of my body. I looked down at my hand. I still felt like me even though my heart was thundering like a horse galloping down a racetrack. There was no detachment but no panic either.

I placed my hand over my heart. This wasn't a side effect of having cancer. This was a side effect of Jesse Taylor's affection.

I pushed out of the exit and instantly breathed in the warm country air. I closed my eyes as it filled my lungs. I could hear Jesse and Chris talking behind me, then an arm threaded through mine, linking me.

"Are you trying to run away from me, June?" Emma said, and I huffed out a laugh. My heart calmed a little as she walked beside me.

"No running," I said and tapped my knee. "Not sure this would hold up if I tried."

Emma laughed. "Hey!" she squealed as Chris ran by her, a bottle of water in his hand. I turned to Emma to see that Chris had squirted her as he passed.

Emma's eyes narrowed. "I'll get you back for that, Christopher." I laughed at the use of Chris's full name.

A tug on the end of my headscarf made me look to the side. Jesse rushed past me, giving me a devastating smile as he did, then chased after Chris.

I watched them as they raced down the trail ahead of us—well, as fast as their weakened bodies would allow. We followed behind them. The sign we passed showed this trail led to several routes through the ranch. Emma's hold on me felt...nice. I'd never had a friend do this to me.

"I swear, all boys are the same. They never mature." Emma shook her head at Chris and Jesse, but I saw her affection for them in her expression. "So, June," Emma said, turning her attention to me. "Tell me about yourself."

Chris and Jesse leaned over a fence in the distance. Longhorn cattle were grazing in the field, and I could hear Chris trying to call them over.

I shrugged. "There's not much to tell. Normal seventeen-year-old from a small town...studious, a little quiet, not much to say."

"Boyfriend?" Emma asked, smirking.

"No boyfriend," I said emphatically.

"Yeah, I hear ya," she said, then leaned in close. "My last boyfriend dumped me when I lost my hair. So fuck him, I guess."

My heart broke. "Emma..." I said, "That's awful."

Emma shrugged. "His loss," she said, pretending to toss her imaginary hair over her shoulder. "I'm fabulous no matter how much hair I have." I laughed and Emma held me tighter. "I'm only kidding, but my ex *does* suck. He wasn't a good guy."

"No current boyfriend for you either?" I asked.

"Nah," Emma said. "I've decided to wait for the man of my dreams. He's in my future; I can just feel it."

For some reason, I lifted my head and caught sight of Jesse. He was leaning over the fence to the longhorn cows still, laughing at Chris trying to feed one a handful of grass he'd picked off the ground. As if feeling my stare, Jesse looked my way, and his eyes softened as they met mine. My heart kicked into a sprint again.

Emma cleared her throat. "Jesse's cute." I whipped my head to Emma, eyes wide. She leaned forward, laughing. "June, you should see your face." She laughed harder. I couldn't help but smile at her. When she recovered, she said, "It's okay to think a boy is cute, you know."

I was quiet as we closed the gap between the boys and us. There was an instant comfort with Emma. Her personality was as warm as her smile, and I found myself revealing, "I've never had a boyfriend." I could see Emma look at me in my periphery, but I kept my face straight forward. "I've never even been kissed."

Emma hugged me closer. "Well, June, I have only known you for the grand total of twenty-four hours, and I can tell you that the boy who steals your heart will be one lucky guy."

My cheeks heated, and I tried hard to ignore the twist in my gut that told me a guy like Jesse would never look at a girl like me. I didn't want to be crippled by insecurity on this walk right now. I just wanted to enjoy this glimpse of pretreatment freedom and make a new friend. "Thank you."

"Now," Emma said, "let's talk about something that doesn't involve boys. We're strong, independent women, who have more to give to the world."

"Okay," I said, chuckling.

"Tell me about your friends," she said, and this request hit me harder than the question about boyfriends. I was too quiet, and Emma noticed. "You okay?"

"Yeah," I said, and cleared my throat. I tried to think of what to say without sounding pathetic. Shrugging, I said, "I don't really have any friends." Emma's arm linked through mine squeezed me tightly. I felt too vulnerable to look at her. "I had lots of people I played with as a kid and spoke to in class, but no one I was really close to. Then after all the treatment..." I trailed off.

Emma was only quiet a beat before she said, "Those friends drifted off, stopped coming around so much, and moved on with their own lives while you were stuck in chemo-and-stem-cell hell?" I couldn't have said it better myself. After I gave Emma a nod, she said, "Trust me, June, I get it."

Some of my embarrassment ebbed. "You do?"

"I do," she said and squeezed my arm again. "I did have best friends, but we grew apart when our lives took vastly different directions." Emma sighed. "I don't blame or resent them." She gestured to her body. "It's this damn disease I resent."

"Who do we resent?" Chris asked, as he came toward us and moved between us to throw his arms around our shoulders.

"You," Emma said dryly, and Chris backed away, pretending to look offended.

Warmth burst beside me, and when I glanced to my left, I saw that Jesse had fallen into step next to me. He was laughing at Chris, who moved ahead of us and walked backwards so he could look at us as he spoke.

"No, really. Who do you resent?" Chris asked again. I could see Jesse tossing the ball back and forth in hands in my periphery.

"Cancer," Emma said. "You know, the disease that is trying to kill us all."

"Ah, Mylo," Chris said. When Chris was only met by a wall of confused silence, he said, "What? I gave him a name." In a flash of seriousness, he added, "Depression hit me pretty hard in the beginning. Snuck up on me until I couldn't get out of bed." Chris shrugged. "I started getting help for it which helped. Still do, though I have more better days than bad now." Chris paused in thought, then said, "I like dark humor, it's how I cope with things—so my therapist says—so I named my cancer: Mylo. He's not the best of guys, and I'm trying to get rid of him while he tries to kill me, but while he's with me, existing in my body, he's Mylo."

"I say this with the utmost affection, Chris," Emma said, "but you're the weirdest person I've ever met."

Chris stopped walking and dramatically placed his and over his mouth, then dropped it to his chest, over his heart. "Emma...that's the nicest thing anyone has ever said to me."

I burst out laughing, as did Emma and Jesse. I wanted to bathe in the sound. It felt just as healing as the pain meds that lessened the aftereffects of treatment.

I liked Chris. And I more than admired the way he was so honest about his depression. It was admirable. I already adored Emma. And as for Jesse...I flicked my gaze up to him. He caught me and said, "You having a good time, Junebug?"

"I am," I said. I truly was.

We rounded the corner and a playground lay before us. Chris ran straight over to the swings and took a seat. Five other swings made up the set, and we all sat down. Emma was to my right and Jesse to my left. I swung back and forth, looking out at the many acres of longhorn cattle. The air smelled sweet, and the temperature wasn't too hot.

"So, Chris?" Emma said. Chris was moving back and forward with a bit more vigor than the rest of us. "What were you like at school?"

Chris tipped his head to the side and said, "Hugely popular. The biggest ladies' man that ever did exist. The best baseball player that the county had ever seen." He shrugged. "But I try to keep humble about it."

I giggled, and Emma threw her head back and laughed. Jesse shook his head but chuckled to himself.

"What?" Chris said to Jesse. "You don't believe me, bro?"

Jesse held up his hands. "I'm not saying anything. I wouldn't want to doubt the biggest ladies' man that ever did exist."

Chris rolled his eyes and smirked. "All right. I was pretty good at baseball, enough to get a scholarship to college. I had a few girlfriends, but every single one dumped me."

"I knew it!" Emma called out.

Chris scowled at her. "But I liked school. I'm bummed that I won't see out my senior year alongside my classmates. But I guess you guys will do." Jesse kicked his foot into the shredded bark that made up the playground's flooring, spraying Chris with it.

Chris dusted it off, then narrowed his eyes on Emma. "What about you?"

"Normal student. Band nerd. No enemies. It was all good," Emma said.

"June?" Chris asked, and my stomach flipped.

I held my notebook tighter to my chest and stared at the ground. "Good student. Probably more reserved than you guys. But I liked school." I felt my cheeks heating, but when I looked up, Chris was nodding.

He then locked eyes on Jesse. "Jesse?" Chris asked, smirking.

"No, I got this," Emma said, butting in. "Hugely popular. And was *actually* the biggest ladies' man that ever did exist. And really *was* the best football player in the county."

I laughed at Chris's expression as he took in Emma's "betrayal." But then his expression eased, and he said, "Yeah, that's probably all true."

When I glanced to Jesse, it was obvious by the look of embarrassment that it was all true. But instead of agreeing, he said, "I'm a man of mystery. I'll just keep y'all guessing." But I could see it. I imagined Jesse was the most popular guy at his school. And if my daddy had heard of him, he was clearly insanely talented at football. And by just the effect he had on me, he no doubt had girls flocking to him.

We couldn't have been further apart in social status if we'd tried.

"We're quite the hodgepodge group," Emma said, but her following smile was blinding. "And I love it!"

I looked to Chris, the humorous one; Emma, the loyal one; I was the book nerd and quieter one; and Jesse, well, he was the all-American boy with the magnetic smile.

"Let's see what else this place has to offer," Chris said, and jumped off the swing. Emma followed. I got off my swing, and Jesse fell into step beside me again.

"You like Emma?" he asked, tossing his ball.

"I love her," I said. "I can't wait to get to know her more." I laughed at Chris and Emma walking ahead, Chris trying to trip Emma on the graveled path. "He was definitely the class clown," I said and pointed to Chris running from Emma as she tried to get him back.

"One hundred percent, not the ladies' man he wants us all to believe," Jesse said.

A spark of jealousy rushed through me. "But you were?" I found myself asking.

Jesse turned to me.

"Mr. Popular?"

His head tipped to the side. "Popular, maybe, though it makes me sound like a douchebag to say that out loud." Jesse turned before me, and I stopped dead. "But not the ladies' man I think y'all believe me to be."

I raised a brow in disbelief.

Jesse smiled wide. "A few girlfriends, max. I promise."

My stomach tightened hearing that. I had no idea why—I had only just met him.

I shook my head as we started walking again. "I'm not sure we would have even spoken if we'd gone to the same school," I said. "I was mostly in the library. I wouldn't have even crossed your path."

"I would've seen you," Jesse said, and every word was said with conviction. I looked up at him and his face was serious. "I would have seen you, Junebug. Believe me." But I didn't—that was the problem.

A familiar sound came from behind me, and when I looked to where Emma and Chris were heading, I saw a field full of quarter horses. A smile spread on my face, and I rushed forward.

"June?" Jesse called out, then ran to catch up with me. When I rounded the corner, a stable yard came into view. It was both the most amazing sight and a punch to the gut. The stables were vast, all painted white, with an outdoor and an indoor arena for training.

I stopped next to Emma and Chris at the fence. I held out my hand as a skewbald quarter horse came toward me. I ran my hand down its face and kissed its nose.

"Horse girl?" Emma asked.

"Used to be," I said.

Emma nudged me. "Maybe could be again." She gestured at the stables, where we could see grooms brushing down and bathing horses through the large, open barn doors showcasing inside.

The thought of just being around horses again brought warmth to my heart. I forgot how healing they could be. "Maybe."

Jesse patted the horse, and it walked away. I burst out laughing when he turned to me with a bewildered look. "What did I do?"

Chris laughed and carried on walking. Emma linked her arm with mine again, and Jesse walked beside us. As we left the stables and went to explore more, Jesse leaned down and said, "There you go, Junebug. As popular as you believe me to be, I'm not among horses."

"Jesse!" Chris shouted, pointing at a barn filled with tractors and other farm equipment.

As Jesse headed off to Chris, Emma squeezed my arm again. "We may be the most random friendship group to ever exist, but we're sure gonna be a fun one," she said.

"That we are," I said, and felt a moment of true happiness. We may have had a mountain to climb here at Harmony Ranch, but if I could climb it with these people, I thought that maybe it didn't seem so hard.

chapter five
Jesse

"Is this gonna be a daily thing?" June said as she opened the door.

I was leaning against the doorframe, smiling. "Mornin', Junebug."

June was wearing a lilac headscarf, black yoga pants, and an oversized, white T-shirt.

"You look lovely," I said, and June's smile faltered just a touch as she dropped her head, breaking eye contact.

I was worried I'd been too bold saying that, but when she uttered, "Thank you," I didn't think I had. I just wasn't sure she believed it, which was crazy to me. Did she not see herself?

"Our last day of freedom," I said. Tomorrow we started our new "miracle treatment"—or so Chris and I called it. As much as the treatment would no doubt suck, I couldn't wait to get started. The quicker I could be in remission, the quicker my goals could come into fruition.

"So what have we got planned for today?" June asked as she pulled on her white Converse.

"Toby, Kate, Cherry, and Silas are in the swimming pool. So grab your swim things. We said we'd join them."

June hesitated for a second, then ducked back into her room. In minutes, she came out with her swim bag, her notebook on the top. She fell in step beside me, and I led the way to the swimming pool.

"How are you feeling about tomorrow?" I asked.

June paused to think. "Okay, I suppose," she said and shrugged. "I guess I'm just nervous. I read it's chemo again with immunotherapy." She sighed. "I *loathe* chemo."

"Same," I said, which was true. Chemo was brutal. Out of everything that they tried with me, chemo was the worst. "But at least we've got each other to get us through, hey?"

June smiled. "We do. But if this cures us, then I'll take as much chemo as they'll give us."

I nodded. "Where are your parents?" I asked, just as we stepped outside, toward the pool.

"They're working from the parents' residence today. I had breakfast with them this morning, but I wanted to hang out with you guys again and they had to work anyway." A blush coated her cheeks. I couldn't say how happy hearing that made me.

Shouts from the pool sailed into our ears, and when we rounded the corner, we saw everybody was already in it. We arrived just in time to see Chris cannonball into the pool, splashing Emma in the process.

I laughed as Emma screamed, then ducked his head under the water. It seemed like it was going to be the perfect last day, and it reminded me of easier times back home with my friends, when life hadn't been quite as intense.

I pulled my shirt over my head and said to June, "The change-rooms are over there."

Her eyes were fixed on the pool, and when she looked to me, her cheeks reddened as her eyes found my chest. "I'm just gonna sit on a lounger for now."

I frowned in confusion. June passed by me and sat on a lounger, smiling at everyone and pulling a paperback from her bag.

I was busy staring at her, wondering why she wasn't getting in when Emma pushed up out of the pool. She toweled herself off and said, "I'll go sit with her."

"Do you think she's upset with me?" I asked, worried I'd done something to offend her.

"No," Emma said. "I don't think she's upset with you." She went to June, and June's genuine smile was back on her face as our friend approached.

"You gonna get in, Romeo, or are you just gonna stare at June like a lovesick fool all day?" Chris shouted from the pool, and I wasted no time diving in and swiping his legs out from under him as I swam underneath the surface.

"Prick," Chris spluttered as we both came up for air.

I immediately sought out June. I couldn't help but worry she wasn't okay. She and Emma were sitting together on the lounger, talking up a storm. My chest pulled tight watching her. I didn't like how nervous and uncomfortable she had just been. And I didn't like having no idea why.

Emma got up and came toward us. She leaned down at the side of the pool. "We're gonna do something else," she said, gesturing back to June.

"Like what?" I asked. Chris swam up beside me, listening.

Emma shrugged. "Don't know. We'll figure it out."

"June doesn't want to swim?" Chris asked. Emma shook her head.

"Is she okay?" I asked, deep concern burrowing inside me.

June was reading a book, not even looking our way.

Emma glanced at her and looked back. "She's great. Just doesn't want to swim."

Then there was no other decision to make: I pulled myself out of the pool and grabbed my towel. Chris followed suit.

Emma straightened with a knowing eyebrow raised in my direction. "Let me guess: you're coming too?" she said, amusement lacing her tone.

"That okay?" I asked, pausing, wondering if June needed space and just wanted to be with Emma, alone.

"Of course it is," Emma said. "I'm going to go get changed."

I dried off, threw my shirt on, and grabbed my football. I walked to where June sat and checked out what she was reading. "Let me guess…buff fairies?" I asked.

June lowered the book and laughed. "Buff fairies?" Understanding dawned on her face. "Do you mean High Fae?"

I shrugged. "I have no idea, but some of my friends back home talked about them all the time." June's eyes sparkled with mirth. "Like, they were low-key in love with mythical creatures."

She closed the book and, waving it, said, "No buff High Fae in this one. *This* one is about buff vampires actually," she said, fighting back a smile, and I nodded, smirking. Sort of called it. June put her book in her bag, then got to her feet. "No more swimming?" she asked.

"I decided to hang with you guys instead," I said just as Chris came over, now dry and with a T-shirt on.

"Me too," he said. "We can't break up the band on day two, June. We're in our bonding stage and must stick together."

"Ah," June said, smiling. "Gotcha." But I saw true happiness in the way she held herself a little bit taller.

Emma returned wearing jean shorts and a blue tank, a blue headscarf on her head. "So, what do y'all wanna do?"

"Game room?" Chris said, pointing to the large barn-like structure behind us.

I looked to June, eyebrow raised in question.

"Sure," she said. We followed Chris, and he opened the door to the game room and June stopped dead. Her brown eyes were wide as she drank in the space. Arcade machines lined the walls. Air hockey and pool tables took up the center, and games consoles of all kinds were set up with the TV in the room, beanbags in front of it.

"We found this on our first day," I said to June, just as Chris turned on country music that filled the room from the state-of-the-art speakers in the ceiling.

"Wow," she said, and placed her bag on the table by the entrance way. "They really have turned this place into a patient's paradise." June turned to me and smiled. "Gone are the days of staring at four white walls and a window with no view."

"I know, right?" I said. "All it took was for us to be knocking on death's door to get it."

June choked on a laugh and looked at me from the side of her eye. "See? Trouble," she said. Heat zapped through my veins at being on the receiving end of her playfulness.

"Says the girl reading vampire smut," I said, and watched June's mouth drop open in shock. I quickly held up my hands. "Which is totally okay and not at all wrong in any way, shape, or form. All art is subjective et cetera, et cetera," I said in a panicked voice.

June pointed at me. "Those vampires could teach you a thing or two, Mr. Ladies' Man." I felt full to the brim with happiness. June was joking around with me. I'd made it through her protective layer in some way. I felt like the luckiest son of a bitch in the world.

June's arms were crossed over her chest. I stepped closer and closer until her pupils dilated a little. Tucking my football under my arm, I said, "How do you know they could teach me a few things?"

June's lips parted slightly, and a rush of breath escaped them.

"Maybe I could teach *them* a trick or two—in a non-blood-drinking way, of course."

The sound of pool balls being set came from behind us. Emma appeared at June's side, but I was still holding her stare. June quickly broke away to smile at Emma. Emma fought to hide her amusement. I was sure she'd heard me. "Pool game? Me and Chris versus you two?"

"You're on," I said, and June shook her head.

"I don't know how to play pool," she said, and looked my way apologetically.

"No problem," I said, and headed to the pool table. June came too. "I'll teach you."

"Oh, here we go," Chris moaned, but I ignored him.

I grabbed a pool cue and added some chalk to the tip. "Who's breaking?" I asked.

"Me," Chris said. He lined up his shot and pocketed a striped ball first. Chris smiled and waggled his eyebrows at me as he lined up his next shot.

"What's happening?" June asked, leaning close to me. Goose bumps broke out on my skin as her minty breath ghosted over me.

"Chris keeps going until he misses. Then it's your or my turn."

"Okay," June said, just as Chris sent another striped ball wide.

I offered the cue to June.

"No, please. You first," she said, holding up her hands.

I pointed at the table. "Emma and Chris are stripes. We're solids." June nodded, watching me like a hawk. I pocketed three solids, only to miss the fourth.

Emma pretended to stretch like an athlete across the table. "Get ready for a master class, boys," she said when it was her turn, and winked at June. June's smile was wide as Emma began to pocket striped ball after striped ball. I leaned on my cue and groaned.

Chris was beaming, watching his teammate annihilate me and June. When Emma—thankfully—missed the eight ball, I turned to June. "Junebug," I said, "not to pressure you or anything, but our victory lies on your shoulders."

June's head dropped into her hands, and she groaned. She peeked at me through spread fingers. "Jesse, we're going to lose. You get that, right?"

"No!" I cried. "Not on my watch." I moved behind June and placed the cue in her hands. "I might be a good football player, but I'm a pretty epic coach too. We've got this, Junebug."

"Okay," June said, voice raspy. It took me a minute to realize that maybe it was because I'd moved closer to her.

"This okay?" I asked, just in case she was uncomfortable.

"Yes," she said, pink bursting on her cheeks.

"Okay," I said, and demonstrated how to hold the cue and position it on the table. "Just…" I adjusted her arm. "Like that," I rasped.

June tried to maneuver the cue as I'd shown her but couldn't quite get it. Before taking her shot, she looked over her shoulder, and said, "Could you help me do it, please?"

Standing at her side, I covered her hands with my own, my mouth close to her ear. My heart slammed in my chest at having her this close. "Draw back," I said, "and then smoothly hit it." When we hit the cue ball, it sailed into the striped ball. I smiled when the ball rolled into the pocket.

June turned to face me, eyes bright, a huge smile on her face. "I did it!" That beautiful smile on that stunning face was a sucker punch to my heart.

"You did," I said, voice hoarse. I couldn't help but add "Could your buff vampires help you do that?"

June's threw her head back as she laughed, filling the room with the addictive sound. When she faced me again, she said, "No, Jesse. I'm not sure they could."

"Then a point to me, I guess," I said, just as a throat cleared.

"Chris?" Emma said from across the table. "Do you get the feeling these two keep forgetting we're here with them?"

"Mmm," Chris said. "Now that I think about it, yes. Happened a few times yesterday too."

I looked up at Emma and Chris to see shit-eating grins on their faces.

Without June seeing, I flicked them the finger. Emma cackled, and June stood up, clearly embarrassed. Nervously looking back to me, she said, "I think I've got it from here. Thanks, Jesse."

Nodding, I stepped back and watched June sink another ball into a pocket.

"And so the student becomes the teacher," she said to me, shaking off any discomfort Emma's and Chris's comments had brought.

I groaned. "I've created a monster," I announced, but secretly, my pulse was racing.

She was, showing her personality more and more the longer we hung out.

Then June missed and turned to me to say, "Or maybe not."

I laughed at the apologetic grimace on her face and hung my head in defeat when Chris immediately pocketed the eight ball.

"Victory is ours!" Chris shouted, arms in the air. He and Emma high-fived and hugged in celebration.

I scanned the rest of the room. "Air hockey, Junebug?"

"You're on," she said.

I beat her five-to-one.

We had just placed down our paddles when the door to the game barn opened. Bailey, a ranch's nurse, came in with a tray of pale orange drinks.

"Hey, guys," he said, and placed the bottles on a table. "I have an immunity drink here for each of you. You have to take it today for the start of treatment tomorrow and the tests that will be performed for the trial."

Chris walked over and took hold of a bottle. He brought it to his nose and quickly wrenched it away. "Nah, man, that's nasty," he said, and Emma, June, and I joined him. He wasn't wrong. The liquid smelled vile.

"I know they don't taste good, but I'm afraid they're required."

Bailey tapped his hand on the table. "I'll be back in thirty minutes. That's how long you have to get it down."

Bailey left, and Emma moved to the circle of beanbags that were set up for gaming. June sat beside her on her on another bag. I sat beside June and Chris took the last one.

"Okay, let's do this," I said, and forced myself to take a sip. My eyes watered as I tried to swallow the thick liquid, fighting the urge to wretch. I coughed and wiped at my mouth as it went down. "Shit," I said. "That's the worst thing I've ever tasted."

Emma blew out a breath. "Not sure I can do this." She brought it to her nose, and her eyes immediately watered.

"Me either," June said, staring at the bottle like it was the most offensive thing in the world. She sighed. "Can't be as bad as some of the other treatments we've all had, right?" Her brown eyes searched us all for confirmation.

"What *have* we all had?" Emma asked.

"I've got an idea," Chris said, and I laughed when the three of us groaned at him. "No!" he said. "It's good, I promise." He tapped the bottle with his finger. "Never Have I Ever, AML treatment edition."

"I can't believe I'm saying this," Emma said, "but it might help us get this down." She checked her watch. "We only have twenty minutes left to get this done."

"I'm in," June said, then with shy eyes, said, "I've never played Never Have I Ever."

"Well, it's better with beer, Junebug, but I suppose this sewage water will have to do," I said. June laughed. Sighing, I turned to Chris. "Okay, I'm in."

"I'll go first," he said. "Never have I ever had chemotherapy."

Closing his eyes, Chris downed a mouthful, his face contorting at the taste.

"That's not fair," Emma said. "We *all* have had that!"

"Exactly," Chris said, voice tight due to the aftertaste. "We have to get this drank at some point."

I turned to June and, lifting my bottle, said, "Bon appétit!" I threw the mouthful in, forcing it down.

June started coughing. "Oh my gosh," she said, and wiped her mouth.

"My turn," Emma said, moving us quickly on. "Never have I ever had radiation."

Once again, the four of us all drank. I looked at the bottle, and it felt like there was hardly any of it gone. "Does this bottle friggin' refill itself somehow?"

The giggle that June let out beside me made my heart flip. "I was thinking the same thing."

"Okay," I said, "Never have I ever had stem cell treatment." I raised my bottle. "But mine didn't work!" I took another sip.

"Didn't work for any of us!" Emma tacked on.

My friends all drank. Turning to June, I waited for her to speak. "Never have I ever had a bone marrow transplant." June drank, but I didn't this time. Emma didn't either; only Chris joined in.

"You didn't?" June said to me after she drank.

"Nope."

June looked to Emma. "You either?"

"Nope!" Emma said, echoing my answer.

It was quiet a moment before Chris said, "Err...that's all the treatment I had before I came here. What else is there?"

"I had targeted drug therapy. Twice," June said, and I felt like I was seeing her for the first time. This girl had been *through* it.

"Whew, girl. You've had it all," Emma said, and June nodded her head sadly.

"And none of it worked," she said somberly, but then forced on a smile. "But this one will," she said, and drank the remainder of her bottle in one go. "I can just feel it."

"Yes, girl!" Emma called out, then holding her hand in the air, finished off the rest of her drink too.

"Hell, man," Chris said to me. "We've been outdrank by the girls." I laughed as Emma tossed her empty bottle at him. Chris tried to do as they had done but had to stop to fight back puking it all back up.

I curled over, laughing. "That serves you right for that shitty comment," I said. "I've got two little sisters who would kick your ass for that kind of talk."

"It was a joke! I was *joking!*" he said, attempting to drink the orange sludge again.

Closing my eyes, I took a deep breath, then finished my bottle off too.

A shiver of disgust ran down my spine just as Bailey came back into the barn. "How did we get on?" he asked.

"Easy-peasy," Chris said, his body still shuddering in the aftermath.

"How often will we be treated to *that* delicacy?" Emma asked.

Bailey grimaced. "I'm sorry to tell you this but daily. The drugs will be hard on your body, and this helps you stay strong."

"Awesome," Emma said, then got to her feet.

Bailey cleared the bottles and left us alone.

Emma held out her hand in June's direction. "June?"

June lifted her head in question.

"I've decided, as your new best friend, that we will have girl time for an hour each day. What do you say?" Emma looked from me and Chris. "I love you guys, I do, but being exposed to too much testosterone in a day makes me twitchy."

June laughed, then got to her feet. She grabbed her bag, and Emma linked her arm through June's. "Boys, we shall see you tomorrow for the start of treatment. I'm taking my girl to the kitchen for something to eat," Emma said.

My heart melted at the look of happiness on June's face. Emma seemed really good for her. As they left, June looked back over her shoulder and met my eyes. *Bye*, she mouthed, and I waved, watching her and Emma fall into easy conversation as they left.

"Screwed," Chris muttered from his beanbag, closing his eyes as if for a nap. "Completely and utterly screwed."

I ignored my friend's jab because it was true. I couldn't get June from my head—her smile, her eyes, her laugh. My chest tightened recalling how much she had been through with treatment, leading me to believe that she'd been sick for a while.

But we were here now. And we *would* be healed. There was no other choice.

And in the process, I couldn't wait to get to know June even more. Because like Chris had said, when it came to June Scott, I was—*happily*—screwed.

chapter six

June

THE TRIAL'S HEAD DOC FINISHED SETTING UP AT THE FRONT OF the rec room.

I nervously played with the tail of my headscarf. I was sitting between Emma and Jesse, with Chris on Jesse's other side. As if it had become a little ritual, Jesse had knocked on my door this morning. I hadn't seen him after Emma and I left the gaming stable yesterday. I'd gone to Emma's room, and we just hung out, ate snacks, and watched trash TV. It was heaven. But I'd often found my mind drifting to thoughts of Jesse and what he and Chris were doing.

These feelings were…new for me.

I had resigned myself to maybe never finding someone I liked. Especially while going through treatment. Now I'd found myself drawn to someone while getting a new form of chemotherapy and immunotherapy.

It was making my head spin.

Silas, Cherry, Toby, and Kate were sitting on the other side of the room. The man at the front of the room looked no older than mid-twenties. He seemed very young to be heading up the entire trial.

"Good morning," the doctor said, starting the introductions. "My name is Dr. Duncan. I am the head doctor in this trial." He pointed at his face. "I know, I seem young. And that's because I am." Muffled laughs trickled throughout the room. "I have been working on this new treatment with an extremely talented team for quite some time. And I am pleased that you are here and that, for most of you, we hope will have great success."

There was a sudden pause in the air as those words left his mouth—*for most of you, we hope will have great success.*

Most *of you...*

Some of us would not see that success. I cast my gaze around the room and caught eyes with the other patients; it was clear they were thinking what I was—out of the eight of us, some of us still might not make it. It was a sobering thought.

"I apologize if that sounds too blunt," Dr. Duncan said. A white-hot shiver ran down my spine. Fear, I realized. As if sensing it, Jesse leaned closer, his arm touching mine, offering me comfort. The warmth immediately took the brunt of that fear away. I didn't look at him. I wouldn't because I knew I would break if I did, and I had to keep positive. I was determined to.

"I have autism spectrum disorder," Dr. Duncan said, pulling focus back to him. "I have a high IQ, and I have dedicated my life to saving people. But I'm afraid I'm better with facts than pleasantries. Science is my language and my strength. People skills are not."

I smiled as he said that. He seemed like a nice man, and I appreciated him opening himself up to us a little. After all, the entire staff here knew everything about us; it was nice to be told something personal about them too.

Dr. Duncan waited for us all to stop shifting or whispering to one another. I felt a hand take mine and looked down to see it was Emma's. I glanced up at her and saw the same frisson of fear I was feeling reflected in her blue eyes. I squeezed her hand back. We had laughed and joked yesterday when we had all been together. But the reality was, there was nothing humorous about our situation.

We were all here because we were *dying*. That realization was always close by to remind us why we'd been given a spot at the ranch. The past couple days of fun had been amazing and had helped us form some friendships. But playtime was over, and we were faced with reality.

"The treatment is invasive, and the medicine is strong, stronger than you will have had before. Being young helps you tolerate this treatment better than people who are older, but the side effects can potentially be many and difficult. It will be uncomfortable for most, if not all of you." Dr. Duncan pointed at the back of the room. I hadn't seen the nursing staff and Neenee enter, but they were standing back there. My parents had come in too, along with what seemed to be everyone else's—except Jesse's.

My heart fell at that.

Jesse was the only one here alone. We were being told the side effects would be awful, and he had no one here to help him through it.

"The medical staff will administer a round of chemotherapy on days one to four in your rooms which are sterile, and FDA approved.

You will have four days rest after that. Then you will receive a new form of monoclonal antibodies through infusion for four days. This will be administered in your room too for about an hour each morning. After that you will be free to move about the ranch. After the first immunotherapy cycle, you will have a few days' rest, then we will repeat the antibody treatment until phase one ends. We will review your results to see how you are responding, then phase two will begin. Adjustments to the treatment's strength may need to be made at this point, but we will assess this on an individual basis.

"You will all be under twenty-four-hour surveillance in case you have any side effects or need urgent help. Frequent blood tests and scans will be done along the way to monitor how you are responding to treatment. Questionnaires will be given to you to fill out." Dr. Duncan pointed down the hall. "Everything we need is on-site, and the nearest large hospital is on standby should we need it for emergencies, though we are equipped for them here too." He gave us a tight smile. "I'll go and set up with the nurses for the pretreatment checks and the fitting of your chemo ports. Neenee will speak to you now about what else you can expect from your time here." He gave us a sharp nod and left the room.

Neenee took Dr. Duncan's spot at the front of the room, and I took a deep breath. It suddenly felt like too much. Emma squeezed my hand, and I let that connection and the touch of Jesse's arm on my own soothe my frayed nerves.

"Before we start pretreatment today, I just want to talk to you about a few things. First, alongside your treatment, you have access to Michelle." Neenee pointed to a lady with long, blond hair and a kind smile standing on the side of the room. She waved. "Michelle is our resident therapist. She will hold some group sessions and meet with you all individually on a regular basis. Your mental health is just as important to us as your physical health."

Neenee gestured to someone else. "This is Pastor Noel. He will be here for any of you to talk to and will also carry out services in the ranch's chapel should you wish to attend." Pastor Noel's smile was warm. "Then, finally, is Mrs. Frank. She will be your educational supervisor."

Jesse groaned loudly, breaking the tension in the room by making everyone laugh—including Mrs. Frank. "We're here for life-saving treatment and we *still* have to do math?" Jesse said but followed up his complaint with a cheeky smirk. We all knew we would be continuing our studies. Many of us had our sights set on college or at least high school graduation. That didn't stop because we were here.

"I believe all of you can make it through this treatment with clean bills of health," Neenee said, conviction in her voice. "So we need you to keep living life normally."

Chills of excitement rushed through me. I glanced behind me at my parents. They were looking at me, hopeful expressions on their faces too.

This was my—*our*—chance at a new start.

Neenee stepped forward and relaxed her stance. She sat down on a chair at the front of the room. "Just a few more words that are a bit off script." I leaned closer, not wanting to miss a thing. "Rely on one another." She pointed at the eight of us. "I have been doing this a long time, with lots of different patients of all different ages. And I have found—and so has scientific research—that if you bond with the people going through this alongside you, it can help get you through treatment and into remission quicker."

I jumped a little when Jesse placed his hand on top of mine. I stared down at it. It was tanned and held the occasional scar, no doubt from years playing football.

I smiled to myself at the feel of his palm's warmth on my skin. Feeling bold, I gently turned over my hand until our palms met. Clearly being the most forthcoming out of us both, Jesse curled his fingers and threaded them through mine. I inhaled. I had never held a boy's hand before. I couldn't stop staring at our entwined fingers.

They fit together perfectly.

"And there is a reason we fought for so long for this ranch to be approved as a hospital," Neenee said, breaking me from staring at our hands. I looked up at her. She gestured to the floor-to-ceiling windows on one wall. "Nature is healing. Studies have shown that those fighting cancer respond better when surrounded by nature." The trees and foliage swayed in the light breeze outside, as if showing us their worth.

It was beautiful, serene. All I knew from hospitals were sterile white walls and antiseptic smells. I felt privileged to be at the ranch. Doing our treatment here would feel vastly different. "We also have therapy horses. Again, studies show that animals can help people heal. We are here for the trial's drugs and new chemo treatments, but don't underestimate how healing the people, the place, and the animals can be for you too," Neenee said.

The fear I had been feeling was gradually trickling away. Emma's and Jesse's hands in mine and the trees and horses outside had given me more hope than I'd dared to let myself have before now.

"Take walks regularly; see the horses, feed them, groom them at the stables—just make sure you tell us where you are at all times so we can monitor you. Like Dr. Duncan said, the price for this new, exciting treatment is the harsh side effects. We need to be sure you are okay, twenty-four seven." Neenee smiled, then moved toward the parents for a chat with them.

We patients were silent, reflective, until: "Jesse, bro, give me your hand." Chris grabbed hold of Jesse's hand and gripped it in his own. "Why am I being left out of the hand-holding train with y'all?"

I laughed along with Emma at Chris's petulant expression.

Jesse turned to him. "Sorry, man. I just don't feel that way toward you."

Chris threw away Jesse's hand and moved to the other side of Emma, taking hold of her free hand. "Fine. I'll hold Emma's, then."

Emma leaned into Chris's arm and rolled her eyes. Their senses of humor matched, and in the past couple of days, they had bounced off one another's personalities perfectly.

I finally let myself look at Jesse. "You can let go," I said softly, and nudged my chin to our joined hands. "The scary talk is over for the moment."

Jesse scrunched his nose up. It was a ridiculously attractive move. "Nah, I'm good." He squeezed my hand and then looked at the clock on the wall. "Did y'all read the welcome info in the rooms? They've put us into groups for the treatment. I'm in group two. What about you guys?"

"One," Emma and Chris said in unison, they released their joined hands and high-fived when they realized they'd be doing treatment together.

"Junebug?" Jesse asked.

"Two," I said, my pulse racing, and watched his face light up. A shiver of happiness ran down my spine at that.

"The schedule said group two has an hour until our scans. Want to duck outside for a while? Emma and Chris are up now," Jesse said.

I glanced across the room to my parents. They were still talking to Neenee. "Okay." A flutter of nerves burst in my chest.

"Have fun, you two," Emma said knowingly, and Chris waved goodbye.

I got to my feet and caught my dad's eye. I pointed outside to let him know where I was going. He nodded, then refocused on Neenee.

I thought Jesse would release my hand as we walked past the other group and out into the hallway, but he didn't. He tucked his football under his free arm but kept tight hold of me. I gripped my notebook to my chest and already felt words building within me. This feeling... it was new—it was... *nice*.

Bailey, one of the nurses, walked past us.

Jesse led us down the hallway and into the warmth of the outside. The smell of fresh air swept over me, and I smiled when the sun kissed my face. Only then did Jesse's hand release my own. As I stepped off the porch and onto the lawn, I looked out to the paddocks where the horses were grazing. The chestnut gelding I had developed a fondness for looked up and started walking toward us.

I made my way to the fence just as he did. The familiar smell of horse danced around me. I knew some people hated it, but it was comforting to me. The gelding lowered his head, and I ran my hand down his face, over his white blaze. I couldn't help the smile that grew on my face. As his head lowered farther, I pressed my forehead to his and just soaked this moment in.

"You *really* like horses, huh?" Jesse's gravelly voice came from behind me.

When I turned, he was leaning against a nearby tree, watching me.

I ran my hand down the gelding's neck and combed my fingers through his silky mane. "I adore them," I said, and tucked my notebook in the back pocket of my jeans so I could pat the gelding with both hands. I chuckled as he bobbed his head for more love when I momentarily stopped. "I used to ride, did show jumping and dressage."

"Used to?" Jesse questioned.

I lifted my leg. "Not long after I was diagnosed, I lost a lot of strength in my leg and haven't managed to regain it." I shrugged. "It impacted how I rode, so I pulled back from it." The echo of that heartache still lived inside me.

Jesse approached. It felt like there was a shift to the air as he closed the distance, like he was a force unto himself affecting the air around me. He reached out and patted the gelding's neck too. "My best friend is a cowboy, through and through. I've ridden a little with him, but I'm far from good."

He leaned over the fence as I kept making a fuss over the horse. He was beautiful.

"I've lost a lot of my strength in my throwing arm," he said, and I looked over at him in concern. He fiddled with his backwards Longhorns cap. "It sucks when your cancer not only takes away your health but what you love doing most too."

My hands stilled on the horse, and I turned to Jesse. He was staring out over the paddocks, to the horizon, and I saw a flicker of vulnerability on his handsome face. This brazen boy had revealed something to me that caused him pain. He turned to me and gave me a pasted-on smile. "But I'm determined to get it back." Jesse presented as a fun-loving jock, and I had only known him a few days, but I could see it was a bit of a mask and there was much more underneath.

But now wasn't the time to push.

I returned my attention to the horse and fixed his forelock that had gone awry. The gelding turned back to the paddock and walked away. As he left us, I wondered if I'd ever get back on a horse again.

"So," Jesse said, leaning back against the fence post. "Are you gonna talk to me about that notebook that's glued to your hands? I've been dying to know what it's about. You haven't even hinted at it in the past few days."

I mirrored his stance against the fence. I was normally reserved about my biggest passion, but with Jesse, even only knowing him a short time...I felt safe to share. When I looked to him again, he raised an eyebrow and tapped an invisible watch on his wrist. "I'm waiting, Junebug, and you know how limited we are with our *time*."

I shook my head at how he joked about cancer so openly, laughing. "We're reclaiming that time with this new treatment, remember?" I replied. When he tapped his wrist again, I said, "I want to be a writer—*no*." I shook my head. "I *am* a writer."

"What do you like to write?" he asked, attention locked on me, as though I was the most interesting person in the world.

I glanced down as I said, "I want to write love stories."

"*June*bug," Jesse said, pursing his lips. "I didn't think you had it in you!" He held up his hands. "Wait, are we talking buff fairies and vampires? Were you reading for research?"

I slapped him gently on the arm and rolled my eyes as I laughed again. "I don't want to write spicy romance, Jesse, though there is *nothing* wrong with that." I admonished him with a harsh stare.

He held his hands up in surrender.

I took a deep breath and really tried to convey my dream. "I *love* love stories—the kind that has your heart leaping from your chest. Ones that change a reader's life. Make them believe in true love. Soulmates. I want to write at least one great, epic love story that lasts through the ages." I felt slightly embarrassed by my confession, but Jesse appeared fascinated.

"You said you *want* to…" Jesse said, an implied question in his tone.

I sighed. "I haven't written a single love story yet. At least, not one like I want to."

"Why?"

I focused on the horses in the distance as I whispered, "Because I don't know what it feels like." I turned to Jesse, to see him frowning in confusion.

"What *what* feels like?"

"Love," I said on a defeated sigh. "I want to write about love, but I don't know what it feels like to *be* in love. Or to *be* loved." My heart fell, and for a moment, I let myself embrace a true fear. "And if this treatment doesn't work…I never will."

When only silence met my ears, I turned to Jesse to see an unreadable expression on his face. He was still holding the football at his chest, but his attention was focused entirely on me.

The tips of my ears burned under his heavy attention. I played with the end of my headscarf and said, "So now you know what the notebook is for," I said. "For the day that something happens and I can begin the love story I believe I was destined to write."

"You have the notebook on hand just in case?" he asked, and I immediately felt silly.

"Stupid, I know," I said, and stepped away from the fence.

Jesse reached out and placed his hand gently on my wrist, stopping me from heading back inside. "Not stupid," he said seriously, which made me swallow my embarrassment. "It's not stupid at all."

A rare serious expression on his face, he opened his mouth to speak again when Bailey opened the door behind us. "Jesse, June?" he called. "Your group is up."

I inhaled through my nose and headed back inside. Jesse caught up to me and put out his fist.

I looked up at him, puzzled.

"Group two for the win!" he said, and I met his fist bump with my own.

"Group two for the win," I echoed, and Jesse took my hand again, leading me inside.

The desire to write something burned through me again. It wasn't the start of a book. It wasn't even an idea. But maybe I could write a few sentences—a few sentences about a boy taking my hand in his and how it caused my heart to swell in my chest.

And if I only ever had that, at least it was something.

It was a start.

chapter seven

Jesse

Six days later...

I ROLLED OVER IN BED JUST IN TIME TO GRAB THE HOSPITAL-issued bucket beside me. I coughed as my body tried in vain to bring up whatever was left in my stomach—but there wasn't anything. Four days of the trial's super-powerful chemo cocktail had not been simply uncomfortable; it had been brutal. Sweat beaded on my forehead, and my throat felt so dry, I could barely swallow.

A knock sounded on my suite's door, and Susan, my nurse, came through. She had a cold, damp cloth and a fresh jug of water in her hands. "How are you doing, sweetie?" she asked. Susan had been my savior these past few days.

I hadn't seen anyone for five days since we'd been sent to our rooms for treatment. I had sat in bed and binged watched TV shows while receiving the chemo through the IV next to my bed. The immunotherapy started in a few days' time, right now we were on rest and I was so thankful that the chemo part of phase one was over. I had increasingly felt worse each day. Today, I felt completely broken. But I was getting antsy being in this room alone.

Everyone except for me had family with them to help them through. I wasn't bitter about it in the slightest, and I knew my mom would be here if she could be, but I was…I was *lonely*. If it wasn't for Susan, I had no doubts that the dark thoughts that were trying to break through would have won. Dr. Duncan had kept me on my antidepressants, and I was trying to be positive—I really was. But when your health declined, it was hard to see the light at the end of the tunnel.

I coughed one more time into the bucket, then sat up. "I'm just peachy. Never felt better," I said to Susan and gave her a wink.

She rolled her eyes, used to my antics by now, but I was also sure she saw straight through them. She helped me into a sitting position and pressed the cold cloth to my forehead.

"That feels amazing," I said, as I prayed that my stomach would calm just for an hour so I could try and sleep. I hadn't slept well the past couple of days.

"Take a sip," Susan said and handed me a glass with a straw. I sipped the water, and it felt perfect as it soothed my scratchy throat and dry tongue. She handed me a small cup of meds, and I knocked that cocktail back and winced as I fought to make them go down. "There was an anti-nausea pill in there too. Hopefully that'll kick in and give you some relief." Susan retrieved the dirty sick bucket like the saint she was and went into the bathroom. As she hummed cleaning out the bucket, tears pricked behind my eyelids.

God, I missed my mom. My mom would hum as she cleaned too. She'd read her book at my bedside while I recovered from the latest round of chemo. I missed my little sisters clamoring for my attention. I closed my eyes and fought back the sinking emotions again. I couldn't break. I *couldn't*. But I was a people person, and I was struggling with all this time alone. One thing I didn't want was time to dwell and think about what would happen if this trial didn't work. Nothing good came from all that time in my own head. And I needed this treatment to work.

It *had* to.

Susan came out of the bathroom and a lump thickened in my throat. As if she could see me fighting back my sudden emotion, she laid her hand on my shoulder. "You're doing amazing, Jesse. You're being so strong."

"Yeah?" I croaked, still unable to open my eyes. A stray tear fell anyway. I felt it escape the corner of my right eye, and the familiar texture of leather was suddenly under my hand. I tried to smile in appreciation, knowing Susan had given me my football. I blinked my eyes open and straightened my shoulders.

As I met Susan's gaze, she said, "Yes."

The sound of my phone vibrating on the bedside table pulled my attention. When a picture of me, my mom and two sisters filled the screen, the heaviness on my chest lifted like a balloon.

"I'll leave you to it," Susan said, tapping my hand. "Buzz if you need me."

"Thank you," I said, as I quickly wiped my eyes and accepted the video call.

"Jesse!" my sister Emily greeted. Her blond hair looked lighter than it did a week ago when I left McIntyre.

"Hey, baby girl," I said, just as Emily screeched at being pushed aside, and my youngest sister's face filled the screen.

"Jesse!" Lucy said. "I've been making you a card—"

"Shh!" Emily hissed. "That was meant to be a secret!"

"Oh…yeah," Lucy said, grimacing. "Oh well!"

I laughed, the sound doing more for my weak body than the meds had just done. The phone was pulled away from the ankle biters and my mom's face came into view. The minute she saw me, her smile fell.

"You're in pain," she said, knowing exactly how to read me like only mothers can.

"I'm okay," I said. It was true. Seeing my family had immediately lifted my mood. They made me feel stronger. Made me remember why I was here. I owed my mom so much.

"Baby…" my mom said, and I saw tears fill her eyes. "I wish I could be there. Maybe…" She trailed off, and I could see she was thinking something through in her head.

"No," I said, and she met my eyes. "I'm okay. You can't lose your job." I hated the way her bottom lip trembled. I couldn't imagine what this was like for her. I knew she thought she'd let me down by not coming to the ranch, but that just wasn't true.

She nodded, but I could see guilt plastered all over her face, along with exhaustion and stress. I hated what my illness and absence was doing to her.

"Y'all are still coming next weekend, right?" I asked.

Mom finally let in a smile and said, "Yes." My sisters were whisper-fighting in the background. Mom shook her head at them and said loudly, "And we are absolutely not surprising you with homemade cards!"

"Or homemade chocolate chip cookies!" Lucy shouted, and I couldn't hold back the burst of laughter that spilled out of me as Emily scolded her.

"Lucy! You just told him again!"

"Oops!" Lucy said, then I heard them running away and caught the familiar sound of the back door being opened and closed. They'd be running to their tree house. I could see it all so clearly in my head, and the homesickness swept in thick and fast.

Mom moved to sit on our well-worn couch and said, "Now tell me how you're really feeling."

I settled back in my bed and realized I still had the cold cloth on my forehead. I pulled it away and placed it on my bedside table. "It's rough," I said. I wanted to protect her, but I also needed to be honest with someone. "This new chemo and the new drug therapy they've got us on..." I shook my head. "But if it works—"

"*When*," my mom said.

I smirked at her tenacity. "*When* it works, it'll have all been worth it."

Mom was quiet for a few moments, just staring at me. "And how are you, in yourself?" Her eyes seemed to bore into my soul. "How are you coping with everything?"

I took a deep breath. "I'm okay. Just trying to keep positive."

She stared at me a touch too long, clearly trying to see if I was lying.

"I promise, Mom. I'm doing okay emotionally at the moment. I swear I'll tell you if I'm not."

"Okay," she said, finally satisfied. "I'm so proud of you, Jesse. I don't think you'll ever realize how much. You've been through so much. *Too* much." Her bottom lip trembled.

"Mom," I said, fighting back my own grief. "I can't wait to see y'all." My voice was breaking, but Mom didn't mention it. She just let me show my emotion. Nothing good came from me bottling it up.

"I'm counting the days until our visit," she said. "How are your friends? Chris and Emma?"

"The same, really. Haven't seen them in a few days. The treatment is hitting us all pretty hard." She nodded, then said, "And June?" There was a different inflection to her voice when she mentioned June.

I raised an inquisitive eyebrow.

Mom laughed. "Jesse, I know when my boy has met a pretty girl, and I can tell when he likes her as *more* than a friend."

"Great place to pick up a girl, Mom. A hospital."

"Love finds us in strange places, Jesse," she said, a singsong note to her voice. "It can sweep in hard and fast."

Her comment gave me permission to think of June. Hell, who was I kidding? I'd been thinking of her nonstop for the past several days. I'd heard murmured conversations through our shared wall and the sound of her throwing up as much as me. I desperately wanted to go next door and sit with her each afternoon when our chemo infusions were done. It gave me strength. I missed company, and it was her company that I was particularly craving.

And I really liked holding her hand.

But I hadn't dared go and see her. I was ballsy by nature but would never intrude on someone when they were on the ropes.

"June is…" I shrugged, unable to find words. "I don't know. Different, I guess?" I felt my lips curl into a smile. "She's the most beautiful girl I've ever met."

"I can't wait to meet her, Jess," Mom said. "She sounds lovely."

Then she changed the subject. "Me and the girls went to the game last night." A pang of jealousy hit me. I gripped my football tighter to my side. "The announcer talked about you, and all your friends and teachers were asking how you were and wishing you the best. Coach most of all. The whole stadium prayed for you."

"Yeah?" I asked.

Mom nodded. "Coach said he sent you the game film for you to watch." I hadn't checked my email yet, so I'd be sure to later. "They're counting the days until you come home," Mom said, full of hope, and it was the lift I needed. She lowered her voice, then added, "And the stand-in QB was no match for you."

I chuckled. "You have to say that."

"I do," she said playfully, "but it doesn't make it any less true."

"I love you, Mom, so much." The past several months, I always told her I loved her. If anything ever happened to me, I wanted her to always know that she was the best mom there could have been, that she had done all she could to save me. When my father left, she'd kept us all standing. I tried to support her as much as I could, but she never let me be anything other than a kid. And she held me up when my daddy's absence crushed me.

"I love you too, Sunshine," she said, and I smiled at that childhood term of endearment. "Let me go get the gremlins so they can say goodbye too."

When I hung up the phone a few minutes later, I took another sip of water and was instantly relieved that my stomach wasn't trying to eject it. The anti-sickness meds were kicking in, and I decided I needed to get out of this room for a while.

I grabbed my phone and downloaded my emails and found the

email from my coach. I put on my slippers and left my room. It was quiet in the hallway for the middle of the day—completely opposite to how the halls were the first few days.

I headed to the cinema room I had yet to visit.

Once there, I sat down in one of the plush chairs. I kept the volume low to not disturb anyone, though in a house this size, I was sure that wouldn't matter, then kicked back the recliner and connected my phone to the movie screen. In seconds, my team was before me. Sipping on the water I had brought with me, a warm sensation burst in my chest at seeing my teammates came on the screen. My school field was illuminated under the Friday night lights. I itched to be there, dressed in blue and white and leading my boys to victory.

I watched Gavin, the junior QB who'd been forced to take my place. When my mom had mentioned him, I'd been riddled with jealousy, but watching him step up and fill in for me made me feel nothing but guilt. This kid was nowhere near ready for varsity, but he was there when my team needed him—when *I* needed him while I healed.

I groaned as, only minutes into the game, our offensive line fell away and Gavin got sacked.

"Ouch!" I heard behind me. When I turned my head, Mr. Scott, June's dad, was standing there watching the screen too.

"Sorry, sir," I said, and quickly paused the game. "I didn't mean to disturb anyone."

Mr. Scott shook his head. "You didn't, son. I was getting Claire a drink and saw that godawful sack. It stopped me in my tracks."

I laughed and said, "That's Gavin. My stand-in."

Mr. Scott moved around the room and took a seat on the recliner beside me. I watched him, my eyebrows pulled down in confusion. He shrugged at me. "June is asleep, and Claire looked halfway there too when I left. I'm sure they won't mind if I'm gone for a little while longer."

The mention of June had my stomach tensing. "How is Junebug?"

Mr. Scott fought a smirk, and I kind of wanted the ground to swallow me up.

I wasn't really experienced with dads. I cleared my throat. "I mean *June*."

Mr. Scott shook his head, clearly amused. "June*bug* is doing better. Had a rough few days there though." He regarded me knowingly. "All of you seem to have had a rough few days."

I fiddled with my cap. "Yeah, but I just couldn't stay in my room alone anymore." The words were out of my mouth before I could stop them. I saw that same flash of sympathy in Mr. Scott's eyes that I hated receiving. But I knew he wasn't pitying me—more just understanding that being sick alone was zero fun.

"I thought you might have been in to see June," he said.

"I didn't want to disturb her," I said.

"Son," Mr. Scott said turning toward me. The word *son* felt strange to hear, especially coming from a father figure. It was like a stab in my heart. Mr. Scott, just talking to me, caring about me, a relative stranger, made me realize what a deadbeat mine really was. "I'm pretty sure I'm right when I say this, but my daughter would not think a visit from you would disturb her in the slightest."

I stopped breathing at that, wondering what June had said to her folks about me. "Erm." I shifted in my seat. "Well, that's good to know, sir."

Mr. Scott smothered his amusement with his hand and pointed to the screen, sitting back in the recliner. "Now, let's get this game restarted." He looked over to me. "I have a wife and a daughter that just don't get football, Jesse." Mr. Scott patted the arm of his chair. "While we're here at Harmony, you might have to be my football-watching buddy. That sound good to you?" he asked, and I could barely speak.

This is what a good dad looks like, I thought. The realization that I was missing out on that was heavy on my heart.

"Yes, sir," I said, my voice gravelly as I tried not to show how his offer had affected me. "It sure as heck does." I pressed Play on the video and lost myself to the game.

And just for a couple of hours, I didn't feel quite so alone.

chapter eight

June

"I DIDN'T EVEN THINK," CHRIS SAID AS HE AND EMMA FOLLOWED me down the hallway. I'd requested sick buckets and water to be brought down to the movie room too.

My stomach turned when I recalled the conversation I'd had with my daddy when I woke this morning. I had thought of Jesse often the past few days—of course I had. In fact, I hadn't stopped thinking about him since treatment began. He was alone in his room, and I hated that but didn't want to impose myself on him.

According to my daddy, in his own words, "*I sat with Jesse for a few hours yesterday. Killed me to see him all by himself. Y'all are meant to be there for each other. No one going through this should be alone. Jesse is a good kid, kind and friendly. If his family can't be here for him, then we will be.*"

My heart had beat in double time when my daddy had said that, conviction on his face. My daddy liked Jesse, I could tell, and that made my heart sing. So this morning, despite the aches and pains and feeling nauseous, I'd gone to find Chris and Emma to see if they wanted to come with me. Neenee had told us that leaning on others in the same position was beneficial, so that's what I was doing. We were on a rest period and needed to rally.

Daddy told me he had already seen Jesse in the movie room again a half hour ago, so that's where I knew I had to be too. As we rounded the corner to the movie room, *Gladiator* was playing on the big screen. Jesse was laid back on a recliner, his glass of water and nutritional drink beside him. I sat next to him, and Jesse did a double take.

"Junebug?" he said in shock. Then looked up to see Chris and Emma taking their seats too.

"Mind if we join you?" I asked.

Chris held out his fist for Jesse to bump.

Emma waved. "Hey, Jesse."

"What are you doing here?" Jesse asked. His green eyes scanned me just as thoroughly as the MRI machine Dr. Duncan made us go in. "Are you feeling okay? How are you coping? Do you need to go to bed and rest?"

He was so considerate. And I noticed that as much as he was asking us all, it was mostly directed at me.

Feeling bold, I laid my hand over his. "I'm okay. Being sick, feeling tired, the usual." I shrugged. "But I—*we*—wanted to be here with you."

Jesse tipped his head to the side as he observed me. Understanding lit his eyes. "Your dad told you where I've been."

I squeezed his hand, blushing when he flipped his hand and linked his fingers with mine like it was the most natural thing in the world. I inhaled a stuttered breath. Why did my body feel this way when he touched me? I couldn't explain the pull. "He mentioned it, but that doesn't mean I haven't been thinking of you too." It took be a whole lot of courage to admit that out loud.

My throat thickened as I watched Jesse's eyes shine with unshed tears. "Thank you, Junebug," he said, his voice barely above a whisper. *You're not alone*, I wanted to add, but I didn't have the courage just yet to express that sentiment. Not with Emma and Chris here too.

"*Gladiator*," Chris said excitedly. "Good choice, Jess."

Jesse smiled. "I figured I'd make use of the movie room until classes start and we're forced to endure both sickness and math." He smiled, and it was the cheeky grin I loved on him. "Though I'm not sure what will make me more nauseous, chemo or algebraic equations."

"Amen to that, brother," Chris said, and pretended to high five Jesse from a few seats away.

"Hey!" Emma said, like she was offended on math's behalf. "What did algebraic equations ever do to you?"

"Err...exist," Chris said, and I burst out laughing. He regarded Emma with incredulity. "Don't tell me you're a math nerd, Em?"

Emma straightened her shoulders. "Mathlete regional champion, three years in a row," she said smugly. I already knew this. Emma had shown me pictures of her and her classmates holding the trophy when I was hanging out in her room.

Chris groaned. "June, tell me math doesn't have your love too."

I felt the heat of Jesse's stare, and he squeezed the hand that was still in his. I didn't think he planned to let go anytime soon. "Afraid not. Words are my drug of choice."

Chris groaned again, making us all chuckle. "I'm not sure that's any better."

Chris motioned from him to Jesse, then to me and Emma. "Jocks and nerds coexisting in Harmony. Who said adversity couldn't unite people?"

Emma grabbed an ice cube from her glass of water and threw it at Chris. He caught it in the air, threw it in his mouth, and began to crunch it with his teeth.

"Pig," Emma said, and earned a teasing grin from Chris.

This was already better, I realized. Being here with friends was already better than being in my room. I loved my parents more than life itself, but they didn't understand what it was like feeling this exhausted, this sick. They didn't understand the fight and what it took just to exist with death a half step behind you.

"Penny for your thoughts, Junebug," Jesse whispered as he leaned in close. Emma and Chris were squabbling about something else beside us. I rolled my head to the left, inching closer to where he was. He had dark circles under his eyes and the skin on his cheeks were slightly cracked, yet he still looked so unbelievably handsome.

I tightened my grip on his hand. "I'm just thankful we have each other." But as I retained eye contact, shivers running in relays went up and down my spine. "I'm…" I swallowed my nerves and said, "I'm real glad I'm here…with you."

Dimples popped in Jesse's cheeks as he brought our hands up to his mouth and grazed the back of mine with his lips. I was breathless, words and feelings rushing through me in a torrent. "Ditto."

"You ever wonder if that's what it's like?" Emma said softly, pulling our attention to her. On the big screen, the main character was walking through fields of wheat, fingertips running over the tops as he made his way back to his family in the afterlife.

"I hope so," Jesse said from beside me. "Or something like it." We all fell silent then, watching a serene depiction of heaven before us, the beautiful soundtrack making my skin break out into goose bumps. There was one thing for certain: when you were diagnosed terminal, what happened after death became a constant wonder.

Jesse lifted my hand again, and butterflies swooped in my stomach as he pressed our joined hands against his cheek. I wasn't sure what heaven was or what it would look like, but while I was here, fighting to live, I thought the ranch may not be so bad if I had this boy beside me, making me feel things I'd only ever read about in my favorite books.

"This is what we have to do," Chris said, pulling us away from the beauty of the scene. He circled a finger in the air, encompassing all of us. "We do this when we have treatment."

Just then, Bailey arrived with jugs of water, the dreaded orange drink, and buckets. Then, Dr. Duncan popped in to monitor our levels before leaving us alone again.

When they'd left, Chris continued. "We come here, together, and fight through this as one—while watching movies, naturally."

"*Naturally,*" Emma echoed sarcastically.

"Like *The Breakfast Club* but for sick kids," Jesse said, that humorous tone in his voice back. I'd missed his jokes so much. He snapped his fingers. "Ah-ha! I have it." He paused dramatically. "Chemo Club, where, just like the John Hughes film, we get up to our own shenanigans."

"And by shenanigans, do you mean puking and cold sweats?" Chris said.

Jesse winked at Chris. "You've got it, bro." Jesse looked to me and said, "Does that sound good, Junebug?" There was almost a nervousness in his timbre, like he was worried I might say no. That I might not want to be part of Chemo Club and retreat to my own room again.

He didn't want to be alone. I was again seeing more of his hidden vulnerability. "It sounds perfect," I said and was given the beautiful gift of a wide Jesse Taylor smile that I knew would send many girls' hearts skipping.

Just at that second, Chris grabbed a bucket and retched into it. Bailey must have stayed close by, as he was there in seconds, helping him through.

Jesse leaned over and held out the fist of his hand that wasn't holding mine. "You still group two for the win, Junebug?"

"Always," I said, and bumped his fist.

When Chris finished throwing up, he said, "We best keep the volume high on these movies, or we're not gonna stand a chance of hearing them when we all start upchucking." We laughed, only for me to suddenly need my bucket too.

Jesse kindly rubbed my back as I wretched.

Together, Neenee had said. We would get through this better if we stuck together, so that's what I intended to do.

The ticking of the clock on my bedroom wall was going to make me scream. Sleep evaded me, an effect of the steroids we'd been given. It was the same every time I had been on them throughout the past year. I looked up at the time and saw that it was just before five in the morning.

I was an early bird by nature, though never quite this early. But I adored sunrises, so I decided to go outside. I needed fresh air anyway. Another week had passed and we were on our break from the antibody treatment. My mama and daddy were in the parents' residence, and I was alone.

Throwing a blanket around my shoulders, I opened the doors to the porch outside. It had chairs and a swing and a sweeping view of the horses in the field. Darkness was slowly lifting, and the sun was rising, bringing a golden glow over the ranch. It looked unnatural, like it was some fancy CGI edit on a movie.

I stepped off the porch and headed to the paddock. Ginger, the chestnut gelding I came out here often to fuss, came toward me. He suited his name—he was as vibrant in color as his namesake spice. I ran my hand down his blaze like he preferred and pressed a kiss on his head.

"You're such a good boy," I said, and patted his neck.

I listened to Ginger's breathing, it's rhythm steady like a meditation. I inhaled and exhaled only to hear, "If I let you kiss my forehead, will I be a good boy too?"

I laughed before I'd even turned around. Around Jesse Taylor, I had laughed more in a week than I had in the past year. I had no idea how he did it, but he definitely made life much more entertaining.

Without turning my head, I patted Ginger and said, "Is the big, bad QB jealous of a horse?"

"Hell yes I am!" he said, and this time, I did turn, only to see him swinging in an egg chair on his suite's little porch, a red plaid blanket over his legs. He was wearing a long-sleeve black top, and this time, his head was free of a cap. I realized I didn't have my headscarf on either.

I froze, and anxiety rocketed through me. I was never without my headscarf. It was silly, I knew it was, but it crushed me to be seen without it. My breathing came fast, and I found myself looking down at my hand. I flexed my fingers to be sure they felt like my own.

They did for now.

"Junebug?" Jesse's voice made me look up and broke me free of my spiral.

I placed my head on my hand on reflex, and Jesse frowned. "I'll just retrieve my headscarf," I said, and made a move to go back to my room. I rushed and, in seconds, was back outside, my headscarf firmly in place and my anxiety settled.

Jesse watched me closely, and I could clearly see the question on his face. But he was a gentleman about it and didn't comment.

I approached where he sat, keeping the blanket around my shoulders for warmth. I was feeling the chill constantly these days. Jesse nodded in the direction of Ginger. "I think he's been waiting to see if you'd come out."

"He has?" I asked, looking back at the gelding who was stealing my heart.

"He wasn't the only one," Jesse said, and I whipped my attention back to him. My blushes had lessened around him, though the butterflies hadn't—not even a smidge.

"How long have you been out here?" I asked.

Jesse shrugged. "A coupla hours maybe. Couldn't sleep."

"Steroids?"

"Bingo," he said, pointing at me, then tipping his head to the side. "You?"

I nodded, then stretched, feeling my aching joints.

Jesse shifted over on the egg seat. "Care to join me?"

"Is there room?" I asked.

"Junebug, you weigh as much as a feather, and I've lost all the muscle I ever had. I'm practically a walking string bean at this point. We can fit."

I studied the chair, assessing.

Jesse tapped the space he'd made beside him. "Plus, I'm pretty sure this egg is a double yolker."

I sputtered out a laugh at that.

Jesse grinned. "Come on, Junebug. I'm cold, and so are you by the look of it. Get warm beside me."

I shook my head at his cheeky expression but found myself moving toward him. I sat down on the chair, ignoring his look that screamed *See? We do fit.* Jesse placed his blanket over us both, then used his foot to swing us back and forth. The motion made me feel all cozy and content, but the woodsy, smoky scent of Jesse kept my body wired.

"Are you warm enough?" he asked. His voice had lowered in volume and held a hint of gravel. I had realized that was how he sounded when he was as affected by me as I was him—it was his tell.

"I am," I said, casting my gaze to the horizon, as the semicircle of the sun began to climb higher into the sky. "This is beautiful," I said, resting my head back against the egg chair.

I couldn't get comfortable, and Jesse offered, "You can rest against my shoulder if you'd like."

I hesitated for just a moment before I followed my heart and pressed my cheek to Jesse's shoulder. It was soft and comforting and made me completely relax. I smiled as Ginger joined the bay mare he obviously saw as his companion in the paddock.

"You looked good without the headscarf, Junebug," Jesse said.

Every part of me tensed, and I reached up to play with the tail of my scarf.

In the stretched-out silence, Jesse said, "You believe that, don't you?"

I shifted when my eyes filled with tears, trying to quickly wipe them dry, but I knew Jesse had seen by the way he tried to move in closer. The truth was, I didn't believe it. Over two years of treatment in, I couldn't see it. My confidence had taken as much of a hit as my health.

"I...I struggle with how I look now," I confessed, shock wrapping around me. I couldn't believe I had admitted that to Jesse. I shook my head. I didn't look at him. It was easier sharing these truths without meeting his face.

"I've never been a vain person, but..." I sighed heavily. "I can't really explain it."

"Junebug," Jesse said, and pressed his cheek to my head. "I mean this with my entire heart: you are stunning." My breathing grew shaky. Jesse's cheek moved against my headscarf. "If anything, your headscarf hides it. You don't need anything, not even hair, to be beautiful."

I stared out at the paddock and my vision blurred. There was no lie in his steady voice. And it made me sad that I couldn't see it in myself. My nerves skyrocketed as, reaching up to my head, I slowly pulled off the headscarf. The morning air kissed my bald head, and it took everything I had not to run back into my room and hide.

I lifted my head, and Jesse watched my every move. I dropped my eyes to my hand. It still felt like mine, but it was trembling.

"Stunning," Jesse said, and gave me the sweetest smile.

I exhaled and felt something I didn't expect—a sliver of happiness that I had just opened up to someone—no, not just *someone*. Jesse. And by the look on his face, I knew what he said was true. For some reason, he really did think I was beautiful.

"You look good too," I said, fighting a blush. I slowly brought my hand up toward his head. "Can I?" I asked. Jesse leaned forward, giving silent permission, and I ran my fingertips along his scalp. It was smooth and silky under my touch. It was curious—I saw true beauty in Jesse that, for some reason, I couldn't see in myself.

But I wanted to, more than anything.

"What color was your hair?" I asked, bringing my hand back to my side and resting my cheek against the cushioned back of the swing so I could meet Jesse's eyes.

"Light brown," he said, and I could picture it in my head.

"Long or short?"

"Longish," he said, then smiled at me. "And it was curly."

"Really?" I asked, wondering how curly. "Do you have a picture?"

Jesse pulled out his phone and searched through it. Finally, he turned the screen, and I was met with a smiling Jesse in his football uniform, loosely curled hair that was a few inches long, enough to give him that just rolled out of bed look. He was stunning in this picture, but… "You're just a handsome without it," I said, surprised by my own candor.

"Well, hair doth not maketh the man," he said, and I giggled at his terrible attempt at an English accent.

"Look at Jesse Shakespeare here!" I teased, and Jesse lifted his hand and ran his thumb over my cheek. My breath paused, and I was pretty sure all the air around us did too.

"You like literature, Junebug. I thought I'd try and impress you and shoot my shot." I swallowed back a spatter of nerves that danced inside of me, and then Jesse lifted his hand toward my head. "Can I?" he asked.

My anxiety slammed back into me.

Jesse must have seen it because he shook his head. "I'm sorry, Junebug. I shouldn't have pushed."

He lowered his hand, but I took hold of his wrist before he dropped it to his side.

His eyes were wide. "Honestly, June, I shouldn't have asked—"

"Please," I pushed out. "I…" I took a deep breath, centering myself the best I could. "I want you too."

Carefully and tenderly, Jesse's calloused fingertips ran over my bald scalp. Goose bumps broke out all over me, and I shivered at how strange it felt. Jesse's hand paused. "I'm sorry," he said, pulling his hand back.

"No, please don't stop," I said, surprising myself. "It just tickles." I smiled and urged him continue by bringing his hand back to my head. "No one has touched my head before."

"Do you have a picture of you before cancer?" he asked.

I reached into the pocket of my pajamas and pulled out my cell. I found a picture my daddy had taken of me while on a trip to the Texan novelist Katherine Anne Porter's home. I turned it to show Jesse, completely self-conscious. I looked so different now. I was thinner, paler, and bald. My biggest fear was that he'd see the me from before and wonder what the heck he was doing here with the me from now.

Jesse studied the picture, taking in my long, dark hair that fell in waves past my shoulders. It was thick and healthy. Then, handing me my cell back, said, "You're just as beautiful without hair now too."

I studied his face to make sure he meant it. There was nothing but 100 percent honesty in his face.

Jesse lowered his hand but took hold of mine and gripped it tightly. We stared in silence at the rising sun, and I thought back to his picture from before cancer.

"How did you find out you were sick?" I asked.

Jesse shifted in his seat. He laid his cheek on the top of my head. His cheek was soft, and I couldn't help but laugh. "What?" he asked in confusion.

"Your cheek is the warmest hat I've ever had."

"Then I'll sit with you as much as you need me to, Junebug. Anything for you." The butterflies swooped and soared in my stomach. Clearing his throat, he said, "By the time we realized I was sick, it was already too late."

I froze at that and traced the small scars on the back of Jesse's hand with my free hand's fingertips. I felt him shiver and couldn't help but adore how it felt to cause such a reaction within him. I'd gone from being terrified to show him my true self to feeling content to sit as the me from now by his side.

"Being a football player, I was used to aches and pains. I trained hard and had to fight to keep my weight on. My fitness was my priority. I'm naturally leaner than I need to be for a QB, so I didn't question why I was losing so much weight or why my throwing arm was hurting—it was always somewhat sore, as I used it so much."

I could see that being the case. Although they weren't my friends at school, anyone could see the football team trained crazy hard.

Jesse sighed. "It wasn't until I collapsed on the field during training that the doc tested my blood. They thought I might be anemic or something, and that was why I was losing color in my face." He squeezed my hand tighter. I pressed my cheek into his shoulder, trying to give silent support. "My throwing arm was weakening, and it was agony. We thought maybe I'd torn something. The doc ran more tests. We didn't know at the time, but he'd seen an anomaly in my blood—my leukemia had gathered in my shoulder and that was what was causing me all the pain.

"Two days later, I was diagnosed with AML, stage four."

I closed my eyes. That had to have been brutal.

"It was only four months ago." I lifted my head in surprise. Jesse circled his finger to indicate the ranch. "That's why I was a good candidate for here. I was so far gone that the usual treatment barely touched me." He swallowed, and I saw a flash of fear shining in his eyes. "I didn't know if I'd even make it to this point."

"Jesse," I whispered. He must have been so scared. The conversation he'd had with my daddy when I'd first arrived now made sense. "That's how my daddy saw highlights of you playing. You really *were* playing with cancer. You just didn't know."

"Yeah," he said on a sorrowful sigh. "It's been hard but not as hard as on my family." He swallowed his emotion back, his Adam's apple bobbing in his throat. "I'm the man of the house, Junebug. Have been for as long as I can remember." Jesse looked up at the brightening sky. "I had a plan, a dream I was determined to make come true. I was gonna go to UT, play for the Longhorns, get drafted to the NFL, and become the next Peyton Manning. I was gonna buy my mom a house and send my sisters to college and just…*live*, you know? Give my mom and family everything they deserved."

He exhaled and his breath shook. "Now, she's stuck with thousands of dollars of medical debt that she can't afford and is unable to leave her job to see me through this trial." A tear fell from his eye and just about broke my heart. "She doesn't deserve this, Junebug. None of them do."

Tears pricked behind my eyelids as Jesse let me see though one of the cracks in his ever-cheery demeanor. I wiped the tear from his cheek with my thumb, then held his cheek, my palm to his damp skin. "Not once, when you were talking just now, did you mention yourself." Jesse searched my eyes. "You're a good man, Jesse Taylor. And one way or another, the world will see that. I promise."

Jesse smiled through his sorrow, and I thought for a moment that he would kiss me. But instead, he asked, "What about you?"

I leaned back against the chair and faced him. "I've been fighting it for a couple of years," I said. "Diagnosed stage two, but the chemo and drugs didn't work on me." I tapped my bad knee. "The leukemia gathered in my knee for me." I remembered the day I felt so weak that my parents took me to be assessed. "I was riding at the barn and didn't have the strength to pull myself up on the horse's back. Then, as I tried, I cried out when an excruciating pain sliced through my knee. It was crippling and I couldn't walk."

"Hello, AML," Jesse said.

"Hello, AML," I repeated. I looked at Ginger. "I didn't get a place here at first," I said.

Jesse placed his thumb under my chin and pulled me back to face him.

"Someone didn't make it, and I got their place," I confessed. My voice trembled when I thought of the person who should have been here but had passed away before they could. I lifted my hand and held Jesse's wrist. "I nearly never got this chance."

"You were meant to be here, Junebug," Jesse said, his voice strong. "I don't know why, but I believe it with every cell in my body—including the too many white cells that just won't fuck off."

I laughed though my tears, my throat sore but heart dancing with Jesse's always-needed dose of levity. I kept laughing until my chest ached. It felt good. Jesse studied me like I was a precious painting. I sobered quickly when he said, "I have something for you."

"You do?" I asked, surprised.

He reached under the egg chair and pulled out his pad of drawing paper. It wasn't until now that I noticed the smudge of charcoal on his hand. He opened the pad, and I gasped, as staring back at me was…*me*.

"Jesse," I whispered, as the most realistic drawing of me lifted off the page. It was after I'd held Ginger's face in my hands, after I'd had my eyes closed as I pressed my forehead to his. My hand ghosting along his blaze. It looked serene; it looked… "Beautiful," I said, wanting to run my fingertips over the intricate charcoal details. I faced Jesse. "Jesse… you are so talented." I shook my head, awed at what I was seeing. "It's so realistic, it looks like a black-and-white photograph."

Jesse shrugged off my praise. "I had to draw you," he said, and my heartbeat raced at his confession. "When I saw you that day with Ginger, before we started our treatment"—Jesse's eyes lost focus, and I knew he was picturing the scene in his mind's eye—"you looked perfect."

Jesse pulled it from the pad and handed it to me. "For you," he said, and I took off him like it was priceless—and it was to me.

"Thank you," I whispered, unable to speak any louder. "I'm honored."

When I looked back up at Jesse, he was wearing an expression I couldn't decipher. He shifted forward, and I held my breath, making me lightheaded. "I've never been kissed before," I said, hating how childish that made me feel.

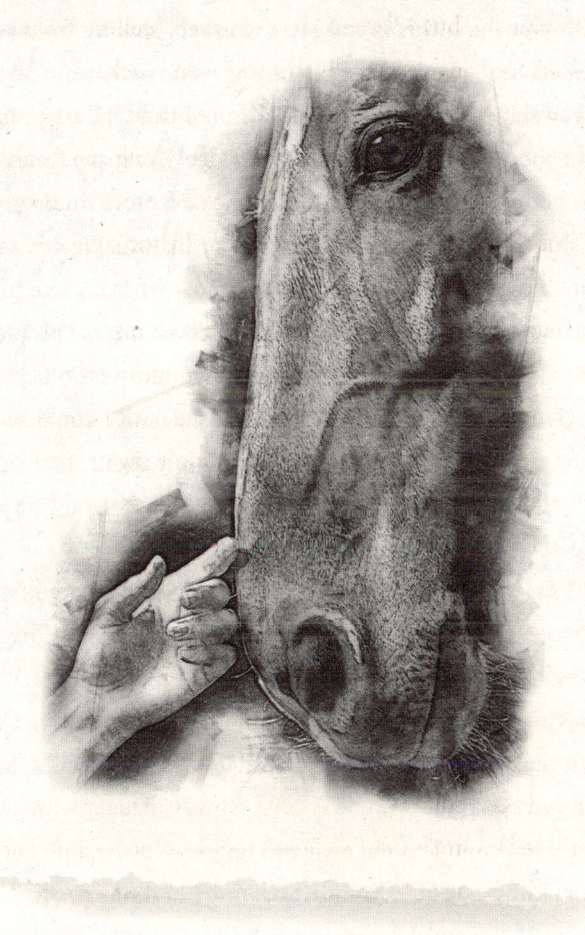

He moved in closer, and I placed my hand on his chest.

Jesse stilled, like I was rejecting him. "I'm sorry," he began to say, moving back.

"No!" I said, and Jesse sat back in our chair, waiting for me to speak. "Do you think this is too fast?" I asked, stalling from what I really wanted too, from feeling his lips against mine, from showing him my true self—including the parts of me I thought were stained. I'd thought about what this moment would feel like many times. Now that it was here, my nerves were holding me back from finding out.

Jesse studied me and, without humor or his usual levity, said, "I might only be seventeen, Junebug, but I know what it's like to have little time left. And as much as I want us to come out of this place in remission, cancer has taught me that nothing in life is too fast. Time is relative. How I feel about you…" He paused, and I could see him trying to find words. "It's not about time. It's not about what right or wrong. It's about connection and wanting to be with you every day." He shrugged. "Does it feel too fast to you?"

"No," I said, shaking my head. Jesse was right. When you'd been told you were dying, a catalogue of missed opportunities played in your head like a movie, showing you things you wished you'd done earlier, making you mourn things you might never get to do. Cancer taught you that death waits for no one, and you had to cling to life's joys while you could.

"Okay," I said, and I curled my hand on Jesse's chest, into his long-sleeved top. I was sure I felt his heart beating fast underneath.

"You sure?" Jesse said, leaning in close.

I nodded, keeping my eyes open until the very last moment, just to be sure this was really happening. Jesse's woodsy scent wrapped around me first, then his soft lips pressed against mine. In that moment, against the backdrop of the Texan sunrise on an idyllic ranch, I let the warmth of Jesse's affection cocoon me.

It felt like magic.

All that I had dreamed was nothing compared to the real thing. Jesse's hand moved to the back of my head, gently holding me against him. I held on tighter to his shirt and embraced every single second of this kiss. My heart swelled, my stomach danced, and my soul sang with joy.

When Jesse pulled back a fraction, breaking the kiss, I brushed my hand against his cheek. No words were spoken, and we both bathed in this newfound closeness, until he whispered, "Write me for you."

"What?" I whispered back in confusion.

Jesse met my eyes, keeping just an inch from me as he searched them. "Write me for you. In your great love story. Fall for me." He pressed his forehead against mine. "Allow me to fall for you. Write me for you."

My pulse raced, as did my breathing. Jesse saying those words... He couldn't... He didn't...

"You would want that?" I asked, dumbfounded. Jesse was beautiful inside and out. He was funny and loved by everyone who met him. And he wanted me?

Jesse smiled, and if there had been anything left within me that could have gotten faster, it would have joined the fray. "Junebug, I'm not sure if I've made it obvious, but you've kind of knocked me off my feet."

I smiled too.

"I'm kinda obsessed with you." He held his hands up defensively. "In the most non-stalkerish and non-creepy way possible."

I laughed loudly, the sound causing birds in the surrounding trees to scatter to the dawn skies. Jesse laughed too as our sweet moment was disturbed by a chorus of shocked avian squawks. When the birds flew away and peace had been restored, I said, "I'm kinda obsessed with you too."

Jesse's smile was blinding. He kissed me again, then held up his fist. "Group two for the win," he said.

"Group two for the win," I echoed and laid my head against his chest.

Jesse wrapped his arm around me, and I was lost to pure contentment. As I stared at the sun, now high in the sky, the beginning of our love story came to my mind...

When I arrived at Harmony Ranch, I knew it would change my life, just not in the way I expected. I expected to be healed, or I expected to die. What I didn't expect was to meet a country boy who would utterly change my life...

chapter nine

Jesse

Several days later...

I TAPPED MY FOOT ON THE FLOOR AS I WAITED FOR THE TRUCK TO come up the driveway. I checked my watch just as the familiar, red, beat-up Chevy came into view.

I pushed myself to my feet. It wasn't as easy as it sounded I was exhausted and every part of me ached—but nothing was gonna stop me from greeting my family. I went and opened the ranch's main doors and made it to the porch just in time for my mom and sisters to reach me. Emily's and Lucy's eyes fixed right on me, and like a double tornado, they ran, slamming into my legs and almost knocking me off my feet with the force. I gritted my teeth from the twinge of pain they caused in my hip but hugged them back.

They squeezed me tightly, only for Lucy to tip her head back to see my face and say, "Jesse, you don't look too good."

I laughed at her forever-honest reviews of my health. Emily slapped Lucy on the arm, then hugged me more gently. "I've missed you," Emily whispered.

I kissed her on her head. "I missed you too, baby girl."

I stepped back as my mom walked up. "Sunshine," she greeted and wrapped her arms around me. The past couple of weeks had been so hard. I'd held it together the best I could, but a hug from my mom had me fighting back tears. She rubbed my back, then pulled back to scan me with her eyes. I could tell she thought I looked awful by her worried expression.

"I'm doing good, I promise, even though it might not look it," I said. "We get assessed again at the end of the month. Dr. Duncan said there should be markers in our blood already indicating how we're responding to the treatment."

"It's too intense," Mom said, worrying her lip.

"It is intense, but I can handle it," I said nonchalantly, and waved them into the ranch to change the discourse. She didn't need to know about the deep pangs of sadness that hit me more and more each day or about the nights I worried I couldn't do the treatment anymore. I needed to be strong for my family. They'd been through enough.

Besides, today was about fun. The day was already getting warm, and we had a cookout later. It was family weekend at the ranch. My mom had managed to get the weekend off work to attend. I couldn't be more thankful.

I walked them through the hallway and to my suite. I passed June's room, but she was at the stables, grooming Ginger with Emma. It was one of their BFF activities. And I knew how much June adored spending time with Emma.

I must have been staring at June's room a few seconds too long as Mom raised her eyebrow, and I shook my head, laughing. We entered my suite, and my mom moved straight to the growing amount of drawings on my wall. There were many showing the rural view from the back porch, the horses in the field, Emma and Chris sitting together on the movie room's recliners—somehow, I'd managed to catch their incessant mockery of one another in the art. There were several angles of the nurses' hands as they changed the IVs and handed me my meds, Dr. Duncan as he studied his notes at the side of my bed, Susan as she brought me in water…then one of June, looking off into the distance, her notebook in her hands, the tail of her headscarf blowing in the mild Texas wind.

Mom stopped to look at that picture the longest while my sisters broke out of the back doors and ran out to see the horses in the paddock.

"She's beautiful," Mom said, knowing exactly who the picture showed.

"More than," I replied, and ran my hand over June's pencil-drawn cheek. I could still feel her warm skin under my fingertips. Something exploded in my chest, a feeling I had never felt before. "She's got me good, Mom."

Mom leaned her head on my arm. "I'm glad you have her, Sunshine. You need some good in your life." My gut twisted at that. Some nights I worried that, even if I did reach remission in this trial, there just wasn't enough time to get healthy enough to play football at UT. Those fears sent me spiraling, so I focused on the road ahead and just kept hold of the blind faith that I could do it.

"I'm glad I have her too," I said, pulling back from my panic.

"C'mon, I'll take you to meet Chris. June and Emma are at the stables, but they'll be by later to meet y'all."

I went outside to the porch and shouted in the miniature tornadoes and led them to the rec room to meet Chris. He jumped up as soon as we entered.

"Mrs. Taylor, nice to meet you, ma'am," he said and shook Mom's hand. I smirked at how proper my clown-like friend acted. Emily and Lucy pushed by Mom to shake Chris's hand too.

We hung out with Chris and his parents until Neenee called us all out for the cookout. My sisters immediately got dressed for swimming and jumped into the pool. Silas came up with a person who was clearly his little brother in tow. The kid must have been about ten.

"What's up, man?" I said, as Mom chatted to Paster Noel and Michelle around the firepit.

Silas put his arm on his brother's shoulder. Silas was slim, wore glasses, and was a gamer. His brother, although he looked like Silas, was the complete opposite. "Richie here is a football player and has dreams of being a QB. I told him about you, and he wanted to meet you."

"Hey, Richie," I said. "You wanna be a QB, huh?"

"Silas said you're going to UT to play for the Longhorns?" he said in response.

"That's the plan," I said, refusing to entertain any other outcome. This was a happy day. A good day. A family day. I would focus solely on that.

"I'm gonna play for the Longhorns too," Richie said as I tossed my football between my hands.

I grinned at his confidence. I'd been like that as a kid too. Hell, most of the time I still was. "Then let's see what you've got, little man." I moved a few steps away and signaled for him to get some space away from everyone. Richie waited for me to throw the ball. I had to grit my teeth when the ache that light throw brought made sweat break out on my forehead. But Richie caught it, and I whooped.

"Good catch, little dude!" I clapped my hands. "Now, back to me." Richie threw it, and even with the pain slicing up and down my arm, I was back throwing a ball. This was me in my element.

An hour passed with me coaching the kid, only for his mom to call him away to get something to eat. I'd missed throwing the ball, but with the sting I was feeling in my shoulder, a break was smart. I would probably pay for it tomorrow, but in that moment, I didn't care in the slightest.

A light round of applause made me look over my shoulder. June had returned from the stables and had been watching me. "Have you been standing over there checking out my ass, Junebug?" I said, and chuckled when her face blazed red.

She walked toward me, pointing at my grin. "You're nothing but trouble, Jesse, I tell ya."

When she finally reached me, I laid my tired arms on her shoulders, still gripping my football in my left hand. June rolled her eyes at me still holding the ball. "Gotta keep tight hold of my two favorite things, Junebug," I said, and kissed her forehead.

June was getting better at letting me show her affection. She'd grown less shy and reserved, and more comfortable and bolder around me.

"Now, now, son. Enough of all that," Mr. Scott said from behind me.

It was my turn to go red as Mr. Scott approached. I immediately dropped my arms and took a step back from June. He threw me a mocking wink. We'd grown closer from watching football together, and it was...nice. My dad up and left when I was only twelve. From then, I'd only had my coaches guide me in being a man. Mr. Scott was a good father. But as nice as he was, at times, it reminded me what I'd missed out on—and I couldn't deny that it crushed me.

"Sorry, sir," I said, and he nodded in acceptance. I quickly searched the cookout and found my mom just breaking from having a discussion with Emma's aunt, who had also come to visit. "Mom!" I shouted, and she turned toward me.

As soon as her eyes landed on June, her face lit up. Mom grabbed hold of Lucy and Emily, halting them from stuffing their faces, and brought them toward us.

June stepped back a touch. By the sudden flush to her skin, she was clearly nervous as all hell. I put my arm over her shoulders to keep her by my side. "Mom," I said, "this is Junebug."

June held out her hand. "Nice to meet you, ma'am."

"You too, June," Mom said, and my chest squeezed tightly. Seeing June meeting my mama seemed to soothe something a little broken inside me.

"Wow. You're so pretty," Lucy said to June, staring up at my girl, blurting out whatever she was thinking as always.

June laughed and crouched down to Lucy's height. "Thank you, sweetie." She flicked her amused gaze up to me. "Your brother pretty much said that the first time he saw me too. I can tell y'all are related."

"I like your headscarf," Emily said next, touching the end of June's green scarf.

June was dressed in black leggings, a white T-shirt, and a green sweater tied around her waist. She dressed casually, but it made her look just as beautiful as a ball gown would have. "Thank you," she said.

I put my hand on Emily's head, then Lucy's. "These two monsters are my little sisters." I addressed my sisters as I said, "Girls, this is June and her mama and daddy, Mr. and Mrs. Scott."

"Are you Jesse's girlfriend?" Lucy asked June, brazen once more.

June's blush was back, and she opened her mouth, then shut it again, clearly not knowing what to say. We hadn't exactly defined what we were. June's wide, brown eyes landed on me.

Without breaking June's gaze, I said, "She is."

June stilled, as though she couldn't believe I'd admitted it, then she smiled a soft smile just for me.

"She's my girl." She was insecure—I knew that now, but I'd made it my mission to always tell her just how beautiful she was until she believed it too.

"Wow," Lucy said dreamily, making us all laugh. I quickly introduced my mom to June's parents, and they went to the food and drink set up to grab something. This day was good for my mom too. She didn't have many people to talk to about what she was going through. June's parents were good people, and I liked that she could talk to them a little, for her sake.

June sat down on a nearby bench, and I took the seat beside her. She seemed a little tired, but her eyes shone with happiness. Our friends were mingling, eating with their families. It was nice. It felt peaceful after the hellish initial stage of treatment.

"Girlfriend, huh?" June said, cutting through the soundtrack of people talking, humor in her voice, though there was a little doubt there too. But I could see contentment in her expression. My chest squeezed tightly. This girl had my heart in a vise at this point. She'd been a hurricane that had just blown into my life without warning.

She stared at me, waiting.

I sat back against the bench. "Well, I've been telling everyone I'm your boyfriend, so it'd be weird if you said you weren't my girl."

"You have?" she said, humor dropped and her nerves showing stronger if the shuffling of her legs were any indication.

"No," I said, smirking, "but I'd like to."

June playfully bumped her arm against mine. She stared down at her hand. I noticed she did that sometimes. She stared at her reflection for long periods of time too. It appeared to me like she was sometimes seeing a stranger staring back at her. I hadn't asked her about it yet. I didn't want to upset her.

We both had issues we hadn't spoken about.

June curled her hand into a fist and slowly relaxed it, then looked back to me and said, "Then I...I suppose we could call each other that."

I placed my hand on my chest. "I felt the love then, Junebug. I'm bowled over by your blatant and enthusiastic affection for me."

June laughed loudly, then, meeting my gaze, said, "You know how I feel about you."

And it was true—I did. But I wanted her to tell me. I had no problem telling June, but she was a lot more reserved than me, and sometimes she left me wondering what she really did think of me—of us.

"And how's that?" I asked, throat raspy.

June inched closer, then whispered, "You're my favorite part of every single day, Jesse."

"Junebug," I murmured, and turned to put my back to the rest of the courtyard, facing her and blocking her from peoples' view. "I think

I'm gonna have to kiss you now. Okay? You can't just say things like that and expect me to not react."

"Okay," she said, fighting a smile, and held her breath as I moved in. She always held her breath, like every kiss was a great, life-changing event.

It was to me, so I understood the feeling.

"Not again!" a voice said behind us. "Emma, you're gonna have to start kissing me too so we have something in common with the Chemo Club lovebirds." Chris—it was always friggin' Chris. I dropped my forehead to June's in exasperation.

"I love you, Chris. But I wouldn't touch you if you were the last man on earth," Emma said, and June giggled. I loved hearing that sound.

I turned back to the bench, and Chris and Emma handed us both a drink. We took the offered waters, and they sat beside us.

"This is nice," Emma said wistfully, enjoying the view of our families talking and spending time together.

"They'll be more days like this," I said, and June leaned into my side, clearly thinking the same thing.

"What you said," Chris echoed, raising his water in the air. "Exactly what you just said."

I heard the familiar click of a door opening and closing and peeled back the plaid blanket from my lap. June came into view, making a beeline for our egg chair and sliding in beside me. I covered us with the blanket and noticed June was holding her notebook to her chest.

"Is that what I think it is?" I asked. I knew she'd begun writing our story, but she'd been shy about letting me read it.

"It is," she replied, then bit her lip.

"You're nervous." I knew her tells by now.

June nodded, then shook her head, like she couldn't decide. I had no idea what she was feeling. She must have seen my confused expression, as she smiled and said, "I wrote about how we met, all of it, up until the moment we came out here and you told me 'write me for you.'" She paused then.

"Okay?" I asked, still unsure what was happening to make her so cagey.

She handed me the notebook, but I went to open it, her soft hand on mine stopped me. My eyes immediately met hers. She swallowed then said, "Then I wrote more." June stared off at the crescent moon. Our five a.m. starts had gotten earlier and earlier until, most nights, we sat out here all night long. It had become my favorite part of the day—just us, on our egg chair, on the porch, under the moon and stars. Everything was quiet and peaceful, and I had my girl right beside me. Illness drifted away from us when we were here—all the sickliness, the pain, the aches, and the fear of getting our first set of results that were quickly heading our way.

Out here, we were just Jesse and June, a couple of seventeen-year-olds falling quickly for the other. It was simple. Easy.

"Junebug?" I said, and she settled back into me.

"I kept going," she said, and I waited for her to go on. June put her hand on the notebook next to mine. "Once I started"—she tapped her chest—"it just poured from me, my heart guiding my fingers until I had written beyond how we met."

I stared down at the notebook, at our hands side by side, like they were protecting our fledgling love story inside.

June sighed. "I'm sick of all the bad days, Jesse," she said. "I want to write about love and laughter and *surviving*. *Thriving*."

She turned to me and her brown eyes were glistening, shining like the garnet crystals my sisters had on their bedside tables.

June took hold of my hand and brought it to her lips. "This book I've begun writing…it's our happily ever after."

My heart began to race so fast, it took my breath away for a moment.

"I *believe* we will make it through this trial," she hastened to add, her open expression imploring me to understand. "I do. But just in case we don't…" She trailed off, a flicker of fear in her beautiful stare as she let that sentence land.

"You wanted to give us our happily ever after anyway," I said, understanding why she had been so nervous to tell me. June's smile was watery as she nodded, and a tear escaped out of the corner of her eye.

"When I'd finished what had actually been our start, I began thinking of us in the near future," she said, "out in the world, cancer free and able to live out our dreams—"

"But together," I interrupted, and she laid her head on my shoulder.

"Together," she repeated. We were silent a few moments before she said, "It's been helping me, writing this book. Helping me keep going—just like you do."

June opened the notebook, and her handwritten story came into view. I smiled and dropped a kiss on the top of her head. "Your handwriting is just as pretty as you are," I said. "How's that possible? My handwriting looks like chicken scratch."

"Well, I can't throw a football, so I'd say we both have our own strengths."

"Touché."

"Read," she instructed. So I did. I smirked, feeling pretty damn proud about how she felt for me in the beginning. But my favorite part...

"I love the chapters from my point of view," I said.

June worried her lip. "Really? I wasn't sure if I should have done that. Put myself in your brain. It's just all my favorite books have the male perspective too. I didn't want to presume how you felt for me or how your inner narrative sounded or—"

"Junebug," I said, stopping her with a kiss. June sucked in a breath just as my lips met hers. I had only meant to stop her spiraling, but once I kissed her, it was like we didn't want to ever stop. When I finally pulled away, I said, "You have my full permission to write my chapters." I tapped the notebook. "You could never get how I feel about you wrong." June exhaled a relieved breath. "In fact, I would say you could kick it up a notch."

"Trouble," she joked, tapping my chest, and I kissed her again. Just reading how she felt—*still felt*—about me blew me away. "You okay?" she asked, clearly noticing my floored reaction.

I swallowed a lump in my throat and said, "I'm just stunned at how *you* feel for *me*..."

June waited patiently for me to continue.

I shrugged. "I just never thought anyone could feel that way about me."

"Why not?" she said, voice strong, like she was offended I could ever believe that.

My mind quickly took me back to my dad, the man who taught me how to throw a football. The man who would take me to all my Pee Wee games, my practices, the one who told me I was his best friend. All these memories came barreling in. I was unable to stop them, as well as the barrage of emotions that quickly followed. "My dad…" I said, voice breaking. "He told me he loved me, but then one day…" I trailed off, trying to not let the pain of that day pierce my heart even more. I was pretty sure there was a gaping hole still there, scarred and tough and unable to close. I'd always struggled with rejection since then.

"You don't have to continue if you can't," June said gently.

I met her eyes. There wasn't sympathy or pity there, but there was understanding…and affection. Such raw affection, it made me want to share this—this deep, pained part of me that I hid from the world. "He left, Junebug. One day he left and just never came home. My sisters were tiny. My mom was shattered, heartbroken. Her childhood sweetheart just up and leaving her." I blew out a long breath. "He told me he loved me, yet he still left. No word, just…gone. We haven't heard from him since." I ducked my head to hide my embarrassment and the pain I knew was etched on my face, but June's hands cupped my cheeks, tilting my head.

She looked me square in my eyes, more serious than I had ever seen her before. "You are so loveable, Jesse Taylor." Heat raced through my veins. "You are kind, you are beautiful…" She searched my gaze more. "And I'm not sure if you have guessed it yet, but you have wrapped yourself so tightly around my heart that you are the first thing I think about in the morning and the last thing I think about before I close my eyes at night."

I slid my hands around June's waist and held her tightly.

"I used to wake up and fear would hold me captive for several minutes before I could move. Now…" she said.

"Yeah?" I whispered, desperate for her to continue.

"I wake up happy. I wake up excited…because I get to see *you*. I go to sleep content because we've spent the night out here, talking. One on one, I have spent more time with you than anyone in my life—my parents excluded. And..." I held her tighter, desperate for her to keep speaking. "I'm falling for you, Jesse Taylor. So hard. And more and more every day."

June leaned in and kissed me. She was never the one to initiate a kiss, too reserved. But she held my cheeks and kissed me, and that kiss made me believe every single thing she'd just said. When she broke away, she said, "Cancer is trying to take me from this world." My heart thudded on the ground. "I despise it. But I will forever be grateful that it led me to you."

I smiled, my cheeks aching with how wide. "It may have taken my hair and every inch of muscle tone, but it led me to you and for that reason alone, I can overlook it...just this once."

June laughed, and it was a damn balm to my soul.

She linked her arm through mine and repositioned her notebook that had fallen down the middle of us. She opened page, and said, "Please read."

So I did.

Jesse

Jesse and June's Happily Ever After

The sun shined through my window, and the birds were singing. I took that as a good sign. Even my body ached less today. The immunotherapy had floored us all again this week, but Chemo Club was still in full force and helping us cope together. We'd debated calling it 'Immuno Club' now that the chemo portion of our treatment had ended, but the original name had stuck, and we felt rather attached to it. We were on another few days' break from treatment, days to rebuild. And today was a big day for us all. Phase one had come to a close.

Today, we got our first month's results back. Dr. Duncan would be telling us if the treatment had started to work or not. I refused to let nerves take hold. It would be working. June's would be working. Everyone's results would come back with positive news. That was the only outcome I would entertain.

I knocked on June's door. She opened it with the same happiness evident on her face that was running through my veins.

"You ready?" I asked, searching the room for her parents.

"They're meeting me in Dr. Duncan's office," June said, understanding who I was searching for. "I told them I wanted to be with everyone else for a while first."

We'd all agreed to meet in the rec room, just to hang out and be there for one another as we got our results. Tucking my football under my arm, I held out my free hand to June, and she slipped hers in mine. I stood straighter, as she did, and even the ache in my throwing arm seemed to not be as bad today.

"You nervous?" I asked June as we headed down the maze of hallways that we were now much better at navigating.

June squeezed my hand. "I'm trying to be positive and keep imagining only receiving good news." She nodded firmly. "We're gonna be okay," she said, and I kissed her on the head.

"Group two for the win," I said, struggling to hold out my fist because I was holding the ball.

"Group two for the win," June said, laughing at my contortion act but bumping my fist all the same.

As we turned into the rec room, I saw we were the final two to arrive. "Are we ready?" I said, loud enough for the other six to turn to us.

"Hell yeah!" Chris said, walking across the room and throwing his arm around me. I let go of June to slap his back.

Emma hugged June, then blew out a shaky breath. "I didn't sleep last night. I could barely eat!"

"Is your mom coming?" Chris asked me, just as the parents who were staying on-site began to trickle in.

"Cherry?" Neenee called. She was clearly up first.

I was distracted as I watched her go, keeping my eyes on the door as I answered Chris. "She couldn't get time off work, but I'll video call her, so she gets the results when I do."

"Cool," he said as I only half listened.

June's slim hand slipped into mine, and she led me to a couch. I watched the clock on the wall, feeling like I was crawling out of my skin. I just wanted these damn results back.

June was talking to Emma, and she laughed—that laugh was enough to pull my attention away from the length of Cherry's appointment and just stare at my girl.

A flash of fear cut down my spine. What if Junebug's results weren't good? What if mine were and hers weren't?

My throat clogged up just at the thought. June must have felt me watching her, as she turned to me. Her eyebrows pulled down, just as the sound of Cherry leaving the doc's office sailed into the room from down the hallway. We all stilled. You could have heard a pin drop—we were that quiet. Cherry's mama's cries came next, and my heart began to beat faster.

Was that a good cry or a bad one?

We didn't have to wait long to find out though because Cherry came in, a wide smile on her face and said, "It's working." She seemed to be in complete disbelief.

I exhaled a breath I hadn't even known I was holding. Mr. and Mrs. Scott came into the room and went straight across to congratulate Cherry and her parents.

"It's working," Emma said in disbelief.

I think, deep down, we had all been too scared to truly believe it could.

"It's fucking working!" Chris said loudly, excitedly, and practically jumped on me in celebration. "Did you hear that?!"

"I did." Excitement took hold of me. "I fucking did!"

"Jesse, can we do without the F bombs, please?" Neenee said, but I saw even she was grinning.

"Anything for you, Neenee," I said, and she shook her head at my cheekiness.

"Chris, you're up." Chris went with his parents, smiling and confident in his steps. Cherry sat with Silas, Kate, and Toby, full of life. Her happiness was infectious.

"I'm so happy for her," June said. Emma echoed the sentiment. We were actively watching people's dreams coming true.

One by one, people saw the doc—Emma, Silas, Toby, Kate—until it was my turn. All with positive results. I took hold of June. I didn't want her to be last, but she rubbed my arms in excitement.

"I'll be here when you're done," she said.

Mr. and Mrs. Scott came over. Mr. Scott put his hand on my shoulder and said, "Do you need anyone in with you, son? I'd be happy to come with you." The way my throat closed in appreciation was instant.

I cleared my throat but said, "No thank you, sir. We're video calling my mom. But I really appreciate the offer."

Mr. Scott nodded, then tapped my arm in support. Mrs. Scott gave me a tight hug, and June blew me a kiss. I followed Neenee into the doc's office in a daze. I quickly video called my mom. Her face came on the screen, and I could see the worry in her eyes.

"I'll get straight to the point," Dr. Duncan said, looking at his computer. Every muscle in my body stilled. "I'm happy to say that your blood and scans are showing that the new chemo and targeted drug therapy are having a positive effect on your AML." I blinked and blinked again as I heard my mom begin to cry in relief. "These are still early days, and we have more to come, but I am very pleased with your initial results."

Dr. Duncan nodded, and I looked down to my phone. "Jesse..." my mom said, searching for words. "I'm so proud of you."

"Thank you, Mom," I said, voice barely there from shock. Since I'd been diagnosed, there hadn't been one bit of good news. This felt foreign. It felt... I didn't even know.

"Call me later, Sunshine," Mama said, and I walked like a zombie into the rec room. June and her folks were the first people I saw, and June jumped to her feet, brown eyes wide.

"It's working," I said, and caught another triumphant whoop from Chris somewhere in the room. June's happiness engulfed her face, and she ran to me, wrapping her arms around my waist. She was petite, but it felt like her embrace swallowed my six-foot-two frame.

I held her back, needing her to get the same news.

"June," Neenee called.

June broke away from me.

"Group two for the win," I rasped, fist held out.

"Group two for the win," she said back and bumped my fist. I cupped her face and kissed her lips, then watched her walk to the doc's room with her mama and daddy flanking her side.

"You wanna sit?" Emma said and patted the seat between her and Chris on the couch. I shook my head. My body was a live wire, waiting for June to be told what all of us in this room had.

"She's got this, you know?" Chris said, but I didn't look to my friend. I kept my eyes locked on that door, hearing nothing but white noise as I stayed suspended in time, ready for when my girl came back through.

I didn't know how many minutes had passed when June left the office and came down the hallway. I held my breath, heartbeat slamming in my ears. But then she turned my way, and a euphoric smile etched on her lips. I didn't wait for her to enter the room. Instead, I ran right into the hallway and picked her up. I held her tightly, her feet dangling off the floor. "It's working?" I asked, pulling back enough to see her face.

"It's working," she repeated, and I kissed her.

I kissed her and kissed her until Mr. Scott jokingly pulled us apart. But June's parents' smiles were huge. Relieved.

The treatment was working. We were going to get through this. And I had my Junebug by my side. Life was only getting better. And it was going to be cancer free.

꒰ ꒱

When the chapter ended, goose bumps had broken out all over my body. June's arm was still linked with mine, but by her sudden stillness, it was clear she knew I'd finished.

"You're so talented," I said, and gently closed the notebook.

June exhaled, then said, "I want that to happen for us all. I want Dr. Duncan to give us all that news."

"You've written it," I said, "so it *must* happen. Right?" My voice held humor, but I wished for it too.

June smirked. "I'm not sure it quite works like that, Jesse."

"You never know. Your pen might have special powers, a direct line to God or the universe."

June rolled her eyes.

"Keep going," I said, dropping my teasing. "I want to know what happens next."

"You do?" June asked. She clearly didn't understand her talent if she had to ask that.

I was hooked. I covered her hand with mine. "Show me our future, Junebug. 'Cause it looks kinda amazing from where I'm sitting."

"Okay," she said, relief in every breath. She cuddled in beside me.

The countdown was on for those results she'd written about. I stared up at the stars and replayed her words over and over in my head, trying to feel that joy that I'd felt as I read that we'd all responded to the treatment and our cancer had stopped spreading.

June laid her head on my chest, listening to my heartbeat. If it all worked out like we wished, she would be listening to my heartbeat, just like this, for many, many years to come.

It sounded like heaven.

chapter ten

June

A few weeks later

"You've already finished?" Chris asked, mouth agape. "Impossible!"

"Guess that's the perk of being a nerd, huh, Chris?" Emma said sassily, and I laughed as Chris batted her hand to shoo her away. It looked like he and Jesse still had several pages of the assignment to go.

As I passed Jesse, he held out his hand and took hold of mine. "Come here, bookworm." Jesse pulled me in and tilted his head up for a kiss. Our lips pressed together and only Emma pulling me away by my other hand broke me from Jesse's mouth.

"I'm stealing your girlfriend for a couple of hours. I'm sick of you monopolizing her," she said. "It's my turn with her now. Best friend privileges."

"You get BFF hour every night," Jesse argued.

Emma flapped her hand in dismissal. "And I thought I'd get more than an hour! But you came along and swept her off her feet." Emma gestured with her head to Chris. "Meanwhile, I get this one to entertain me when you sequester June."

"Hey!" Chris said, in complaint.

Jesse playfully gestured to his body. He wore his usual T-shirt and jeans. "Junebug can't help it, Em. She can never resist me when I look this good." Jesse was messing around, but his words had never been truer. I fell for him harder and harder every day.

Emma pretended to gag, and Jesse winked at me as we left the education room.

As promised, classes had started, but they were flexible. We couldn't exactly write papers when we could barely move off our beds. But just like Chemo Club, our foursome had decided to do it together and that had helped us immensely.

"Should we just go to your room? It's closer," Emma said, heading down the hallway, linking her arm in mine. We mostly hung out in Emma's room, as it was closer to the kitchen and the rec room.

"Sure," I said. As we walked, I replayed what she had said about not spending as much time with her as she wanted. It made me feel guilty. I adored Emma and loved spending time with her. But she wasn't wrong; I did spend a crazy amount of time with Jesse. Especially of late. But now, it was my plan to make even more time for her.

As we entered my room, she stopped dead as she saw the picture Jesse had drawn of me and Ginger on my wall. My mama had bought me a rustic wooden frame to protect it, and it hung opposite my bed, so I saw it every time I laid down.

"Erm…who drew this?" she asked. In the beginning, I'd kept Jesse's drawings to myself. But the more he drew, the more I believed they needed to be seen.

"Jesse," I replied, and Emma's mouth dropped open in shock.

"Well…damn. Guess he's not just football brawn and terrible jokes."

I laughed and waved her over to my bed. I switched on the TV, ready to continue the series we'd been streaming.

Emma made herself comfortable beside me, but her eyes kept drifting back to the pictures. "How are they so lifelike?" she asked, and I paused the episode that had just started playing. "It's so detailed, it could be a photograph." Emma's eyes narrowed. "Are we sure it's not photoshopped?"

"Emma!" I said, tapping her hand in admonishment.

"What?" she said, playfully pushing me away. "It's just we've been here awhile now, see each other every day, and I've never seen him draw."

I shrugged. "He does it in private. He sketches most nights while I write." Only a silence met me. When I looked up at Emma, her eyebrows were raised.

"Oh, we're talking more about *this*," she said. "At night? At *night*? When at night?" Heat rushed to my face as I realized what I'd said. "Oh, no," Emma said. "Don't go all bashful on me now, princess, not when you're running around in the midnight hours with your beau." Emma batted her eyes, teasing.

I hadn't meant to say it, and I didn't keep secrets from Emma. But…I didn't know. I supposed my and Jesse's time outside, when the world was asleep, seemed like our personal slice of time, when it was just him and I and the art that made our hearts sing.

"My beau?" I cackled at that.

"I'm waiting," Emma said when I didn't answer her actual question.

The truth was, I found myself now wanting to share this with Emma. If I was honest about why, it would be because sometimes, I couldn't believe that it was true. Why was Jesse so drawn to me? I felt like he could have any girl he wanted. And as much as I tried to understand that it was me he was falling for, there was a barrier of insecurity that still made me doubt why.

"We sit outside every night," I said, feeling Emma's impatience. "The few times we haven't is when one of us has been hit badly by the treatment." I flicked my eyes to hers. "And even then, we sneak into the other's room, so we can be there for the other."

"June Mary Scott, I didn't think you had it in you."

I stilled and met Emma's blue eyes. "My middle name isn't Mary."

Emma flapped a hand in front of her face. "That's of no consequence. I'm only interested in you and Jesse." Her head tilted to the side as she regarded me. "Anyone can see how close you are. So do you see it lasting beyond Harmony?" she asked.

"Yes," I said. I knew it was true for both Jesse and me. It was pathetic how gone for that boy I was. "I can't explain it," I confessed to Emma. "I don't know if it's because of the position we're all in being here, being terminal, but everything is amplified."

"I get what you mean," Emma said. "Like everything just feels *more*. The sun seems brighter now. The heat more intense. Your favorite smells are sweeter."

"Yes," I said. I stared at the sketch on my wall, the one of my face. Jesse *actually* saw me like that. When I looked in the mirror, that wasn't the girl in the reflection. Jesse's picture made me look…

beautiful. I could barely believe that was how I looked to him: *beautiful*. I had never thought of myself that way, but his sketches showed me *me* through his eyes, and it was beautiful.

"Em?" I said, and Emma met my eyes. My gaze dropped and my heart raced at what I was about to ask. I hadn't told anyone of my insecurities, but I loved Emma. She truly was the best friend I'd always dreamed of. And I knew she wouldn't judge. "Do…do you think I'm…*enough*, for Jesse?"

Emma stared at me in silence a touch too long. I looked down at my hand. It still felt like it was mine. "June," Emma said, pulling me from my stupor. "Please look at me."

I did as she asked and felt my throat clog up. Emma's face was serious. She looked fierce, when she said, "I mean what I'm about to say and you need to hear this: you are point-blank the best girlfriend I have ever had. You are sweet and kind and have the inner strength of an entire Roman legion." Tears filled my eyes and Emma took hold of my hands. She gripped on tightly. "And you are stunning," she said, emphatically. "Beautiful, utterly gorgeous, *banging*."

I laughed through my tears as she listed those off.

Emma sobered and said, "I've seen how you look at yourself, babe. I know you didn't swim that day before treatment because you don't like how you look. But I am a brutally honest person—just ask Chris. And I am telling you, you're a fucking ten."

I laughed again, and Emma released one of my hands to wipe the tears from my cheek.

She tipped her head. "Do you believe me?"

I breathed deeply. "I'm trying to," I said. "I was never one to care that much about my looks. But when I lost my hair and my skin reacted to the treatment and the steroids changed my body and everything else that comes with fighting cancer..." I shrugged. "I guess I lost my confidence somewhere along the way."

"I understand. I have days where I feel like that too."

"You do?" I asked. Emma always seemed so sure of herself. "I never would have guessed."

"How could I not? For all those reasons you've just listed. But..." Emma trailed off.

"But what?" I said, clinging to her every word.

She smiled. "But I know my worth and what I've fought to still be here, on this earth, breathing. And that reminds me of what I've always known."

"What's that?" I asked.

Emma's smile turned into a grin. "That I'm fucking fabulous."

I laughed—I laughed so hard that Emma joined in and we faced each other on the pillows.

When our laughter faded, Emma said, "Jesse adores you, June. I mean, look!" She pointed to all his drawings.

"I imagine his previous girlfriends were cheerleaders with perfect hair," I said, feeling my chest squeeze. My insecurities were still there.

"But they weren't you, and it's you who he adores."

"I often wonder, though, that if it wasn't for us both being here at the ranch, would he have ever even looked at me? And that worries me," I confessed.

"Babe, that boy would tackle everyone in the world to find you if he'd known you were out there."

"I'm pretty sure quarterbacks don't tackle," I said, fighting a smile, but feeling my soul being soothed by this talk.

Emma rolled her eyes at me. "Then I'm sure he'd make an exception." Emma dropped a kiss on my cheek, and said, "Face it, June, Jesse Taylor is gone for you. You have that boy whipped." My body filled with warmth.

Before I knew it, words were spilling from my mouth. "When I met him, it was like I felt a shimmer in the very fabric of the universe. Like, *wow, I think I've just found my person.*" I paused and met Emma's gaze. "You know the meaning of soulmates? The story that God split a being into two and they had to find one another on earth again?"

"Yeah," Emma said softly.

"It feels like that for me. Yes, it's quick. But a month ago, we all thought we were going to die. We might still. We don't exactly have the luxury of taking our time to find happiness." I smiled to myself. "And with Jesse, I'm not sure I would have been able to not fall for him so fast, even if we were well."

"You love him," Emma said—not a question but a statement.

"I'm falling for him, Emma. So hard," I confessed.

She launched forward, knocking me back on the bed. "I can't breathe!" I said as she wrapped me up tightly.

"I don't care," she said, planting another kiss on my cheek. "I'm just so happy for you."

I playfully pushed her off me. Emma cackled, then righted herself on the pillows. "So what about you?" I asked. "Do you like Chris?"

"As a friend," Emma said firmly, and I knew that was true. They were platonically perfect for one another, but there didn't seem to be any spark of romance. Emma went quiet, then said, "In all seriousness, June, I hope I get what you have one day. It would be nice to know what it feels like."

"You will," I said, squeezing her hand. Emma stared out of my window, lost in thought. "Are you nervous about tomorrow?" I asked after a couple of silent minutes.

"Yeah," she said. "I know Neenee and Dr. Duncan said to try and be positive, but it's hard to always stay in that space, often detrimental as I just want to *feel* what I'm going through without the forced optimism. Sometimes, I can't help but worry the treatment won't be working. I want to feel the fear, the dread. Let's be honest, we've all been told that before, hence why we're here. We're not unused to bad news."

"I know," I said, running my thumb over the back of her palm. "But I'm trying my best to only imagine the good things from now on. And that is helping me. *This* has helped me. More than you know." I smiled at Emma, and she returned it. "And I see us all in the future, still best friends. You visiting me at UT and telling me you've met that boy you hoped for and are madly in love."

"That sounds nice," Emma said, and her eyes glazed over a little. "In fact, it sounds perfect."

chapter eleven

June

My heart seemed to rattle in my chest. We were all in the rec room like we'd agreed. Our parents were here too. So far, Silas, Toby, and Chris had all been to see Dr. Duncan, and just like I'd written, the treatment was working for them.

It was happening.

What we had all dreamed of was *happening*... It seemed surreal. My leg bounced as I waited for Emma to come back in. Jesse's hand was clasped in mine. Neither of us had been in yet, and my stomach was in knots.

My mama and daddy were sitting together close by, and every time one of my friends came in with a smile, I saw my daddy's back straighten in confidence and excitement begin to glow on my mama's face.

"June," Jesse said, and I looked up to see Emma heading our way.

Her smile was wide, and she was staring right at me. Her arms came out and I got to my feet. I released Jesse's hand and Emma crashed into me.

"I'm so happy for you," I said and felt Emma shake in my arms. The joy I felt for her was like a tidal wave.

"Thank you," she said and pulled back. "That's all of us so far." She was right, and I couldn't help a fission of excitement wash over me too. We could all have this. We could all be heading for remission.

"Jesse," Neenee called out. I snapped my head to Jesse, and he met my eyes.

"Here goes nothing," he said.

I reached up on my tiptoes and kissed him. "Group two for the win," I said first this time and held out my fist.

Jesse chuckled and met my fist with his own. "Group two for the win." He followed Neenee to Dr. Duncan's office, and I couldn't keep my eyes off the doorway waiting for his return. Just like the chapter I had written for Jesse, everything faded away but for my singular focus on waiting for my boyfriend to return.

Boyfriend—it sounded too reductive for what we were.

"I'm just running to the bathroom," Chris said, and rushed out the rec room. "I wanna be here when Jesse comes back."

Minutes and minutes passed. It felt longer than the others had taken, and I began to worry. Or had it not taken as long? I didn't know if it simply felt like it was longer because this was *Jesse*.

The sound of footsteps approaching had my heart leaping to my throat. Even my parents got to their feet. Chris came through, a wide smile on his face. My shoulders dropped. *What was taking Jesse so long?*

"Why are you smiling like that?" Emma asked. Yes, Chris was

obviously happy that he had received good news, but he looked ecstatic. I tried to search for any sign for Jesse over Chris's shoulder, but the hallway was still empty.

"I've just seen Jesse," Chris said, and all my attention fell on Chris. My heart began to thunder in my chest.

"What did he say?" I asked, a nervous tremor to my voice.

"He was on the phone," he said. "To his mom, I think. But he flashed me a smile and big thumbs up."

The relief was instant. "Her did?" I said, my voice stronger now. Chris nodded emphatically and Emma through her arms around my shoulders in celebration. She squeezed me tightly and happiness drifted over me. Jesse…it was working. The treatment was working, and he was going to be okay. I didn't realize how much I needed to hear that until this moment.

"June?" Neenee said, and I felt my mama's hand on my back.

"We need to go in now, sweetie," my mama said. I searched the hallway again for Jesse, wanting to see him before I went in, but he must have still been on the phone to his mama. She would be so happy. *He* must have been so happy.

As I linked my arms with my mama's and daddy's, I felt it: I felt the good news coming my way. I could see the orange glow of attending UT in the distance. A dream I had thought would never occur was now in my grasp again.

My daddy dropped a kiss on my head, and I knew he was silently sharing my excitement. We walked into Dr. Duncan's office, and Dr. Duncan avoided our eyes as he looked at his computer. "I'm so sorry to tell you this, June, but our initial findings are showing that the treatment is not working as well as we'd hoped for you."

His words were a bucket of ice-cold water poured over my head. My heart stuttered from shock, and I heard my daddy whisper, "What?"

My hands began to shake, and my mama reached over and gripped them tightly.

"You've only had treatment for one phase, but this new form of monoclonal antibodies are intense and you should already show improvements. Our results tell us that your AML has progressed."

I was still, like my body was locked in a cage I couldn't climb out of.

"Phase one has not been successful for you, but we still have phase two. And we have hope that this may still work with another round of treatment."

My mama seemed to be just as shocked as I was, silent and trying to digest this unexpected news.

"What are the chances?" my daddy asked. "What are you predicting the chances will be of recovery in phase two?"

"When this was tested in a lab, it was never more than ten percent," Dr. Duncan said, straight to the point. "But that was not in humans, so we don't have conclusive evidence. It could be more or less. We don't know until we trial the next phase."

I swallowed.

"And if there's no improvement by the end of the second phase?" Daddy asked, and I braced myself.

"Then the trial's treatment would be deemed unsuccessful for June," Dr. Duncan explained. "And June's cancer will keep progressing. After this next phase, if there is no improvement, June will be moved on to palliative treatment. We will do all we can to make her pain free, but there would be no need for more chemotherapy or immunotherapy."

All I could hear was the slamming of my heart against my ribs. One more phase. I had one more phase for this treatment to make a difference—which seemed unlikely—and maybe only a few more months left to live if it failed.

Nausea swirled in my stomach, and I jumped up from my seat. I stared Dr. Duncan right in the eyes and said, "Am I going to die?"

"As I said, I don't have that data yet," he replied.

I shook my head. That wasn't enough of an answer for me. I could feel myself unraveling with panic. "In your opinion, do you think the treatment will begin to work in the next phase?" I knew I was being direct, making him repeat himself, but I just...I just needed to be told again. I needed it to sink in.

"As I said, lab results show around ten percent. It's not great odds, but we must continue, as humans may take to the treatment better. We will increase the dosage of the immunotherapy and monitor you to be sure your body can withstand it. There is hope, June. It's small, but it is there. We mustn't give up yet."

Ninety percent. There was a ninety percent chance that this treatment would fail.

Mama moved before me. "June?" She had tears streaming down her face.

My daddy stood too, his face looked stricken. Then I thought of Jesse—of his smiling face, of how excited he would be that his treatment was working, that I would hopefully be receiving the same news as everyone else.

My dream of us being at UT together evaporated. The idea of walking out of this ranch cancer free seemed like a fool's dream now rather than a likelihood.

I left the office and stood in the hallway. I could hear laughter coming from the rec room. I couldn't face it. My feet were planted into the ground.

"Come on, sweetie. Let's go to your room," Mama said, but I shook my head. I didn't want to go to my room. I didn't know *what* I wanted.

And I couldn't face Jesse who would be back in the rec room by now—couldn't face Emma and Chris and everyone else. Oh God, Jesse... My treatment had failed. His was working; he was going to be okay, but he was going to be moving on without me.

"I need to be alone," I blurted out, and backed away from the office and toward the door that led outside. My daddy tried to follow, but I held out my hands. "Please," I said, my bottom lip trembling. "I just need to... Please don't follow me. Just give me space." I fled the building and was met with a warm breeze. Still, I was freezing.

Shock, I thought. I pulled my sweater from around my waist and put it on, walking as fast as I could, ignoring the pain in my leg. It suddenly seemed more pronounced somehow.

I sped up, Dr. Duncan's words swirling around my brain like a tornado.

Ten percent. I might only have a 10 percent chance that the treatment would work from here on out. I slowed, tasting salt on my lips, and I realized tears were falling from my eyes.

It wasn't fair. Why couldn't my body just accept this new treatment? Or the old treatment for that matter? What was it about me that rejected any kind of cure?

I felt like my heart was breaking with every step I took. I only stopped when I found myself at the stables.

"June?" Olivia, the stable manager, came over to me. "Are you okay?"

"Can I groom Ginger?"

Olivia's concern was evident on her face, but she nodded. "Let me get his halter." When she retrieved it, she said, "Do you want me to get him for you?"

I looked down at my shaking hands. "Yes, please," I whispered. As Olivia went straight into the paddock to retrieve him, I stared at my hands, that feeling of detachment tumbling back. I clenched my hands into fists, but they no longer seemed like mine.

My brain was back in protection mode—but nothing could protect me from this.

My eyes roved over the paddocks, distantly watching the trees surrounding them sway in the light breeze. I inhaled the comforting smell of horses and felt the hard ground under my feet. I needed to be grounded, to be back in my body. I needed to still feel like I was here, alive.

The sound of horseshoes on the hard ground made me lift my head. Olivia tied Ginger's lead rope to the grooming stall and brought me the brushes. She gave me a sympathetic nod, then left me alone with Ginger. Like he knew I was racked with emotional pain, Ginger turned his head my way and I laid against his neck. He didn't even move when my tears soaked his coat. It was like he was giving me a hug.

Forcing myself to calm, I reached for a body brush and began running it over Ginger's body slowly and steadily, willing my heart to calm. I worked on my breathing. As I did, I tried to shift my thoughts, to hold on tightly to the 10 percent. Minutes passed, and numbness spread over me. The monotonous motion of brushing Ginger had lessened the shaking in my hands and soothed my frayed nerves.

"Junebug?"

My back was to the front of the stall, so I hadn't seen him coming. I froze, stock-still. I couldn't turn and look at Jesse. I couldn't face telling him that we may be taking different roads.

"June?" he tried again, his hand softly taking hold of my elbow.

A fresh wave of fear came over me—not of dying but of not getting more time with this boy who had swept me off my feet.

"Please...look at me," he begged.

With a long exhale, I turned and there he was. In his faded orange Longhorns T-shirt that was baby soft with so much wear, his jeans, and his backwards cap, I wanted nothing more than to melt into his embrace. He was staring at me with fear in his deep green eyes.

"It's not good news," I whispered, my voice trembling on every word.

Jesse paled and tried to step closer to me in comfort.

I held out my hand to stop him. He couldn't touch me—if he did, I'd break. "Jesse." I shook my head. "They've only given me a ten percent chance of the treatment working in phase two." I gave him a watery smile. "I...I..." I ran my hand down Ginger's neck, turning away from Jesse's pained face and toward Ginger's chestnut coat instead.

"June," he tried again.

"I think this is where we have to part," I said, hating every word that was pouring from my mouth. But I wanted Jesse to thrive. I wanted him to live. Hitching his wagon to mine would only slow his progress. He didn't need that in his life.

"June—"

"You have a chance at beating this," I said, cutting him off again. I was still avoiding his eyes. I couldn't face him. I had fallen for him too hard, and this felt like splitting open my own chest and ripping out my heart. "You have a chance at making it to UT, at achieving your dreams. And you need to put all your attention into that." Finally allowing myself to face him, I lifted my head and said, "You have a *chance*, baby."

Jesse took hold of my arms gently, softly, and with all the adoration I knew he felt before me. It almost shattered me. I had finally allowed myself to believe that he could want me just as I had to lose him.

When I met his eyes and gave myself permission to become lost in them just one last time, Jesse said, "I do have a chance…about ten percent."

My eyebrows pulled down in confusion. "What?"

Jesse looked out into the distance, then, facing me again, said, "My chance at beating this," he said, voice husky and broken, "is about ten percent too."

I shook my head. "I'm so confused…"

"I didn't receive good news," he interrupted.

My body went statue still. I struggled to breathe. "But Chris…" I shook my head, trying to clear it. "Chris said you smiled at him in the hallway after you'd been to see Dr. Duncan. You gave him a thumb's up. Made him think your treatment was working."

Seeing I was struggling to comprehend what had happened, Jesse said, "I wanted to tell you after your appointment, so I was going to wait out in my room until you were done. But then I saw Chris coming out of the rec room. I pretended I was on the phone to my mom to avoid him. But he saw me and was studying me for news. So, I gave him a thumbs up as I wanted to tell you when we were alone, from my own lips, not from Chris."

"No…" I whispered, my happiness for him immediately morphing into fear.

"The treatment isn't working for me either, Junebug. At least that's what Doc Duncan said." He gave me a sweet smile, and I tried to make my sluggish brain catch up with what he was saying. "My cancer has progressed. I'm doing another round of treatment, but if that doesn't take…"

"Then you'll be on palliative care," I said, repeating the conversation I had had with Dr. Duncan.

"Bingo," he said, then studied me. His eyes saddened.

"Jesse?" I asked, seeing him so forlorn.

"I knew I wouldn't be able to face seeing the expression you're wearing right now, the one that is telling me how destroyed you are for me." He swallowed loudly. "I wanted you to be happy and focused and keep getting better. I wished for it with my entire heart."

I ran my fingers down his cheek, heart swelling as Jesse leaned into my touch, as if our contact was limited and he wanted to advantage of it as much as he could. "The look you're wearing now too," I said, "over *me*."

"Yeah," he rasped, then pulled me into his chest. Jesse's arms wrapped around me so tightly, I could barely breathe. But I didn't care. He was holding me, and I was holding him and we both… Lord, we were both hanging on to life by mere threads. "I wanted you to get good news so badly," Jesse said, and I felt the truth of his words all the way down to my bones.

"I wanted that for you too," I said, head against his shirt, holding him even tighter. He felt so warm. He felt *alive*.

Jesse pulled back and held my face in his hands. It was only then that I noticed he didn't have his football. He always had it with him, but not right now—not in this life-altering moment. My heart broke anew. Was this Jesse accepting that his dream of being a UT QB was fading? Or was it something else?

Inhaling a shuddering breath, I said, "My pen must not be magical after all. Not for us two at least—the last chapter I wrote didn't come true."

"Not in this life anyway," Jesse said. He looked at me intently, then said, "I love you, Junebug. I have for a while. But I love you, and I need you to know that."

All of the fear and pain that was surrounding us fell away as those words came from his mouth. And the detached feeling that had taken me in its hold disappeared, and I hurtled back into my body.

I love you.

"Jesse," I whispered, my heart flipping from lead to helium in seconds. Pressing my hand to his cheek, I stared into his evergreen eyes and said, "I love you too. So much that it aches."

Jesse's gaze always held a flicker of pain—a sign that he had a sadness inside of him that he never set free—but that flicker of pain wasn't there now, in this moment. I was choosing him, and he was choosing me for whatever time we had left.

We breathed each other in, and then Jesse stepped back, holding out his hand and said, "Let's go."

"Where?" I asked.

"The rec room."

I shook my head, that happy bubble of ours bursting. "I can't…" Then a thought occurred to me. "Does everyone have their results now?"

He nodded.

"Are they all doing better?"

Jesse nodded again. Sadness was back in his eyes. And I somehow knew that the sadness this time wasn't for him—it was for me.

"It's just you and me, Junebug," Jesse said in a raspy voice. He held up his fist, dark humor replacing the sadness in his gaze. "Group two for the win." The irony of that motto shouldn't have been funny, but it was.

Despite all the sadness, the shock, and the knowledge that the mountain we both had to climb was now Everest sized, I couldn't help but laugh out loud and bump his fist with mine. "Group two for the win."

As my laughter left me, I still felt the heady mix of being both shattered and elated, swinging between numb and feeling every bit of Jesse's love.

Like the balm he was, Jesse had soothed me. He *loved* me…and the universe had made sure we were still here, side by side, fighting the exact same battle. It felt like there was some kind of bigger plan to that, something almost unworldly.

Placing his hand in mine, Jesse led me from the stall. Olivia gestured to us that she would turn Ginger back out in the paddock. We walked slowly and silently back to the rec room, building our collective strength to do this.

When we entered, everyone stopped talking and turned our

way. Tears built in my eyes when I saw my mama and daddy were here too. They must have been waiting for me to come back. Tears still swam in their eyes, but there was belief and determination there too. It might have only been around 10 percent, but I still had a place in this fight—Jesse and I both did. Together, we were even stronger.

"You both okay?" Chris asked tentatively, like he knew we were anything but.

Jesse squeezed my hand. "Our treatments aren't working," Jesse said, and I saw the surprise and sorrow on our friends' faces—none more so than Emma's and Chris's. Tears immediately fell from Emma's eyes and Chris appeared stunned.

"I misled you earlier, Chris, not wanting to tell anyone but June first. Not until we were alone, but…" Jesse looked to me, making sure I was okay to share my news.

"My treatment isn't working either," I said. I saw Emma's parents move straight toward mine, along with Paster Noel, who my mama spoke to often.

"Is there still a chance?" Emma asked, her voice small. She was frozen, her pain plain to see on her face. My first best friend and this threatened to tear us apart.

Jesse turned to me, and I turned to him. "Ten percent," we said, in unison, then laughed, which must have looked completely inappropriate. That caused a range of confused expressions to be thrown our way. They must have thought we'd gone mad.

"We're not done fighting," I said, feeling the truth of those words travel through my veins and take up residence in my heart. "We're going to change the odds."

"We're not done fighting yet," Jesse echoed and then dropped a kiss on my head and put his arm around my shoulders.

Our chances of survival were slim. But we had around 10 percent. And with Jesse beside me, that 10 percent felt like 100. I'd never wanted to fight for something harder in my life.

chapter twelve

Jesse

"Jesse?" Mom said as she answered the call. "I can't see you. Why aren't you video calling?" She inhaled shakily. I could hear her panic in that simple breath. "Did you get your results?" Mom hadn't been able to get free from work when I'd had my appointment. I'd promised to call her as soon as she was free.

I chased the lump from my throat, and said, "We got them." I opened my mouth to talk, but nothing more came out.

"Jesse," Mom whispered, "you're scaring me. Please put me on video call. I need to see your face."

I wiped my eyes, then tapped the screen to connect the camera. My mom's face immediately came into view, and I crumbled. My shoulders shook, and I covered my face with my free hand. I didn't want her to see me break.

"No, Jesse," Mom said, despair in her voice.

I shook my head, still trying to speak. Minutes passed until I could. My mom stayed on the call, being there with me, even though she was miles and miles away.

"It's not working yet, Mom," I managed to say.

"What did Dr. Duncan say? Tell me everything he said, as best as you can."

"My cancer has progressed," my voice came out a little stronger. I met my mom's eyes through the screen. "They don't really know what happens from here in terms of survival as this form of antibodies hasn't been tested on humans before, but previous lab results stand at about ten percent." My heart skipped a beat at that.

"Sunshine," Mom whispered, and her face became engulfed with sadness. But she didn't crack. Mom was strong and I knew she wouldn't break in front of me.

"So there's a chance. But if there's no improvement in this next phase…" I didn't even want to say the words. I pictured June in my head, holding my hand as we walked through downtown Austin; I pictured myself wearing the UT orange football uniform and felt those dreams inch just that little bit farther and farther out of reach.

"You're still in the game, Jesse," Mom said, voice brooking no argument. "You might be down some points, but don't give up yet. Okay?"

"Yes, Coach," I rasped, but felt some of the heaviness lift.

Mom's lip curled into a small smirk. "I mean it, Jesse—" She stopped for a moment. "Wait, are you the only one?" She swallowed heavily.

The pain I still felt over it being June was raw and almost unbearable. "Junebug," I pushed out. "Only me and June."

"Oh, son," Mom said, and her voice hitched with deep emotion. My mom adored June. They chatted over video call a few times when Mom called and June was with me.

I glanced out the window, then met my mom's eyes. "We're gonna fight this together, Mom. We're gonna try our best to win."

"You'll do it," she said with confidence. "If anyone can do this, it's you two." Mom tried for a smile. "You're meant to be, you know that, son? You and your Junebug."

My heart swelled in my chest. "I do," I said, knowing it was true. "Whatever happens, we're gonna do it together."

I sighed. "Is it okay if I didn't talk to the girls tonight? I'm worried they'll see something's wrong."

"Of course," Mom said. "Call tomorrow. Or anytime. You know you can, right?"

"I do."

"I love you, son," she said, and the lump was back in my throat.

"Love you too, Mom. I'll call you tomorrow." I hung up and peered out of my porch doors. There was rain lashing at the panes, which felt fitting. When I'd gotten back to my room, I'd seen Olivia and the stable hands hurriedly bringing the horses in from the fields to the safety of the stalls. Then darkness had set in, and the storm raged on.

June was with her parents. After we had made our announcement in the rec room, they had asked her to go with them. They'd wanted to be sure she was okay. They'd asked me to go with them, which had stunned me, but I declined. It was something they needed to do alone.

That thought made me think of the call just now. My mom was

crushed at my news, and I hated to see it. But I was determined to take our 10 percent chance and turn it into gold.

I cursed the rain outside. I needed a night on the porch with June like I needed my next breath. I just wanted to talk to her, be next to her. I didn't want to be alone right now. Sadness was trying to take hold of me, no matter how much I was trying to keep my head above water. I was trying so hard to not find my plan for the future impossible. I was still holding on to recovering quickly and having enough time to get fit and healthy to play m next year. It would be near impossible, but I felt I could do it. The coach from UT had told me they were holding my spot. As long as it was mine, everything was still a possibility.

Sitting on my bed, I returned to my most recent sketch. It wasn't the drawing I'd hoped to be working on tonight. But this image had been clawing its way out of my soul since this morning, and I needed to put it down on paper. It was of June, in the very moment she realized I had been given the bad news too.

I smoothed my finger over her cheek, smudging the charcoal into her skin. Her cheeks were tearstained, eyes glassy with sorrow. But it was the desolate expression on her face that destroyed me. In this moment, the sadness for her own failing health wasn't what had her so distraught. It was learning that mine was failing too.

Ten percent.

As brutal as this moment had been, it also showed how much she cared for me. That her own pain had been eclipsed by mine. If I had ever doubted how much June cared for me, this image...it would be ingrained into my conscious for life.

A soft knock sounded on my suite's door, and I closed my

sketchpad. I quickly opened the door, praying it was her. "Junebug," I said, my voice laced with relief, and moved aside to let her inside.

She ducked into my room, and I closed the door.

I turned to see her moving to my bed, notebook in hand. Instantly, I felt calmer having her with me. I tilted my head as she sat on the edge of my bed. "I didn't know if I'd be seeing you tonight." I gestured to the rain outside and the bolts of lightning that were flashing across the sky. "Thought the storm would keep you away. And I didn't know if your parents wanted to be with you after today."

"I told them to go back to the parents' residence," she said.

A smirk broke out on my face. "Junebug Scott, did you tell them that so you could sneak into your boyfriend's room?"

June didn't blush; instead, she met my eyes straight on, and with confidence in her posture, said, "Yes." Her demeanor took me aback. I had never seen her like this, with no doubt or insecurity in her body. I liked it. More than liked it.

I reached the edge of the bed and looked down at June. The corners of her lips tugged up, and she held my gaze. "You naughty, naughty girl," I said, and June burst out laughing.

"What can I say? You're a bad influence," she said, her voice laced with both humor and exhaustion. It had been one hell of a day.

When she stopped laughing, I placed my finger under her chin and tilted her head up. I leaned down and kissed her. Any unease in my body melted away when her lips were on mine. When I broke away, I said, "Well, I won't ever apologize for that, not if it brings you to my lair."

"Lair?" she sputtered.

"Room of love?" I said, breath catching at the laughter in her brown eyes.

June's hand landed on my arm. "Let's stop while we're ahead. *Please*." I shrugged and June pointed at my sketchbook and the charcoal smudges on my hands. "You've been drawing?"

"Yeah," I said, and sat on bed too, leaning against the headboard.

June frowned. "What did you draw?" My stomach flipped. I didn't think she'd want to see it. I didn't want her to be sadder than she already was. I shrugged again, and June asked, "Can I take a peek?"

I hesitated, but June's stare was bold. Unable to say no to her, I reached for the sketchpad and opened it to the page. I handed it to her, searching her face for any sign that it was upsetting her.

"When was this from?" she asked quietly.

"Today," I rasped, "the moment I told you the treatment hadn't worked on me too."

June nodded and ran her hand down her portrait's tearstained cheek. But she didn't seem upset—rather, in awe. Raising her gaze to meet mine, she said, "I don't think I've ever been so scared as when you told me it hadn't worked for you."

My heart slammed against my ribs. "Same," I said, and still felt the shivers that had accosted my body when June shared her news. Still felt the utter unfairness at how my girl might not be saved. How we felt for one another turned to static in the air between us.

"Come here," I said, and held out my arms. June placed the sketch, along with her notebook, beside her, then crawled up the bed. She fell into my arms and her warmth sank into my bones. I wrapped my arms around her and June tucked her head into the crook of my neck.

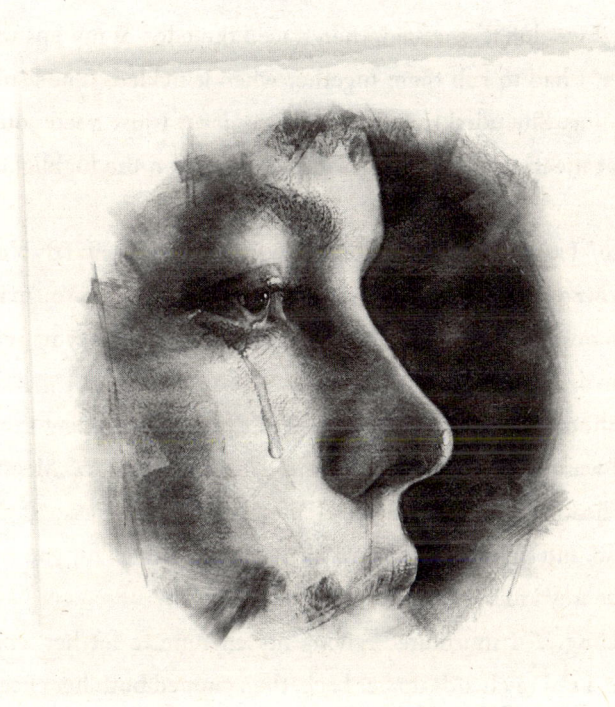

I ran my hand over her scarf-free head. She was dressed in white pajamas and fluffy, pink socks. I was in an old pair of lounge pants and a threadbare McIntyre football training shirt.

"Jesse?" June asked, just after a huge crack of thunder came from outside.

"Yeah?" I said, kissing her smooth scalp.

June lifted her head until she met my eyes. "I have loved every minute of being with you." My stomach sank, because although the words were heaven to my ears, her tone was sad.

"We'll have more," I said, wishing it could be a promise instead of a wish. "*Many* more."

"But if we don't," she said, then traced the edge of my lips with her finger. I had to rub them together when it tickled. June's smile was blinding. She quickly sobered. "If we *don't*, I just need you to know that meeting you…being with you has been the highlight of my life."

"Ditto," I said in lieu of a better response. I didn't think I'd able to say them even if I'd had them. A few moments later, I said, "You're not giving up on me are you, Junebug? These things you're saying seem kind of final."

She shook her head. "Never, but I'm done with holding things back. If I want to say something to someone, I'm going to." Meeting my gaze head-on, June confessed, "I've fallen for you, Jesse Taylor. Hook, line, and sinker. And I know I will continue to fall for you even more. The way I feel for you…could be endless."

"Junebug…" I murmured, giving myself time to let her words penetrate. I ran my hands up her back, then cupped both her cheeks. Making sure I had her full attention, I said, "I *am* irresistible. A total fucking *snack*."

June burst out laughing, and I couldn't resist kissing her lips. I pulled her in, and she quickly parted her mouth. I kissed her deeper. I didn't know if it was the news we'd received today, or the sharing of our ever-growing feelings, but this kiss felt different. It was all-consuming and wrapped in love.

June mirrored my hands and put her palms on my cheeks. She kissed me back like there was no tomorrow. When we broke away, she smiled at me, and it shattered my heart. She was so beautiful. I kissed her one more time, and when she leaned her chin on her hand, watching me, I said, "I'm damn glad your dad didn't see that kiss. He'd have been after me with his shotgun. My ten percent chance would have dropped to zero."

June threw her head back and laughed harder than before. Every laugh from her lips was a shot of tonic I so desperately needed. We *had* to live. Both of us. I could entertain no other outcome.

Something caught June's attention across the room. "You didn't have your football with you at the stables today." She pointed to where it sat on the chair in the corner, then turned to me. "I don't think I've ever seen you without it."

"I don't remember the last time I didn't have it in my hands," I replied. It seemed like she was trying to read my face, so I said, "When I realized you hadn't gone back to the rec room, I went out searching for you." I ran my hand down my face. "I didn't even know I'd left it behind until I came back to my room and I saw it on the chair." My stomach turned with nerves as I said, "My goal has always been football. Getting to UT, the NFL et cetera." I glanced at the football, then concentrated back on June. Her brown eyes were wide as she waited for me to go on. "Today, I knew something had happened to you. In that moment, for once, I didn't even think about my football not being in my hands. And I came to realize something else."

"What?" June whispered.

"That my main goal is no longer football."

June took in a deep breath.

"Instead...it's *you*. Being with you. Surviving this with you."

"Jesse," she said, eyes shining and laid her head on my chest.

I was sure she could hear the beat of my racing heart. But it was true. Football had paled in significance today when June hadn't returned to me with a smile on her face. I had felt in my soul that she had been given the same news as me. We were strangely linked that way. We mirrored one another, and that meant I had to keep strong—not just for me but for June too.

I wanted a shot at our forever.

That made my attention go to June's notebook. "Have you written any more of your story?" I asked. June stiffened on top of me. "June?"

She lifted her head, resting her chin on her hands again. I ran my hands over her head, her cheeks. Hell, this girl had me completely under her thumb. "I don't think I'll continue with it," she said, shocking me to the core.

June had come *alive* writing our happily ever after. Fulfilling her passion had made her glow. As much as the ranch was a nice hospital, a happy place, death always hovered close, and falling back into depression's waiting hands was only one piece of bad news away. Her writing had given her a purpose.

Reading the story of *us* making it through…it had given *me* hope.

"Why?" I asked carefully.

Sorrow filled June's eyes. "It feels like too much," she said, "writing our happily ever when we're here, just scraping by."

"That's exactly why you *do* need to keep going," I said, and she fixed her eyes on me. "Give us the story we should have, Junebug."

"But what if…" She drifted off, and a tear escaped her eye. *What if we don't make it?* she meant.

"Then we live within the pages."

June's lips twitched at that. She liked how that sounded as much as me.

"Anyway, I have this theory," I added casually, trying to lighten the mood.

The grin June had been fighting began to win out. "Oh, I can't wait to hear this," she said, sass in her Texan twang.

I narrowed my eyes. "Junebug, jocks can have good ideas too." She rolled her eyes. "What if the Jesse and June in your book are out there, in a parallel universe, waiting for you to breathe life into their story."

June's head tilted to the side. She was intrigued, I could tell.

"What if the June in that world is writing a book too, only in that version, her story is the you and me of *this world*—us here, on the ranch, clutching our ten percent with both hands."

"A parallel universe? Look at you pulling out the big guns," June joked, but there was interest in her expression. I could almost hear her mind ticking with excitement.

I took one of her hands in my own. "I want us to live, June. If the only way we get to do that in the end is in your book, then at least I'll have the comfort that somewhere, out there, in a parallel universe, we are really making a go of it. And that even though life has roughed us up a bit, we've turned it around and made it our *bitch*."

June dropped her head forward and giggled at my word choice. But she understood the sentiment. I knew she did. Her body had relaxed against mine. When she lifted her head, she said, "I like that, the idea that my words, my story—*our* story—is just the narration to an already-existing life in another world."

Excitement built within me. The spark writing brought to her soul was magnetizing. I kissed her fingers, just needing to be close. "What is your dream with writing, Junebug?"

Her eyes lost focus as she thought through her answer. When she met my gaze again, a small smile on her lips, she whispered, "I want to leave my fingerprint on the window of the world."

"Wow," I said, feeling those words hit me. "That's beautiful. I'm not sure I have that type of depth or the capacity to have that effect on anyone." She was incredible. How could she ever doubt why I loved her?

"Jesse, you have a deep soul, full of love and kindness. Your art leaves everyone who sees it speechless." June kissed my hand this time. Looking me dead in the eye, she said, "And you make me happy. Truly happy." Her eyes shined. "I'm quite literally dying, yet you make me feel so ridiculously alive. That is who you are. And *that*, Jesse, is gift from God."

My throat clogged at her words. I made her happy. I didn't think there was an accolade in life that was greater than that.

I hooked my hands under June's arms and lifted her to me. I kicked back the comforter, placed her beside me, covered us back up, and dimmed the lights. We just stared at one another, holding each other's hands.

"If I die," I whispered a while later, "I want to go just like this—with you next to me, holding my hand." June's lips trembled. But she nodded, making me that silent promise. "Write our story, Junebug. Let our parallel-universe selves live the best lives they can. We deserve to have our happily ever after, even if it's in another life."

"I will," she whispered, then her beautiful, brown eyes began to drift close. "I love you so much. Good night, Junebug."

"I love you too, Jesse. Sleep tight," she murmured, half asleep.

I closed my eyes too, content in knowing that I had at least several weeks left with the girl I had fallen madly in love with.

chapter thirteen

June

Jesse and June's Happily Ever After

The room looked strange now that all my things were packed. The wall opposite my bed was bare, free of Jesse's many drawings of me, of us, of Ginger, and all of us Chemo Club members together in the movie room. They were some of my most-prized possessions and were tucked safely in a folder in my suitcase.

I exhaled a long sigh. We had all come here dying, with mere months—maybe even just weeks—left to live. But the ranch had become a place of healing, of laughter and love, and now we were all cancer free and graduating from high school and from the new treatment that had worked so well on us all.

I took my headscarf off the bed and ran my hand over my scalp, the feeling of hair growing back again making me smile. I'd gotten used to the smoothness. I moved in front of the mirror, finally recognizing the girl before me. She was a warrior, and she was perfect. Though I adored seeing my new dark-brown fuzz.

I fixed my headscarf in place and smoothed my hands over my dress. It was the sage-green one I'd worn my first day here—I knew it was Jesse's favorite.

A familiar knock on the door filled the room. When I opened the door, my mouth parted seeing Jesse Taylor on the other side. Gone was the boy who lived in T-shirts and faded jeans, and instead, he wore a linen button-down and navy-blue shorts.

"Jesse..." I said as he leaned his arm against my doorframe. In the past several weeks, Jesse had begun building up his muscle mass and weight. In mere weeks, he would leave for preseason training at UT. I would follow after that, when the nonathletic freshman class arrived. Jesse had done it. He had taken his short window to get fit and turned it into gold.

We had made it. We were in remission, and we were going to UT.

I chuckled when I saw that, in typical Jesse fashion, he still wore that damn backwards Longhorns baseball cap that he never took off. Like me, his hair had begun to grow back; he had tufts of light-brown hair that I couldn't wait to see begin to curl.

"Junebug Scott," he said, voice awe filled. Jesse held out his hand and I took it. "Give me a twirl, darlin'," he said, voice hoarse, and spun me around on the spot. "Beautiful," he said, then pulled me to his chest. Bending me back a little, Jesse leaned down and kissed me.

"You're in a good mood," I said against his lips, which felt like such a redundant thing to say. Our entire group was practically euphoric. The only thing that had dampened our spirits was Dr. Duncan's farewell talk, where he mentioned that at our age, we were 50 to 85 percent likely to relapse in the next five years.

Jesse and I had decided not to concern ourselves with that and only focus on what we could control and what was happening now. Cancer had at least taught us that living in the moment was the only way through this life.

Jesse kissed me again, and just like all the many times before, I melted against him. He wrapped the tail of my headscarf around his hand, keeping his mouth on mine. Smiling against my lips, he said, "Soon I'll be able to do this with your ponytail." I blushed so hard, I felt on fire. "Now, won't that be kinky," he teased.

A throat cleared behind us. "I heard that, Jesse Taylor. Now kindly release my daughter."

Jesse stilled, muttered a barely audible *shit*, then stepped away from me. I straightened my dress and saw my daddy in the hallway. Jesse stepped beside me and took hold of my hand. I fought back a laugh. Daddy's arms were crossed over his chest. He wore a shirt and tie and looked really handsome.

"Hey, sir," Jesse said in an overly polite tone, squeezing my hand twice.

Daddy regarded Jesse in silence for a while, then said, "We're getting started in ten." He walked away, but if I wasn't mistaken, I saw his shoulders shaking with laughter as he made his way down the hallway. His favorite pastime seemed to be teasing my boyfriend. But we all knew my mama and daddy loved him to pieces.

Jesse groaned and turned to me. "I can't wait until we're at college and your daddy can't keep popping out from behind corners every time I kiss you."

I pulled him in the direction of the rec room. "I wouldn't put it past him to follow us."

Jesse pressed me against the wall and kissed me again. "Not a chance. At college we get to be us alone—no chemo, no antibody treatment, just Jesse and June taking on the world." Jesse lifted his fist. "Group two for the win."

I met his fist with my own. "Group two for the win."

He kissed me again, then said, "Not sure how I'll survive not seeing you for the next couple of months."

"I know," I said and ran my finger down his face, committing every inch to memory. We had been here now for several months, together every single day. The ranch was our own little world, where everything we did felt more, bigger, brighter. Several months here felt like years in the outside world.

I wasn't sure how we were going to go from our little cocoon here to the big, wide world. Plus, we would return to our small towns miles and miles from each other for a while first. I was going to miss him so much.

Jesse kept a tight hold on me as we entered the rec room, which was now decked out in balloons and a banner that read, Graduation. All of us had missed our high school graduations, so we were getting our own version of that today.

"I have to say, there better be a medal or something for us," Jesse remarked. "Surviving both high school and terminal cancer surely must be better rewarded than a handshake from Doc Duncan and a piece of paper pretending to be our high school diplomas."

Chris came from behind and put his arms around our shoulders. "We're getting sprung, guys. What a glorious fucking day!"

Emma linked my arm with hers and laid her head on my shoulder. "I'm happy, but I'm so sad to be leaving y'all," she said, echoing my feelings. "What will I do without my besties?" She glanced over to Chris. "Well, without my June and Jesse."

"Pssht," Chris muttered. "I got you through this place, Em. And you know it."

Emma rolled her eyes, and smiling, I laid my head against hers. Emma had become incredibly important to me—a true best friend who had been by my side through thick and thin.

"You'll come to UT to visit, and I'll come to College Station to see you too," I said. "We have a deal." UT and Texas A&M weren't too far apart, so seeing Emma and Chris there would be doable.

"Chemo—but no more of the chemo part, please God," Chris said making us all laugh, "Club for life!"

"Chemo—but no more chemo—Club for life!" we all said and broke into hysterics. The air felt charged with happiness.

"Shall we begin?" Neenee said and took to the makeshift stage. Dr. Duncan stood with our diplomas. As Neenee made her speech and began to call our names, it almost felt surreal. None of us had expected to get to our graduation. Yet here we were, feeling almost brand-new.

I was leaving the ranch changed. I had best friends and the love of my life. My passion for writing was more pronounced than ever, but I wanted to write something true, something real. I wanted to write about my greatest fear—about not having more time with Jesse, not having a future at all. Even as I sat there, my hands itched to write. I had begun to put my writing onto a public platform under a pseudonym, chapter by chapter, and it was receiving so many reads that my head spun.

I was doing it. I was writing a love story and people were loving it.

"Penny for your thoughts," Jesse said quietly and bumped my shoulder with his. There was no pain as I did, no aches. My knee still gave me a slight limp, but that was all.

"I'm just so happy that we're here." He put his arm around me and held me close until our names were called, one after the other—S and T were beside each other in the alphabet.

Destined.

Jesse's mama and sisters hooted and hollered as we climbed the stage, and my parents whistled and cried.

This day was about gratitude—something I had in volumes.

Next was college, and a new chapter of our story would begin.

chapter fourteen

Jesse

University of Texas

Jesse and June's Happily Ever After

I ran off the training field and into the showers. I had barely been in there maybe thirty seconds before I was out and throwing on my clothes.

"Why's your ass on fire?" Sheridan, my wide receiver and roommate, asked as I ran my fingers through my hair instead of a comb (I had a sprinkling of hair again!).

I threw on my sneakers and bolted out the door. "Taylor?" Sheridan shouted, eyebrows pulled down in confusion.

"My girl gets here today!" I said and fled as fast as I could out of the locker room. As I got closer to the dorms, the streets were teeming with freshman arriving with their parents.

My heart was slamming in my chest, and it had nothing to do with my pace. I got to see my Junebug after too much time apart. Preseason had been intense, giving me zero days off. So I had been on a countdown to see my girl for what seemed like forever.

Mr. Scott had texted me to say they had arrived. I wanted to surprise June and help her settle in. I could feel the curious stares of people as I rushed by them, but I didn't stop until I reached June's dorm. Out of breath, but thankful to have most of my fitness and strength back, I grabbed ahold of the front door that someone had just walked through and began my ascent.

I heard her voice first and I nearly stumbled. God, how had I made it these past few months without her? The sound of Mrs. Scott's voice came next, and as I rounded the corner and approached her door, I saw Mr. Scott in the hallway.

He spotted me and gave me a wide, welcoming smile. I knew I looked so different from the last time he'd seen me. I had more hair, for one, but I'd also filled out more, gained some weight, and put on some muscle. I wasn't where I needed to be yet, but I was getting there.

Mr. Scott came toward me and shook my hand, then pulled me in for a hug, and my chest tightened. The way Mr. and Mrs. Scott had taken me in would always be a shock to me.

Mr. Scott ruffled my hair, and I playfully pushed him off. He pressed his finger to his lips, then called out, "June, could you come and help me with this box, please?"

I held my breath, keeping my eyes fixed on the doorway. Then she appeared and just about split my heart in two. June was wearing faded jean shorts and a simple white shirt tucked in to the waist. My eyes dropped to her feet, and I smiled at the beat-up brown cowboy boots she wore.

But that wasn't the biggest shock. The shock was the long brown hair that fell to the middle of her back. June opened her mouth to speak to her daddy when she saw me leaning against the wall with my arms across my chest.

"Mornin', Junebug," I said, wincing as my voice shook. I couldn't help it. I was finally reunited with my June after too much time apart—a lump clogged my throat and tears flooded my vision. Seeing her again felt like a goddamn gift.

"Jesse..." June said, her voice breaking just as she launched herself into my arms. She was still light as a feather, but I loved that she had put on some weight. She was healthy and filled out and a complete knockout. Her long hair tickled at my cheek as I pressed her to me, and her hold around my neck was so tight I wasn't sure if she would ever let go.

June reared back and I saw tears trickling down her cheeks. Her big, brown eyes were raking over me, and she smiled when she saw my hair. She ran her hands through it. We video called every day, several times a day, but seeing how each other had gotten healthier in the flesh was a damn revelation.

"Your tiny curls," June said, and pressed her hand on them. I just knew they were tight from the humidity.

I leaned in and kissed her, unable to not have her on my lips for one more minute. I cradled the back of her head with my hand and was content to stay like this all day. Even Mr. Scott didn't interrupt this time.

When June final pulled back, she laid her forehead against mine and said, "We did it, baby. We're here."

I smiled so hard, I felt like my face would crack. I moved my hand into the small gap between us and clenched it into a fist. "Group two for the win."

June bumped my fist. "Group two for the win."

I took my fill of my girl. I didn't want to miss a moment now that I had her back. "Your hair seems to have miraculously grown overnight, Junebug," I said, and ran my fingers down her long, dark-brown strands.

"Mama treated me to hair extensions last night as a starting-college gift," she said, blushing a little. "My natural hair isn't much longer than yours." She sighed.

"What?" I asked.

June put her arms tighter around my neck. I knew I should set her down, but I hadn't had enough of holding her yet. "I wanted to come here and have a new start, you know?" Keeping her voice low, she said, "I didn't want to be Cancer Girl. I want to be like everyone else. Just a freshman starting college."

Understanding washed through me. "You look incredible," I said, making sure she knew that every word I spoke was true. "But you are beautiful with hair or without, you always have been. And I fell for you when you were Cancer Girl and I was Cancer Boy." I frowned. "Wait, why did that make us sound like superheroes?"

June threw her head back and laughed, and it sounded like heaven.

"God, I've missed you so much, Junebug."

"I've missed you too," she whispered back, then kissed me again. When she pulled back, she released her legs from my waist and said, "Come and see my room."

I walked inside, where Mr. and Mrs. Scott were putting June's things away. Mrs. Scott had already made up June's bed. "Jesse!" she greeted and gave me a tight hug. "We've missed you so much!"

"I've missed y'all too," I replied. I had. They were family at this point. My mom and sisters loved them all as well.

"Hi," a new voice said. I turned behind me to see a tall, red-headed girl. "I'm Sydney, June's roommate."

"Jesse," I said, shaking her hand. "Love of June's life, the boy who showed her the true meaning of happiness, and the bringer of all June's fun."

Sydney looked to June a little wide eyed.

"Don't worry," June said. "You'll get used to him in no time at all."

Mr. Scott emptied the final box and said, "That's the last of it, honey. You're all unpacked." His eyes glistened, but he covered his rising emotions by saying, "Let's go for dinner before we leave." He pointed at me. "And you're coming too, son. I want to hear all about preseason and how y'all are looking."

June slipped her hand into mine, and I squeezed it twice. We were here at UT, we were healthy, and I couldn't wait for this chapter to begin.

chapter fifteen
Jesse

"I'd forgotten what the outside world looks like," I said, as I took in the sprawling sight of Zilker Park. To get us out of the ranch before we started phase two of the trial, Neenee had organized a trip to Zilker Park in downtown Austin for the day.

I loved the ranch. They really did have everything there for us. But just being here, out in public and doing something normal, was very much needed. We'd been living in our bubble now for what seemed like an age. It was actually strange to see other people going about their day.

"You make us sound like we've just escaped a cult compound or something," Chris said, and I smiled. The sun felt good on my face.

Emma unlinked her arm from June's and said, "Stand back, everybody. There're sporty, half-naked boys everywhere I look, and I have a feeling my soulmate might be in this park somewhere."

Chris pretended to gag. "Em, please, for the love of all that's holy, I cannot face seeing you flirt today. The next lot of immunotherapy is gonna make me plenty sick soon enough. I don't need you to add to it."

Emma lifted her hand to her ear. "Did anyone else hear that annoying buzzing sound?" She shrugged. "Oh." She looked at Chris. "It was just your whining voice."

June giggled, and I pulled off my shirt and tucked it in my shorts. Neenee would kill me if she saw me. We were under strict rules to keep covered at all times. We weren't allowed much sun exposure because of the meds, but I had to do it to make my joke work. My comedy deserved the sacrifice.

I pointed at Chris. "Emma, I'm offended," I said. "Me and my boy here are sporty AF and walk around half-naked a ton at the ranch. Have we not been an absolute feast for your eyes these past couple of months?"

Emma gagged this time. "Now *I'm* nauseous. Thanks, Jesse." Emma looked at me, studying my body. "Okay, I'll concede. *You're* hot, Jesse, you know you are. June waxes lyrical about it all the time—"

"What?!" June said, shocked, cheeks quickly blazing. "No, I don't!"

"Junebug!" I said and pulled her back when she playfully tried to walk off. "Tell me more about how hot you find me."

June's lips pinched as she tried to not find humor in the moment. "No, thanks," she said mock moodily.

I winked at Emma. "Thank you for that information about my girl, Emma." I threw my arms around June's shoulders and kissed her cheek. "It is most useful." June eventually reached up, held my wrists, and sank into my chest.

"But a feast *you* are not," Emma continued, now speaking to Chris. "More like an average appetizer that never quite satisfies."

"Ohh, burn," I muttered, as Chris narrowed his eyes at Emma.

"You're lucky I love you, Em," he said.

"Love you too," Emma sang, and scanned the field again. There was a lot of people here. Groups playing frisbee, some chilling on blankets and baking under the sun. Some were running, and in the distance, I saw a couple of guys throwing a football back and forth. I threw my shirt back on, knowing I did have to be careful not to get burned, and sunblock could only do so much. I wrapped my arms around June again.

Suddenly, June stiffened in my arms as Emma said, "This is what it must feel like to be famous." I frowned, then I realized people were looking at us. I guessed it was obvious that we were all in cancer treatment. The girls wore headscarves while Chris's and my ballcaps didn't exactly hide that we were hairless too. I had seen Silas, Cherry, Toby and Kate walk off in the other direction, so all attention was solely on us.

It had never bothered me before—didn't now. I'd always been confident in how I looked. But feeling June shrink in my hold showed me just how vulnerable the attention was making her.

I put my mouth to her ear. "Are you okay, baby?"

She turned in my arms and tucked herself into my chest. If she could have disappeared, I'm sure she would have in that moment. "I hate attention," she said. I knew June felt insecure at times, but I was surprised by just how much she didn't like eyes on her.

"Junebug," I said, "I've got you."

Chris seemed as unbothered by people's curious glances as I

was. People weren't being malicious. More than anything, it seemed like sympathy that was bring projected our way. I wrapped my arms around June, hiding her from the world.

"Let's go find somewhere private," I said to my friends.

Emma pointed to a large cropping of trees in the distance, not too far from the guys playing football. "There, it's pretty empty and the trees will protect us from the sun."

"Anyone else feel like Bubble Boy?" Chris said. It was an accurate comparison. As much as we were getting this day to get a break from the ranch, we still had a list of rules we had to follow. Chris carried a cooler full of meds and bottles of the orange sludge that we had to take at various times today. Neenee and Bailey were also here with us, along with a couple of nurses we had to check in with several times a day.

June kept her head tucked into my chest as we walked. She didn't look up until the crowds of people thinned out. "You can come out now," I said into June's ear.

She cautiously lifted her head and looked around us. Seeing I was telling the truth, she exhaled. "That was awful," she said, her tight voice carrying the stress the attention had brought to her.

Emma reached out and took hold of June's hand. "You really don't like attention, huh?"

June shook her head. "I never have." Her expression was earnest. "I'm not completely introverted, but being in the limelight just makes me shudder."

Chris frowned. "You know you're dating Jesse Taylor, right?" He put his hand on my shoulder. My stomach fell.

June's eyebrows were pulled down in confusion. "Okay?"

Chris balked. "June, you're from Texas. Surely you know what kind of attention a quarterback gets. Especially one as good as my main man here. He's *Jesse Taylor*. A once-in-a-generation-type player."

June looked up at me, but I could feel the tension still thrumming in her body. Her brown eyes searched mine, but what could I say? Chris was telling the truth. If we got through phase two—*when* we got through phase two—and I managed to make it to UT and play for the Longhorns, the attention I received would be…a lot.

"I guess I never thought about it," June said, her voice suddenly guarded. I hated how it sounded.

"It'll be fine, baby," I said, trying to reassure her. But I could see a seed of doubt had been planted in her head, and her obvious apprehension didn't sit well with me.

"If anyone gives you shit, June, just call me. I'll come down and whoop their asses for messing with my girl," Emma said, making June smile.

June exhaled, but I couldn't say that I wasn't shook by her reaction.

We were determined to make it, to take our 10 percent and turn it into 100, but now I was a little worried about what came after. My priority was getting to UT with my girl. Playing for the Longhorns and getting to the NFL was a close second. Every day, I told myself I would get there. I never even entertained that June and playing football wouldn't mesh.

"Taylor?"

The sound of my surname being called from somewhere to my left pulled me from my thoughts.

A wide smile spread on my face when I saw that Matthew Banks, a guy from my high school, was heading toward us. "Banks?" I said, and June stepped away so I could go speak to him.

"We'll head to the trees," Chris said, and June, Emma and Chris kept walking, settling under the shade of the trees across the field.

"Shit, bro!" Banks said as he reached me. He held out his hand. I took it and he pulled me in and slapped me on my back. Banks was a year older than me, a linebacker, who now played for UT.

When he pulled back, his smile faltered as his gaze swept over me. Sympathy flooded his expression, and my stomach rolled. For a second, I understood how June had felt when she'd caught people watching us.

"How are you doing?" His hand squeezed my arm. "I heard you were sick. I'm so sorry, Jesse. That sucks. I guess that's why Coach recruited another QB in your place."

My entire fucking world seemed to stop.

"I can't believe I won't be playing with you next year," Banks said, and my vision shimmered as his words sank into my brain. *Coach recruited another QB in your place...*

That wasn't true, was it? I hadn't been told anything about it. My mom hadn't said anything, neither had my coach from back in McIntyre. Every strain of muscle in my body began to tighten until it ached.

Clearing my throat, I said, "I still intend to come to UT."

Banks stilled. "In the future?" He frowned like I was speaking another language.

I shook my head, feeling myself begin to unravel. My hands began shaking.

Coach recruited another QB in your place...

"No, this year," I said, and Banks's gaze swept over me again.

He rubbed the back of his neck. "I was told...I was told you'd gone to a hospice."

"I didn't," I said, a bite to my voice. I was never an asshole, but I knew I sounded like one in that moment. "I'm in a clinical drug trial. I'm gonna get better. And I'm gonna play for UT." I didn't care if my new coach had recruited another QB; there were always a few recruited. I'd still rise to the top.

Banks was quiet again. Then said, "Preseason is brutal, man." I stared at him, but I felt like I wasn't in the moment. My heart was slamming in my chest, my hands were clenching into fists and I felt like I couldn't breathe.

"I know," I said absently.

Banks looked behind him, and I saw a guy I recognized. Jason Williams. He was a UT defensive tackle. He was watching me and Banks with curiosity. His face...I realized he thought he was watching a walking dead man. A QB star that should have had it all until cancer came and ripped it all away.

"I'm gonna reach remission and get to UT this year. I'll get my weight back on and my fitness up. You'll see," I said, and I could hear the desperation in my voice. I wanted to tell myself to stop talking, but it all came spilling out. "I'm gonna play for the Longhorns, Banks. So, get ready. I'll be there in the summer for preseason."

Banks stepped away, and I could tell he just wanted to get the fuck away from me. "That's great, bro," he said, then pointed his thumb over his shoulder at Williams. "I'd better be getting back." He backed away farther and farther until he said, "It was good to see you, Jesse. I hope the treatment goes well."

Banks turned and ran back to Williams—who should have been my future teammate too.

Coach recruited another QB in your place...

Banks talked in low tones to Williams. They looked over at me, and I turned and moved toward my friends. But I was shaken. Rocked.

Preseason is brutal, man…

I *knew* it was brutal. I *knew* it would take all I had to get there and be able to participate. But I could do it. I knew I could.

But Banks didn't. He looked at me like I was *insane*.

I glanced down at my hands. They were shaking, and for a moment, they didn't seem like mine. Is this why June did it? Did she no longer feel like herself in those moments?

I couldn't get my heart to calm down. But as I approached my friends, I forced a smile.

"Jesse!" Chris said and waved me over. "*Die Hard*. Christmas film or not?"

I lowered to the blanket they'd laid out, sitting beside June. I jumped when her hand touched my leg. I met her eyes and saw concern quickly fill their depths.

"You shocked me," I said, hoping I sounded normal. But when I turned back to Chris and felt June's attention remain on me, I knew she'd seen through me. She always did.

"Christmas film," I said, trying to not let myself fall into the sinkhole that was opening up inside of me. My throat was thick with emotion, and it took everything I had to not crumble and let the tears flow.

Banks was told I was gonna die.

Coach had lost faith in my remission.

The feel of June lifting and threading her hand through mine was almost my undoing. She laid her head on my arm. But I couldn't talk. I couldn't even look at her, because then she'd know. She'd know I'd just had the rug pulled out from underneath me.

"It is not!" Emma shrieked. "Just because it's at Christmastime, a Christmas movie it does not make! Ugh!" She turned to June. "June, tell me you agree."

"I haven't seen it, sorry," June said, trying for normalcy too. But I heard the worry in her voice. Worry that something was wrong with me.

There was. It was all wrong—everything was going so fucking wrong.

Ten percent suddenly felt *impossible*.

"June, you're no help, girl," Emma said, and the conversation around me faded.

I froze, trapped in the hell that was my plummeting determination.

Who was I if not a football player? I had June, I wanted June, but I needed football too. I wanted both.

"Baby?" June said, rubbing my arm. I looked to June, seeing Chris and Emma shooting concerned looks my way too. "We're gonna take a walk. Are you coming?"

"Nah," I said. My eyes found Banks and Williams. They were casually throwing a football back and forth. I rotated my arm and had to grit my teeth at how much it hurt.

I couldn't throw a football at all now. I'd tried to accept it over the past few weeks, but now it was smacking me in the face. I wanted to play for the Longhorns, and I couldn't even throw a damn ball.

"I'll stay too," June said.

"No!" I said a bit too forcefully.

June's brown eyes widened in shock.

I pasted on another smile. "Go, Junebug. Take a walk. I'm…" I picked at the grass beside me. "I'm just tired."

"Then we'll all stay," Chris said, nodding at me.

Suddenly, my anger fell away and all that remained was gutting desperation. "No," I rasped. "Please, go."

June nodded, and Emma and Chris got up and walked to the trail that would take them through the rest of Zilker Park.

June inched closer, putting her hand on my shoulder. "Jesse?"

"Please, Junebug," I said, fighting back tears. "Just go for a walk. I'm okay."

"No, you're—"

"*Please*," I begged.

Her hand froze on my shoulder. When it slowly slipped off, I wanted to grab my girl and crush her to me—tell her everything that happened and beg her to make me feel better. Because I was sure only she could.

But I was falling the fuck apart, and if I did, I would finally have to reveal all of me and explain, that at times, I was all kinds of fucked up.

"Call me if you need me," June said and got up. I watched her walk, and a flicker of pride sparked in my chest for my girl when she kept her head high, even walking past people who stared at her—at the most perfect girl in the world who was fighting with all her strength just to make it to eighteen.

When June turned back and looked at me, the expression on her face cut me. I gave her a small wave, one of reassurance, but my girl wasn't reassured about anything.

Laughter sailed from behind me and I turned to watch Banks and Williams shooting the shit, not a care in the world.

And I stayed that way, wondering what that kind of cancer-freedom would feel like. I couldn't remember anymore.

I just watched them from my place under a copse of trees so my chemo-wrecked skin wouldn't burn.

Bailey found me and ensured I drank the orange sludge. I didn't even taste it as it went down.

When Chris, June, and Emma returned, I laid down and closed my eyes, feigning sleep. They had to have known it was bullshit, but they didn't say anything.

An hour later, we loaded onto the bus. June didn't say a word as she sat beside me and held my hand. I leaned my head against the window and closed my eyes. If June saw a tear escape and fall down my cheek, she didn't say anything.

"We going to the rec room?" Chris asked when we got off the bus.

I shook my head and walked to my room.

"I'll go with him," I heard June say. Her footsteps sounded like thunder behind me. I just needed to be alone. I needed to speak to my mom and my high school coach. I needed to know what was happening.

"Jesse," June called as I walked into my room. She slipped inside, but when I turned to her and saw her worried face, I couldn't cope.

"I need to be alone," I said.

June reared her head back—I'd stunned her. I never wanted time apart from her, and I didn't now. I just didn't want her affected by the emptiness that was trying to pull me down.

"Jesse, please," she begged. "What did that guy say to you?"

"June," I whispered, "please leave me alone."

"I don't want to," she said boldly. "I don't think you should be."

"I need to be!" I said, my voice slightly raised.

This time, her mouth dropped open in shock. I felt like the

world's biggest dick. June was perfect, and I'd just shouted at her. But I couldn't help it. I was drowning, and I didn't want to pull her down with me.

"Just go... I'm begging you," I said, and June's eyes filled with tears. She waited for me to change my mind, but when I just stared at her, she nodded and slipped out of my room.

The sudden silence was deafening. Pulling my cell from my pocket, I called my coach. "Jesse?" my high school coach answered. "How are you doing, son?"

"Has UT recruited someone else in my place?" Loud silence was Coach's only response. I sank to my bed. "Why didn't you tell me?" I whispered.

"Because we didn't want it to break you, son. We didn't want you to lose your will to fight." I looked out the window at dusk settling in. Everything felt dark now. "Your spot on the team is still there, as is your scholarship, but the UT coach needed to make sure he had the depth he needed in his quarterbacks. You're not out for the count, Jesse, but he had to make sure his team is as strong as possible for next season."

"It was always impossible, wasn't it?" I said. "A pipe dream. I was never gonna be able to recover in time for next season. I was foolish." I released a self-deprecating laugh. "And y'all knew it and let me pretend."

"We all need something to get us through, Jesse. You were determined." Coach cleared his throat. "You're the most talented player I've ever had the privilege of coaching. And maybe it is too late for you to get healthy for next season. But you're only seventeen. There's the season after. And I know Coach Higgins. He believes in you as much as I do—as much as we *all* do."

Tears tracked down my cheeks.

"Son, you're a football player. And a damn good one at that. You know it's not over until it's over. And the Jesse I know would keep fighting. You hear me?"

"I only have a ten percent chance of survival," I said, my heart feeling really heavy. It was hard to always be positive. "The treatment isn't working—might never work and then I'm all out of options."

"You can do this, Jesse," Coach said, and I knew that my mom must have told him already.

But I nodded, needing to hear it. My chest ached. It was times like this when I really wished I had a dad, that my dad had loved me enough to stick around and help me through rough waters. My old friend rejection infiltrated my veins. "Thanks, Coach," I found myself saying. "I'm gonna go now."

"You're gonna be okay, Jesse," he said. "I believe it."

"Thanks," I said. "Bye." I hung up and laid down on my bed. I pulled the comforter over me and switched off my lamp. I couldn't move and just wanted the world to disappear for a while.

No, that wasn't true. I wanted Junebug. Guilt clawed at my conscience. I'd chased her away. The first person except my mom and sisters to ever love me unconditionally, who had fought for me, chased after me to make sure I was okay—and I'd sent her away.

Getting to my feet, I pulled my comforter with me and went onto the porch. Ginger was staring at me like he wanted to jump the fence and sit with me some. But there was only one person my soul was crying out for. So I sat down at her porch door to wait until she came back.

I'd beg for her forgiveness, but at this point, I felt like June and her love for me was the only thing that was tethering me to this world.

chapter sixteen

June

EMMA OPENED HER DOOR, AND HER EXPRESSION FELL. "I'M SORRY, babes," she said, and pulled me inside. I was thankful her parents weren't here. I just needed alone time with my best friend at this moment.

I fell into her arms and let my emotions out. Emma held me tightly. "He won't tell me what happened," I said. Emma directed me to her bed, and we sat.

I wiped at my face and Emma rubbed my back. "He was a football player, wasn't he?" Emma said, referring to the guy Jesse had been speaking to at the park.

"I think so."

Emma shrugged. "Maybe it hit him, you know? The reality of it all. Of maybe not being well enough to play next season. Of just how much effort it will take him to get game-fit again."

"I know," I said, and sighed deeply. I thought of his face when he came to us under the trees. He was devastated. Jesse Taylor was fun and extroverted. The boy who sat beside us was anything but.

I'd always seen a sliver of sadness in Jesse's soul, and I had a feeling that sliver had been cracked wide open today. "He asked me to leave him alone," I told Emma, and my heart broke. "He's never asked me to leave."

Emma laid her head on my shoulder. "This is the reality of being terminally ill, isn't it?" Emma said. "Having days when darkness shrouds your sun. When the future and dreams you had taken for granted, come crashing down."

I nodded. I didn't have words. Jesse had kept me going this entire time, waiting at my door each morning with his cheeky smile and sunshine personality. He had held my hand through treatments and showed me his talent with his drawings. He'd been my rock.

"Give him time," Emma said. "We all break, don't we? I know I have."

I had too. Many times. And I realized, if I loved someone, I had to love every part. Including the parts that were darkest.

I held Emma's hand and squeezed. "I'm going to my room to wait for him. I just need to know he's okay." I hugged her. "Thank you for always being here for me. I really don't know what I'd do without you."

"Forever, babes. We're besties for life."

I laughed, and it broke through the heaviness in my heart. "Good night," I said.

As I passed Jesse's room, I pressed my ear to his door. It was silent inside, and I wondered if he'd fallen asleep. I wanted nothing more than to walk inside and hold him. I wasn't afraid of his broken parts, but I understood needing time alone. The ranch was amazing, but there was no doubt we were in a pressure cooker. Sometimes we needed to simmer and just rest.

I entered my bedroom and turned on the lamp beside my bed. I turned to go into my bathroom to get ready for bed when I jumped out of my skin. My hand covered my mouth in shock, as on the other side of my porch doors, was Jesse, wrapped in a comforter.

My heart raced as I went to the door and unlocked it. Jesse looked up as I opened the door. "I'm sorry, Junebug," he whispered, and for the first time since I'd met him, Jesse lowered his head and sobbed.

The pain that engulfed me was absolute. I threw myself into Jesse, wrapping my arms around his neck, and I cried with him. I held the love of my life in my weak arms, yet just being here for him, like this, made me feel like the strongest person in the world.

"I've got you," I whispered. "I'm here."

Jesse reached up and grabbed my arm like he needed me to ground him. I kissed his head, over and over, running my hand over his cheek.

"I love you," I said as I rocked him. "I love you so much."

That only made Jesse sob harder. I squeezed my eyes shut. I could barely stand to see him like this—my magnetic charmer, reduced to tears. Yet I felt like the luckiest girl in the world to be the one he could fall apart with.

We were one another's other halves. In good times and bad.

We sat there until Jesse's chest hitched and jumped in the aftermath of his tears. Then he lifted his head, his eyes swollen and face mottled with redness. He didn't speak, but I saw gratefulness shone on his face.

Standing, I held out my hand. "Let's go inside," I said, and Jesse got to his feet, bringing the comforter with him. I led us to my bed, and we laid down facing each other. I held both of Jesse's hands between us, bringing them to my lips and kissing them.

Jesse closed his eyes, his lips still trembling with his sorrow. Finally, he inhaled a stuttered breath and said, "UT has recruited another QB in my place, for next season."

My heart cracked. "Baby," I rasped.

"Of course they have," he said. His desolate eyes met my own. "I feel like..." He trailed off only to add, "I feel like I'm losing everything."

I inched closer and kissed him again. I wanted him to get things off his chest.

"I was naive, Junebug." Jesse swallowed hard. "I was never going to be able to play for UT next season, not even if the treatment had worked during phase one." He sighed. "I'm so depleted of strength and energy. Especially now the immunotherapy isn't working."

"Yet," I added.

"Yet," Jesse repeated, a curl of his lips telling me his emotional fog had lifted a touch.

I released one of his hands and pressed mine against his cheek. He turned into my touch and kissed my palm. My heart fluttered. "Jesse Taylor, you are the most incredible boy I have ever met." He smiled a fraction more. "I believe that, even if playing next season is not in the cards, you will work hard to make the season after happen."

He sighed. "I'll be put on the injured list, and will have to work so hard to get off it."

"We will get you through this."

"We?" Jesse said, peace settling over him.

"What?" I questioned.

"You said we," he said.

I smiled at him and melted when one of Jesse's dimples popped on his cheek. "Of course," I said. "It's group two for the win, remember?"

I lifted my hand and held it out for a fist bump. But Jesse covered my fist with his hand. His smile fell and, imploring me to listen with his gaze, said, "I get so sad sometimes." My stomach fell. But he was just putting into words what I had always suspected. I nodded at him for him to continue. "It's rejection, Junebug. I just don't handle it very well."

"It's understandable," I assured. "You've been through so much." Jesse blinked away tears, but a few escaped. I leaned over and kissed them away.

"It swallows me. The guilt of not being able to do what I'd dreamed for my mom and my sisters. So much that my doctor back home put me on meds for depression."

"That's nothing to be ashamed of," I said, voice stern. "A lot of people with cancer struggle with their mental health. We are constantly thinking and talking about dying, Jesse. That's not an easy thing for anyone to cope with."

Jesse nodded. "I think…" He paused. "I think today, seeing Matthew Banks—the guy I was talking to—it just hit me."

"What did?"

"That my plan that I've had for so long won't work. Even if we go into remission in this next phase, my body has been through a lot. Maybe too much to achieve those dreams."

"Jesse," I said, shifting so close we shared the same air. "I haven't known your mama that long, but I can tell you, with one hundred percent certainty, that all she wants is for you to be happy. If that means still working to achieve your football goals, great. But if it doesn't, I guarantee she would support that too."

"I know," Jesse said, body relaxing like he was releasing what looked like years' worth of stress.

I leaned in and kissed him. I could taste salt on his lips from his tears. When I pulled back, I said, "I love you without expectation. I love you with all my heart because you are the sweetest, kindest boy I know." I smiled. "You make me laugh and show me that life is more than I thought it was. I adore you. And I don't care what you do with your life as long as I'm beside you."

"You will be," Jesse said, and I heard the truth of those words all the way down to my soul. "It's you and me, Junebug. It's you and me forever." He kissed me again. "I love you. Please forgive me for pushing you away."

"There's nothing to forgive," I said, and pulled my comforter over us both. We stared at one another until sleep began to pull us away.

And when Jesse fell asleep first, he seemed lighter somehow, but my heart felt the weight of all he had been holding. His father leaving had thrust him onto a path no child should have to travel. But I decided to make it my mission, for the rest of our lives, that I would be his reprieve when he put too many expectations on himself. I would be his gravity, grounding him, and I would be his sun, chasing away the dark clouds that would inevitably come.

I would be the girl who would cradle his heart until my very last breath—and even beyond.

chapter seventeen

Jesse

"You ready for this next round?" Susan asked.

"That depends," I said. "You got the sick buckets ready and waiting?"

"You know it," she said, untying the tourniquet from around my bicep and placing my blood samples away for testing. Round two of immunotherapy began tomorrow. And I was as ready as I'd ever be. June had gone to see her parents in the parents' residence while I got all my vitals checked and my blood taken. After our talk the other night, I felt better. I'd allowed myself to take some of the weight off and just *be*. That, and I'd arranged to start talking with Michelle, the on-site psychologist. It couldn't hurt and it was probably long overdue.

"See you tomorrow, Susan," I said, and left Susan's office. I gritted my teeth at the ache in my legs and reminded myself to get more pain meds later if I wanted any chance at sleep tonight. In the past few weeks, my pain had stepped up a notch, but then I guessed that was a side effect of my cancer progressing.

June's door was still closed, so I knew she wasn't back yet. I had a few images circling my head that I wanted to sketch, and as I opened the door to my room and stepped through, I heard "SURPRISE!"

I jumped and my eyes widened at my teammates and the cheerleaders from McIntyre all standing before me, smiles on their faces. There must have been about thirty people in my room. My suite had been completely decked out in blue and white, with get-well posters and pictures of me and my friends.

"Wh-what?" I stuttered. "What are y'all doing here?"

Michaels, my best friend and teammate, stepped forward. "We've come to see you and wish you luck for the next round of treatment," he said.

I noticed his smile dip a little as he looked me over. It made my stomach fall. "I know I look like shit," I said, and Michaels snapped eyes up to me.

"I-I-I..." he stuttered.

I slapped him on the arm. "I'm messing with you," I said, just as Josie, my friend and head cheerleader, handed me a gift bag.

"Jesse, it's so good to see you," she said and gave me a hug.

I sat down on the bed, trying to not let my tiredness show. I opened the gift bag and pulled out a home jersey. All my teammates had written messages of luck and get-wells all over it.

"I love it," I said, voice tight. When I looked up, all the cheers had died down and everyone was looking at me a little awkwardly. I felt like a fish in a tank. Standing, I said, "What are y'all standing there for? Come say hi." The tension lessened as I hugged my teammates and friends one by one. They were all wearing their football sweats, and the cheerleaders were decked out in full uniform, even down to the pom-poms in their hands.

As they all settled around the room, sitting on the floor, cushions and seats, Michaels led the conversation about the current season and the many losses they were having. As I listened to them all tell me about their games and parties and gossip, I felt completely detached. They talked of our rival teams and game days, but that life seemed so far away.

"When are you coming back?" Gavin, the stand-in QB, asked. A self-deprecating laugh bubbled out of him. "I'm dying out there, man." His eyes widened so much that it made me laugh. "I didn't mean to say...I'm so sorry," he sputtered.

Dying. Such a taboo subject.

"It's okay, man," I said and laughed again. But that laughter turned to dust in my mouth. I loved them being here and appreciated how far they had all traveled to see me, especially after what had happened at Zilker Park. But they were treating me differently. They were trying, and I loved them all for it, but there was an awkwardness that just wouldn't leave. That was the problem with dying or fighting a disease that was trying to destroy you—people didn't treat you the same; they saw you as breakable and fragile. Banks clearly had.

"I'd love to say I'll be back soon, but..." I shrugged. "I've got more treatment to get through." Surprisingly, that felt good to say, to not have to be so intent on my future.

"But you *are* coming back, right?" Michaels said, and I could have heard a pin drop with how quiet the room had grown. Only my mom, sisters, and coach knew about the results I'd been given. My friends were in the dark. I tried to think of what to say, opening my mouth to give them a response when my door suddenly flew open and my nerves instantly lessened as June barreled through.

"Jesse!" she said, eyes locked on her notebook in her hands. "I've written more..." Slowly, she came to a stop and lifted her eyes, taking in the people in my room all now focused on her. Her cheeks flushed, and I watched her swallow her nerves.

Thirty sets of curious eyes assessed my girl as she stood there in black leggings, fluffy socks, slippers, and an oversized black sweater. She was wearing a red headscarf today, and it made her brown eyes look like the leaves in fall.

June snapped her head to me when no one said anything.

"Junebug," I said and held out my hand.

It took her a second to move, shyness taking her over, but she took my hand anyway, and I pulled her into me. Immediately, any awkwardness I was feeling vanished as I wrapped my arm around her waist.

Facing my team, I said, "Guys, this is June. My girlfriend."

I saw the shocked looks on their faces, saw people assessing June and clearly seeing she was a patient here too. Michaels stood up first. "I'm Michaels—James—but everyone calls me Michaels. I'm Jesse's best friend."

"Hi," June said, and shook his hand. Then she shyly waved at everyone else. "Hey. Nice to meet y'all."

June faced me. I explained,. "My team wanted to surprise me with a visit before going into phase two." Her shoulders relaxed and I could see the pleased expression on her face.

"That's so nice," she said. She'd been my rock the past couple of days, and I could see she was genuinely touched by my team doing this for me.

"Coach has been setting up a barbeque outside for us all." Michaels nodded at June. "He's inviting everyone here too. You should come."

"Thank you," June said politely, and I pulled her closer. "I'll leave y'all to it," she said, attempting to get away, but I held her close.

"Actually," I said, facing my team, "I just need a quick word with June, then I'll be right out."

My team left, one by one, waving and saying goodbyes as they jostled each other on the way out. When the last person had left and the door was shut, June turned to me. "Well, that was embarrassing. I wouldn't have barged in if I'd known you had company."

I got to see the decor my team had put up unobstructed. It was…a lot. I was grateful, but…I didn't know what I was feeling.

June followed my eye line and her gaze moved to the posters now stuck on my wall, the balloons tied to chairs, and the signed helmet that now sat on my desk. June looked at every poster, especially the ones with old pictures of me.

"They really love you," she said. When I didn't respond, she looked at me. "What's wrong?"

"I don't know," I whispered, and felt my chest get tight. My throat felt dry. I tipped my head forward and laid it against June's chest. She removed my ball cap and smoothed her hand over my scalp. I inhaled and exhaled, focusing on how her touch felt. "It…it just doesn't feel the same anymore."

June waited for me to continue, giving me time to put my thoughts into words.

"They're my teammates, my best friends. I've known these people since I was a little kid." I wrapped my hands into June's sweater. She was always cold, even when it was hot outside. "But seeing them today and after seeing Banks at Zilker Park...it feels different. *I* feel different. Like maybe we aren't the same anymore." I met June's eyes. "Does that make any sense?" My head was still a bit all over the place.

"Of course it does," she said and rubbed her thumb soothingly along my cheek. "Because you're *not* the same anymore. As much as we wish we were, it's impossible to be. We're here, fighting for our lives, and they are back home, lives unchanged. No one is at fault or to blame, but our realities are so vastly different, there must be some kind of distance there now."

"There's not with you," I said, and held on to her tighter. June was my lifeline.

She smiled. "That's because we're bonded by group two and membership in the Chemo Club. We're exclusive like that."

I threw my head back and laughed. "I'm meant to be the joker, Junebug."

"Meh," she said. "I have my moments. Especially when you're down."

"I'm so friggin' happy I met you," I said and took her hand, kissing her palm.

"In which universe? This one or our happily-ever-after one?" she teased.

"Both," I said, meaning it 100 percent. "In any universe or lifetime, for no matter how long."

June stepped back and, still holding my hand, pulled on me. "Let's go and see your teammates. They came a long way to see you. It'd be rude to leave them waiting any longer."

"You're staying with me, yeah?" I said.

"Always," she said and led me to the courtyard. "I'll be here for as long as you need me."

Forever then, I thought as we stepped outside.

Forever.

A few hours later, I waved to my teammates, Coach, and friends as the bus left the ranch and disappeared down the road. The smell of the grill's smoke still permeated the air.

June's arm was around my waist, and she laid her head on my chest. "Let's go back to our rooms," she said, but I knew she meant for us to go back to the egg chair. The night was warm, the sky was darkening, and the stars were beginning to awake.

I kissed her at her door. "I'll see you outside soon."

June nodded and ducked into her room to take her nighttime meds and change into her pajamas. I did the same, swiping the Polaroid Michaels had given me off my bedside table.

It was of me and June, hand in hand, smiling at each other. He'd brought the camera to get some pictures of us all and had made another poster of the pictures for me before they left. The cheerleaders put it in my room, but Michaels had handed me this privately as I'd said goodbye to him alone.

"She makes you happy, man," he said. Then his smile had dropped. "You're not doing good, are you?"

I clung on to the picture of me and June and shook my head. Michaels breathed out a long sigh and I caught his bottom lip *wobbling. I put my hand on his arm.* "You've been a good friend to me. I miss you, man."

"No goodbyes, remember," *he said, voice cracking. Since I'd gotten cancer, it had become my thing. I hated goodbyes. They always felt so final.*

"No goodbyes," *I repeated.*

"Michaels!" *Coach called out.* "We need to get going, kid." *Coach's eyes were sad when he looked at me and I didn't think I could take much more.*

"I love you, brother," *Michaels said, then grabbed me for a hug. It was tight and we both knew it could be the final hug we ever had.* "Call me. Talk to me. I'm here for you."

"I will," *I said. He backed away and pointed at the Polaroid.* "I'm glad you've found her."

I was too.

Taking my sketchpad outside, I sat on the egg chair and began to draw. I didn't know how much time had passed when the egg chair swung and the blanket was lifted as June sat down. We didn't speak at first. I just continued to sketch and she wrote. I used my foot on the ground to rock us back and forth. Eventually, the moon high above us, my arm began to ache.

When I looked back at the sketch, my heart swelled against my ribs. It was just like the picture Michaels gave me. But I felt my and June's connection more with this drawing. Could feel June's hand in mine, feel the stretch of my lips as I smiled at her.

"I love it," June said, and then took the photograph off the table beside me. She was quiet until she said, "I like the way I look at you." She lifted her eyes to me. "And the way you look at me."

"Ditto," I said, and June chuckled quietly at my one-word response. Now she knew it was when I was feeling too much but didn't know what to say. I'd dropped all acts around her since our talk. June now got all of me, he real me—the rawness and scars.

It was liberating.

The rocking of the egg chair was hypnotic as June said, "If we hadn't come here…" She trailed off briefly, and I rolled my head on the cushion of the chair to look at her. She met my eyes. "If we hadn't come to the ranch, do you think we ever would have met?"

I frowned. "I like to think so…why?"

June looked out at Ginger. "As much as we connect, you're a football player and I'm a bookworm. Outside of this ranch, we exist in very different circles. Even at UT, you would be in the athletic dorms." June took a deep breath. "Girls like Josie would have been the ones to garner your attention, not ambiverted wannabe creative writers like me." She shook her head. "I don't know, sometimes I wonder if we weren't in this place, if we would work."

I hated the words coming from her mouth. "We would." I shifted in our seat and took hold of June's hand. "I adore you, June." I cleared my throat, my pulse beginning to race. "You're my soulmate."

Her eyes shimmered, pools of chocolate in the moonlight. "I think that too—I know it. But sometimes, when my insecurities get the best of me, I wonder if that's always enough."

I didn't know what to say. We had told one another we were in love. We'd bared our souls as much as we could.

"I've been writing about us being together at college," she said in explanation, and my focus immediately went to the notebook. I wanted to read it. "If we get to UT—or hopefully *when*—you play football and I write, how will we work?" June faced me again. "You'll be at football parties I would struggle to enjoy. I'll be in writing groups." June exhaled a defeated sigh. "I don't know, just writing what I have been, then seeing your teammates today, it's reminded me that outside of this ranch, we are completely different people."

"Opposites attract," I said, and June's sadness lifted a fraction. "Look at me," I said, and she did. Maybe it was her turn to have a wobble now. I held her hands tighter. "I get that we may have problems, issues, fights even." I pretended to shudder at that, and June smiled a little. "All couples do. But I will tell you one thing that I know is fact." June tilted her head. "I will choose you every time, in every universe. I choose you for me completely." I nudged my chin at her notebook. "Write us falling out, struggling, but don't for a second believe that that would be it for us. Will it be difficult at times? Yes. But nothing has been as difficult as fighting cancer, and I think we're doing a pretty fucking epic job at that—despite the immunotherapy not working and our cancer progressing, that is."

June burst out laughing at my dark attempt at humor.

I wanted to be sure she understood me though: "If you need to express your feelings, worries, and doubts about our happily ever after by giving us tough times in your writing, that's fine. It won't upset me in the here and now. But know that I will never give up on us. In this life or the one you are creating in this notebook." I brought her hand to my lips and kissed it. "Okay?" I rasped.

"Okay," she said and then, releasing my hand, gave the notebook to me. "Then read," she said, and tucked herself up in the blanket and cuddled in beside me.

Sitting back in the chair, with my heart in my throat, I began to read.

chapter eighteen

June

Jesse and June's Happily Ever After

I came out of class and walked into the quad. People were lounging on the grass in groups. I pulled out my cell to call Jesse and ask where he was when his familiar laugh sailed into my ears.

Scanning the quad, I found Jesse with a large group of his teammates. I smiled, just watching him thrive as center of attention, when I caught sight of a group of girls walking toward the football team, two of them beelining for Jesse. One of them laughed at something he said and touched his arm.

Jesse immediately pulled away, but the way my stomach dropped and jealousy took me in its hold was all-consuming. I told myself to go over there and see him. But I was still struggling with all the attention Jesse garnered here at college. Whenever we were together, I could feel the judging stares. And as much as I'd been better about my insecurities, at times, I was paralyzed by feelings of inadequacy. Jesse loved me. I knew he did. I loved him and believed we were meant to be together. But I couldn't help feeling unworthy sometimes.

I hated feeling this way and tried to make myself not care. But that just wasn't who I was, and being in the spotlight was never going to be something I was comfortable with.

Jesse checked his cell, began typing, and a text came through to my phone.

Jesse: Where are you, baby? Do you want to meet up?

I tried to step forward, to just be brave. But when Jesse lifted his head, searching the quad for me, I turned and rushed back toward the library instead. I couldn't face all those people right now. I'd try again another day—at least that's what I'd tried to convince myself.

The street was crowded as Sydney and I walked up it. Music blared from the house on our right, and people spilled out onto the front lawn, stumbling and shouting, enjoying themselves. Sydney's arm tightened in mine. This was neither of our scenes, but I had promised Jesse I would come and Sydney told me she would keep me company.

Today, Jesse had been brought on the field. The second-string QB was injured which gave Jesse his first game on the bench. When the first-string QB had been injured too, Jesse was given his shot. He had killed it, and I couldn't have been prouder.

We hadn't expected Jesse to get any game time this early in the season. I wasn't sure if he was quite ready after last year's treatment and was worried his body wasn't as strong as the others in the team. But I was wrong—so wrong.

And I also realized I'd been living completely in the dark. Seeing the crowd's reaction to Jesse, who looked nothing short of perfect with his charming smile and incredible talent as he flashed up on the Jumbotron, made me realize just how much of a big deal he was going to be and how vastly I had underestimated how popular football players truly were.

By the way he had played, the spotlight was now firmly on him.

I had video called Jesse's mama, so she could watch some of the game on her break from work. It had made her day. But when I had tried to call Jesse afterward to meet him, the coach had him doing some interviews. He had exploded onto the college football scene, and everyone suddenly seemed to want a piece of him.

I had agreed to meet him tonight at a football party at a frat house, but now that I was here, I was second-guessing myself.

"Wow," Sydney said, as we watched a tall guy upchucking into potted plant beside the front door. Nerves swam in my stomach. I'd never attended high school parties, and this seemed like a baptism by fire.

I'd texted Jesse, but he'd yet to reply. "We'd better go in and find him," I said, clutching Sydney like she was my lifeline. We walked through the front door into utter chaos. The music was so loud, I could barely hear myself think, the floor was sticky with spilled drinks, and smoke was thick in the air.

I had missed a creative writing session for this. I had been attending a small creative writing club at a coffee shop for several weeks now, and besides Jesse, it was the best thing in my life. My online story about Jesse and I was more popular than ever, and I loved college and my classes. But there was one thing missing—more time with my boyfriend. Between football and classes, our time together was limited, and it broke my heart.

I felt a pull between us taking us in different directions. It terrified me. Looking around this party now, filled with his friends and people I didn't even know, the differences seemed glaringly obvious.

"June!" Sheridan, Jesse's teammate and close friend, saw me from the stairs and waved me over. He had a red Solo cup in his hand, sloshing the beer or whatever was in it all over the floor. We made our way toward him, and he threw an arm around me. "You seen your guy yet?"

"I was just looking for him," I shouted back.

"What?" Sheridan bellowed, then shook his head. "I can't hear you." He pointed to the kitchen. "He's this way."

I clutched Sydney's hand as we followed Sheridan into the kitchen. People bashed into us from all sides, and I held my breath until we entered the kitchen and I saw him.

Jesse was stood with his teammates, a beer in his hand. He wasn't a drinker, but I guessed he had a lot to celebrate tonight. The moment my eyes found him, my heart raced. I didn't think there would ever be a time I didn't look at Jesse Taylor and feel lightheaded. His hair was longer now, curling around his ears, random curls flopping on his forehead in the most adorable way. He had gained more muscle, the evidence obvious from the sleeveless Longhorns shirt he wore right now, showing his defined biceps.

As if he could feel me watching, Jesse lifted his head, and a huge smile broke out on his face. Despite not seeing one another as much as we'd like, when we did, it was like the moon and stars aligned and all was right again in the world.

Jesse didn't even let his teammate finish whatever he was saying. Instead, he rushed straight for me and, wrapping his arms around me, lifted me off the floor. I put my arms around his neck and let the party fall away until it was just us in our own little world.

"Junebug," he whispered, then kissed me so thoroughly that the even the tops of my toes tingled with the sensation. When he broke away, he pressed his forehead to mine. "You came."

"You were amazing today," I said, running my hands through his curls at the back of his head. "I'm so proud of you."

His smile lit up the room. I hugged him tighter, then he put me down.

As he did, I noticed a group of girls glaring our way. My stomach churned. That was another part of our life here I hadn't expected—the attention Jesse got from girls. I trusted Jesse 100 percent, and I knew I was naive to not have expected it. But the disbelief on girls' faces when they saw us together bothered me. I was embarrassed to say it, but it did. I knew that if he kept getting time on the field like he had today and he played as well as he did today, it would only get worse.

"Hey, Syd," Jesse said to Sydney and gave her a quick hug. "Do you guys want a drink?"

"A soda, please," Sydney said.

"And a water for you, Junebug?" I heard a few snide comments from those girls nearby again but tried to ignore it. I didn't drink. After getting through terminal cancer, I tried to be as good to my body as I could. I let myself have treats, of course, but both Jesse and

I knew the odds on relapse, and we did our best to give ourselves the best shot.

"Taylor!" someone called from behind, just as Jesse handed us our drinks. Lockwood, a Longhorns defensive tackle, was waving Jesse over.

Jesse shook his head. "I'm with my girl." He wrapped his arms around me, keeping me close. "Sorry I couldn't see you after the game. Things got crazy."

I smiled at him. He was so happy, he seemed euphoric. Cupping his cheeks, I said, "You were incredible."

Jesse kissed me just as someone else called his name. He groaned and dropped his forehead to mine. "I shouldn't have come here."

"Of course you should've," I said, and was truly touched by how many people wanted to celebrate him tonight. He'd fought hard for this moment. His dream was coming true.

"Go," I said, and pointed to the players trying to get his attention. "I'll wait here."

"You sure?" he asked warily.

"Go," I said, laughing as he kissed me again, then made a heart with his hands as he walked away in the cheesiest move known to man. I turned to Sydney, who looked like a deer in the headlights. Now that Jesse had left the kitchen, it cleared out pretty quickly, leaving us alone.

"It's like he's famous," Sydney said, watching as everyone flocked to him.

"He's always been this magnetic," I said, recalling the day I'd arrived at Harmony Ranch, the way everyone surrounded him, including myself. Girls moved to him again, hands trying to touch his arms, his back—just anything to get closer.

"Does it bother you?" Sydney asked, clearly seeing the same thing.

I wanted to say no, but it did. "Yes," I answered honestly. My stomach turned as a very pretty girl threw her arm around Jesse's neck. Politely, because that's who he was, he pushed her off. Then he turned to me and caught my eyes. I don't know what he saw there, but he made a move to come to me, only to be intercepted by another group of guys.

"I need the bathroom," I said to Sydney. "You wanna come?"

"Yeah," she said. We left the kitchen and made our way up the stairs. We only had to wait a few minutes for the bathroom to empty. "You go first," Sydney said, leaning against the wall. "I really just needed a break from all those people."

Understanding exactly what she meant, I went into the bathroom, locked the door, and just breathed. I closed my eyes, trying to push away the image of that girl with her arms around Jesse. I loathed jealousy. It was a toxic emotion, but it was like seeing all my fears about our differences come true.

I went to the sink and washed my hands. I stared at my face, determined to not slip back into negative thoughts about myself or my appearance. I gave myself an internal pep talk, then went to leave, just as I heard, "I have no idea how they're together."

"Sheridan said they were at the same hospital or something, fighting cancer. That's how they got together." Every muscle in my body froze.

Me.

They were talking about me and Jesse.

"Explains the limp," one of them said, laughing cruelly, making my heart fall.

"And the godawful hair extensions," another said, and despite my best intentions, tears built in my eyes.

"Let's be honest," the first girl said, "if they weren't trauma-bonded, he wouldn't look at her twice. Jesse Taylor is gorgeous. An eleven out of ten. She's a five at best. I guarantee he's only with her because he feels bad about dumping her after they made it out alive. It's sad really. By the way he played today, he is going places. He won't stay with her for long."

I felt as though I'd been punched in my sternum. My heart beat a million miles an hour, and every insecurity I carried was brought to the fore. I had survived terminal cancer. We had won. Yet I was still susceptible to cruel words. At times, the world could be such a nasty place.

Placing my shaking hand on the door handle, I opened the door only to be faced with the same girls from the kitchen who had been glaring my way. Their mouths dropped as I came out. I cursed my limp as I walked past them, desperate to keep my head high.

"Bitches," Sydney hissed as she took hold of my hand. "If you had any idea of what she's been through, you'd be groveling for forgiveness. And as for Jesse, you're just jealous that he worships the ground she walks on and won't give your skanky asses the time of day."

Tears began to spill down my cheeks. I just wanted to leave. I wiped my face, leaving behind no evidence that I was upset, and once we got downstairs, I searched for Jesse in the crowd.

"What do you want to do?" Sydney asked, rubbing my back.

"Let's just go," I said, and headed to the front door. When we were outside, in the house's driveway, I said, "Don't tell him what happened, please."

"Why not?" she asked. "He'll want to make sure you're okay and give those girls a piece of his mind."

"No," I rushed out. "I want him to enjoy this night. He deserves it, Syd. You have no idea how much." My mind took me to the days he'd fought to rebuild his strength. He'd worked tirelessly to be fit enough to play this season.

Today had been the culmination of all that effort.

"You know none of what they said was true, don't you?" Sydney said, then grabbed my hands. "June? I need you to believe me. You're gorgeous, and they're just bitter and jealous that you're better, kinder and more beautiful than they could ever dream to be."

"I love you, Syd," I said, hugging her, thankful for her support. She had sliced through those girls with her words to defend me. The only problem was they had sliced through me with their words too—with perfect precision.

"Junebug?" Jesse's voice sailed out of the house as he came through the front door.

I moved away from Sydney, making sure I was pulled together, and gave him a smile.

"Where did you go?" he said, coming over to me. He searched my face, his eyes narrowing.

"I just needed fresh air." I hitched my thumb over my shoulder. "I think I'm gonna head home though. I'm tired."

Jesse paled, and he swallowed. "Is it because that girl touched me? I swear I pushed her off me, June." He cupped my face, and I wanted to cry. He was such a good person, but as I stood here, a house of football players and fans behind us, me and Syd on the outside, I couldn't help but see the obvious divide.

"I trust you, Jesse. You know that." I did. Without fail.

"Has something happened?" His voice was tinged with worry. "Junebug?"

"No, honestly. This," I said, gesturing to the house, the party, "it's just not my thing, baby. But you should stay. Enjoy your night, your win."

"I'm not staying without you," he said empathically.

"I'm going home to bed," I said. "We both are." I pointed to Sydney. "You should stay. Bond with your team. It's a big day for y'all."

I could read the conflict on Jesse's face. "I'll see you tomorrow, okay?" I kissed him again.

Jesse tried to search my face. He knew I was holding something back, but I would not spoil this for him. "You sure?" he asked, just as Sheridan called his name from the door.

"Don't drink too much," I said, and that same wash of fear I tried to keep down deep inside rose to the surface.

"I haven't touched a drop," Jesse said, a soft smile on his face. "I just hold the beer and drink water when no one is looking."

"You'd better go," I said when I saw Sheridan was still waiting.

Jesse hesitated, then said, "Good night, Junebug."

I fought back tears, as I said, "Sleep tight."

Sydney linked her arm in mine and led me back to the dorm.

Jesse and I would get through this; I knew we would. We were meant to be, soulmates. I just had to ignore that fissure of doubt that had appeared in my heart—and the internal scars those girls' word had caused.

chapter nineteen

Jesse

Jesse and June's Happily Ever After

One thing was clear. June was avoiding me.

One week. It had been a week since the party, and I knew something happened that night. I hadn't been able to find out what, but that was because June was avoiding me. My stomach turned.

The truth was, I was petrified. I no longer knew who I was without her in my life. She was my everything. I was killing it in football. Henderson, the senior QB, was still out, along with most of his backups, and Coach had been giving me more and more playing time in practice. I was playing the kind of football I had always dreamed of, having an unbelievable freshman year.

But that no longer seemed to matter in the way it always had.

June had come to the last game but made an excuse to not hang out afterward. Things seemed strained, and I had no idea why.

I had to leave for an away game tomorrow morning, and I knew June was at her creative writing club tonight. I needed to see her and try to mend this chasm between us.

The only reason I knew she still cared for me was due to the chapter she had published about us—the story of us that had our treatments failing...the one that gutted me.

But even though she was writing us trying to find our way through an impossible situation and the love we shared, hell, it felled me. And those kinds of emotions only came from one place—her heart. Her heart that I knew still wanted us, wanted this.

And if she couldn't see that, then I had to convince her.

Entering the coffee shop, I searched the packed place until I found a cluster of students at the back. A few people stared at me. It was amazing that since getting game time and helping my team get a W, I had become a kind of campus celebrity.

A journalist had heard about my story, of surviving terminal cancer by being in a clinical trial for a new form of monoclonal antibody, and it had gone viral overnight. People seemed to see me as some kind of reborn athlete.

I didn't care for any of it. All I wanted was my girlfriend back. A week was too long to go without her.

I pushed past people who were muttering in low tones about my presence in the shop and stopped right at the cluster of tables that housed the writing group. I found Junebug in seconds. Dressed in jeans and a pink shirt, hair in a messy bun on the top of her head, June was engrossed in what somebody was saying, brown eyes bright and showing her interest.

Some guy I didn't know, one who was sitting far too close to my girl, looked up and saw me standing here. I could tell by his raised eyebrows that he knew who I was. "Er, hi. Can we help you?"

The person who was reading their work paused, and June looked over to see who the guy beside her was talking to. She shifted on her seat the minute she saw me. Her cheeks paled, and I wanted nothing more than to reach across the table to kiss her and remind her that she was my girl and I was her guy, that we were Jesse and his June.

"Jesse," June murmured, looking nervously around the table. "What are you doing here?"

"I came to see my girlfriend before I leave for Clemson tomorrow," I said. I made sure I had her undivided attention when I said, "I missed you, Junebug." I heard the strain in my own voice, the one that told her just how much of what I was saying was true.

The guy beside June turned to her. "You're dating Jesse Taylor?"

The guy's attitude was shitty, but I ignored him, still too busy holding my breath waiting for June's response.

"I am," she said to him, then got to her feet. She gathered her things and came to where I stood. "Let's go outside," she said.

I followed her out. Hell, I'd have followed this girl to the ends of the earth. As soon as we got outside, June turned to me. She had her satchel crossed over her chest like a shield, her stance was defensive, and she could barely look at me.

"Junebug?" I whispered. "What's happening?"

She stared off into the distance. When she faced me again, her expression was lost, her big, brown eyes sad. "I think…" she said, shaking her head. "I feel we're just going in two very different directions, Jesse."

I felt my heart shatter into a thousand broken pieces, slowly, one excruciating smash at a time.

"What?" I rasped out desperately. "What do you mean?"

Tears filled June's eyes. "You have football. You have your dream, Jesse. And I'm so happy for you. But I clearly don't belong in that world." She pointed at the coffee shop behind her. "I have my writing group and Sydney and my online story. I stay at home and read books for fun. You play in front of tens of thousands of people in stadiums and have parties thrown in your honor."

"So?" I said quickly. "That's all just white noise. I only care about you and me."

"You care about football too, Jesse. And you should. It's all you've ever wanted. You're doing it, what we prayed we would be able to do when we didn't think we had a future."

"You're my future, June!" I anxiously ran my hand through my hair. "What's really happening?" I asked. "You don't have to come to the parties. I won't go if that's what you want."

"I wouldn't do that to you, Jesse. Don't you see?" Tears fell down her cheeks. "You deserve all the acclaim, all the attention that's coming your way. But I can't handle it... I can't take the attention."

"What attention in particular?" I asked, completely confused.

June suddenly quieted and completely shut down, her expression shuttering.

"Junebug, please," I said, and stepped closer to her. I wanted to wrap my arms around her, but she looked broken-spirited and frail. "Did something happen? Last week at the frat house, something happened, didn't it? That's when you began pulling away."

June was silent for so long, I didn't think she was ever going to speak, but finally, she said quietly, "They were making fun of me."

I froze, and my hands started to shake.

"A group of girls who were all trying to get your attention."

My blood went ice-cold and turned sluggish in my veins. Her haunted gaze met mine.

"They were mocking my limp, Jesse, my hair…" Her words may as well have been razor blades to my heart. "They couldn't understand why you are with me and said it was only because we fought cancer together, that you felt obligated to be with me now."

"But that's not true," I said. Gone was the coldness. Anger, hot and potent, built within me so much I felt like I was made of fire. I stepped closer to June and put my hands gently on her arms. "Baby, you must know that." The tears falling down her cheeks were twin rivers that I needed to stop.

"It's stupid. I shouldn't care what people like that think, especially cruel people who want nothing more than to rip others down. But it just made me feel so damn inferior, Jesse."

"You're not," I said through clenched teeth. "Never think that, Junebug. You're beautiful, amazing. God, June, you're the reason I'm alive right now, the reason I have this. Without you by my side, I don't care about football."

June stared at the ground. My heart joined that stare. She was done—I could see it in her defeated stance. "I don't have a thick skin, Jesse. And maybe they're right, maybe we wouldn't be here if it wasn't for the ranch. Maybe we held on to each other through the cancer and just didn't know when to walk away."

She could have shot me, and it would have hurt less. "You don't mean that," I said, voice shaking with fear. She had me terrified right now. June didn't say anything in response. I stepped back. "So, what? You're walking away from this, from us? After everything?"

June's shoulders sagged. "I think we should spend some time apart. Just take a breather, focus on ourselves for a while. Just… breathe."

"You're breaking up with me?" I whispered, feeling like the earth had given out beneath me.

June's eyes snapped up to meet mine. "Never," she said vehemently, and it was the only comfort I'd gotten from her in this entire messed-up conversation. "But I just…I need to not be so in the spotlight for a while, need some boring in my life." She shook her head but kept my gaze. "The past few years have been a roller coaster. For us both. I just need calm for a while, to find my feet here at college without the fanfare and judgment."

"And I'm not calming for you?" I asked. I was beginning to feel numb. Torn.

June stepped forward and put her hand on my cheek. I leaned into her soft, warm palm. "Please…just a small amount of time," she said. "I promise. I…" Her breathing hitched. "I feel overwhelmed, and honestly, what those girls said…I don't feel like I'm strong enough to deal with that kind of scrutiny just yet. I'm still recovering emotionally, and I know you are too. I just…"

"I understand," I said, and I did. June was more introverted than extroverted. She liked the comfort of her small group of friends, her passion that was the personal connection between her soul and the page. I was loud and loved being in the center of the stadium. I loved the thrill of football, of laying everything on the line.

What those girls said had clearly shredded her. I knew she was self-conscious about her hair, about her limp. She had struggled when we first got together. But I'd never seen her as anything less than perfection. The fact that they had caused her this much pain made me want to scream.

"I understand," I repeated and kissed her palm. Then I leaned in and kissed her lips. They were soft and still had the taste of cinnamon that she sprinkled on her coffee. "Just don't be gone too long, okay?" I said, voice hoarse, and kissed her again. "You're still my girl, my soulmate…my Junebug."

"Thank you," she said, clearly relieved that I wasn't fighting back.

With tears in my eyes, I raised my fist. "Group two for the win."

June raised her fist and bumped it against mine, bottom lip trembling. "Group two for the win."

I gave her a sad smile. "Good night, Junebug," I said and walked back in the direction of my dorm. I had to leave now, or I'd drop to my knees and beg her to stay. But I couldn't be selfish. I had to give her this time alone, even if it broke my soul to do so.

"Sleep tight," she whispered, but I didn't turn back around.

I was pretty sure I left both my heart and soul in her hands. She would come back to me soon. And I'd wait for that day to arrive.

I'd wait forever if I had to.

chapter twenty

June

I COUGHED AND COUGHED UNTIL NOTHING ELSE CAME UP, AND Jesse rubbed my back. Immunotherapy, phase two was well underway, and the effects this time were far worse. We were on higher doses, and we could tell.

As if on cue, Jesse began to vomit into his bucket.

"You're doing good, guys," Chris said, from his recliner, like our very own cheerleader.

Jesse threw him a thumbs-up in response—that even sweating and uncomfortable, he found time for humor, made me smile.

I looked at Emma, who had grown quiet over the past hour. "Are you okay, Em?"

"I'm just *aching everywhere*," she said, but her cheeks were bright red, and she didn't look well. "I hate this." She breathed out a sigh, and we were all quiet as Bailey came for our sick buckets and made sure we were okay.

He felt Emma's forehead and frowned. "I'll be back in a minute," he said, and Jesse and I shared a look of concern.

The other group had stayed in their bedrooms for this cycle so far, but Chemo Club was determined to remain strong in our movie room. *Lord of the Rings* played in the background, and I did my best to focus on one of my favorite film franchises. But then Bailey came back with a thermometer.

When it beeped loudly, he crouched and said, "Time to get you to your room so Dr. Duncan can check you over, Emma. You're running a fever and we need to monitor you closely."

"Great," she said, and I reached for her hand.

She was scalding to the touch. "Are you okay?"

"You know the drill, June. Meds and sleep and I'll be back tomorrow for *Return of the King*. Sorry I'm missing our BFF time." I waved her off and smiled supportively as Bailey helped her to her feet. We watched her walk back to her room. Fevers were just another side effect of the treatment.

"We'll check on her later, when she's settled," Chris said. He rubbed his head. None of us were feeling great today.

I was calling it. "We need to break up Chemo Club for today," I said, just as Jesse began to wretch again.

Chris looked at Jesse worriedly but then nodded. "I'll see you both later. We can regroup and see Emma in a few hours, yeah?"

"Sounds like a plan," I said, as Jesse gave Chris another thumbs-up. Putting his bucket down, Jesse shifted off his recliner. I joined him, and slowly and painfully, we made our way down the hallway, hand in sweaty hand. But Jesse didn't stop at his room; instead, he followed me into mine. I raised a playful brow at him.

"Your mom and dad are away tonight…" He trailed off.

I squeezed his hand, and we walked into my room. We laid on my bed.

"Junebug, I think this is the kinkiest thing we've ever done," Jesse joked, pointing to our bedside sick buckets. I wanted to laugh, but as soon as my head hit the pillow, my eyelids dragged down, and I fell asleep.

Suddenly, I woke with a start. The room was pitch-black. My heart was beating fast, and I quickly leaned over to turn on the lamp. Jesse was beside me, and he blinked awake with the glare of the light.

When I heard footsteps running along the hallway outside, I knew that must have been what had awoken me. Jesse sat up in alarm. We could hear the muffled sounds of people frantically shouting orders. As quickly as I could, I threw the blanket off me and got to my feet. Jesse did the same and rushed for the door.

As we popped our heads into the hallway to see what was happening, we saw Chris rushing toward us. One look at his face had my heart dropping.

"It's Emma," he said, and I felt like the world came to a halt. Just those two words were filled with dread and fear and apprehension all rolled into one.

I couldn't speak, fear wrapping around me. We all began walking as fast as we could down the hallway toward her room.

"I woke up and couldn't get back to sleep, so went to see if she was okay," Chris said. "But when I got there, it was mayhem." He swallowed, gasping for a steadying breath, and I felt like my heart was being crushed in a vise. "There were doctors and nurses, and then…" Chris choked on his words, and I tried to stop him from spiraling with my hand on his arm.

"They called her parents, June. The doctors. And they were… *distraught*."

I wrapped my arms around Chris, and he collapsed into my arms.

A heartbreaking wail echoed down the hallway…from Emma's room. I felt like my heart stopped beating when another sounded, and I walked, a boulder in my throat, to Emma's room. The wail came again, and when I looked inside, it was to see Emma's parents standing over her on the bed. Her mama was screaming, and her dad had his forehead pressed to the back of her hand…a hand that was limp.

My vision blurred. Emma had a tube down her throat and IV wires coming from her arms that must have been filled with fluids to help her. Dr. Duncan was in the corner of the room, hand on his forehead as he stared at a chart. Susan and Bailey saw us in the doorway, and one look at their faces told me everything I needed to know.

She had died—Emma, my best friend…was dead.

"No," I whispered, shaking my head, refusing to believe the truth before me.

Emma's mama lifted her head, and her devastated expression would live in my mind for eternity. "She's gone, June. My baby has *gone*." I shook my head over and over in. Just hours ago, we had been joking and watching movies. I'd told her I'd see her later. We'd missed out on our BFF time.

"No," I said again, then fell backward just as someone caught me. I knew it was Jesse. I would recognize the comfort of his arms anywhere.

"Junebug," he whispered, his voice thick with emotion. I turned to him to see him crying too. Then I turned to Chris. He was still, locked in the nightmare before us.

"Chris," I said, but he couldn't hear me. He was just staring at our friend, unmoving on the bed.

"I came to make sure she was okay," he said numbly. "To sit with her some while she got over her fever." Chris turned to me, desolation in his expression. "She wanted to watch *Return of the King* tomorrow. She was looking forward to it. She'd never seen it before."

A pained cry ripped from my throat, and I felt my knees give out beneath me. Bailey and Susan rushed toward us and helped Jesse get me to the nearby living room. Bailey placed me on a chair, and Jesse sat beside me.

Chris was still in the doorway, staring at Emma on the bed.

"She isn't gone," I whispered, denial coming in thick and strong. "It's a mistake. She can't be gone. She was getting better. Her treatment was working. She's my best friend."

I turned to Jesse, whose face was pale, his forest-green eyes glassy. He wasn't saying anything.

I grabbed his hand. "She was getting better. Emma was responding to the treatment. She was going to *live*." My voice broke on that word. "She was going to live," I repeated, hands shaking. I held on to Jesse like I would never let go. His grip was just as tight in mine. "We were going to go to college and visit each other."

"Baby," Jesse whispered and pulled me to his chest.

I broke then. In Jesse's safe hold, I shattered, my chest raw with how much I was crying. The chair dipped beside me, and when I looked up, Chris was there, staring at the wall. I threw my arms around him—and he broke then too.

With the sound of Emma's mama and daddy crying over her still body, the three of us crumbled from the loss of our friend. Susan and Bailey didn't leave our sides, silent supports.

Sometime later, Chris's parents turned up, and they all ended up on the floor, Chris in their arms. Time stilled in our bubble of shock and grief. I didn't know how many hours passed, but Jesse held me through them all. Strong and solid and letting me fall apart.

"June, Jesse, Chris?" Susan moved before us.

I blinked up at her. My eyes felt swollen, my throat sore, and my body exhausted.

"Emma's parents have left for a while, to take counsel with Pastor Noel."

Emma's door was closed, a candle lit outside to signify there'd been a loss inside. I hadn't even noticed her parents leave.

"They wanted me to let you know that if y'all wanted to, you can go on in and say your goodbyes."

Neenee appeared beside us. "I'm so sorry," she said, and I could see that she too had been crying. Emma was so loved.

"What happened?" Jesse asked.

"She had sepsis," Neenee said. "With her immunity compromised from treatment, when she got this infection, she couldn't fight it. Her passing was quick."

I couldn't make myself believe it.

"You should go and say your goodbyes," Chris's mama said. "You'll be glad you did."

Neenee held out her hand for me, helping me to stand. As I did, she crushed me to her chest. I hadn't even noticed feeling sick or tired, as shock, adrenaline, and sorrow had kept the effects of our treatment at bay. Fresh tears trailed down my cheeks as Neenee held me. When I pulled back, Jesse took hold of my hand. He was shaking. I cast him a watery smile. Chris walked behind us as we approached Emma's door.

Jesse opened it, and we stepped inside. The room was still and quiet. And I didn't know how to explain it, but it already felt like her soul was no longer there. There was no vibrancy, no life to the air, not even the distant echo of her sweet laugh.

Chris shut the door behind us, and I finally let myself turn to the bed. Emma looked so beautiful, like she was just asleep. Her head was free of her headscarf and her face was clean. The tube in her throat and the wires in her arms were gone. She was dressed in clean cream-colored pajamas.

She looked at peace.

My sobs came thick and fast as I sat on the edge of the bed and took hold of her hand. It still felt warm, but there was no holding my hand back, no squeeze and no smile stretching on her lips. I lowered my head and kissed the back of her hand.

"You were meant to live," I said. "You were winning, Em. You were racing toward remission." Chris sat on Emma's other side, holding her other hand, and Jesse sat behind me. He put his hand on her leg, and all of us were holding her—just like we'd been doing for each other since we'd arrived.

We sat that way for a while in silence. Then Chris spoke.

"You are my best friend, Em," he said, his voice breaking. "Who's gonna bust my balls now? Who's gonna meet my sarcasm in only the way that you can?" He choked on his words, then kissed her hand. "We're gonna be Aggies together." He gestured at me and Jesse with his head. "Rivals to these two at UT."

I laughed, but it turned to sobs.

"Not sure how I'll get through the rest of this without you," Chris said. His head bowed and his shoulders began to shake.

Jesse said, "I'm gonna miss you, Em. It shouldn't have gone this way. It wasn't meant to have gone this way." I turned to him and the tears tracking down his cheeks. I leaned against him and melted into his chest.

Holding tightly to Emma's hand, I began to speak. "I'm going to miss you, Emma. So much that I can barely cope." I took a deep breath, then simply whispered, "You were meant to live."

We sat with her for two hours, until Neenee opened the door and told us it was time to leave. I held on to her until the final minute. I didn't want to let go because then this would be real. I wanted it to be just a nightmare.

When Neenee came in, I stood to kiss Emma's forehead. "Thank you for showing me what a best friend is, Emma," I whispered into her ear. "You were a blessing to me."

Then Emma's mama and daddy came back and gave all of us a hug. It was real. This was real.

She had gone.

My best friend had gone.

And I wasn't sure how I'd ever move on.

chapter twenty-one

Jesse

Neenee didn't say anything as I climbed in bed next to June. I'm sure she called June's parents to make sure it was okay, but I didn't care. I wasn't leaving her alone. Chris was with his parents in his room. Emma's body had been taken into the room of rest in the chapel.

I blinked into the dark night, knowing the sunrise was not too far off. I couldn't make sense of what had happened tonight. My arms were wrapped tightly around June. My chest was wet from her tears. I felt numb. I had no words to say. It just all seemed so unfair.

June slowly moved back, and I took in her tearstained face. Red blotches mottled her skin, and her eyes were bloodshot and swollen. She stared at me for a long time, like she was committing me to memory. "I love you," she whispered. "I love you so much that I don't know how I'd ever exist without you."

Every word sank into my soul, and any pain I had in my body washed away like it was being bathed in golden light.

"Junebug," I murmured and cupped her cheek. She was telling me just in case. "I love you so much, I can barely contain it." Her eyes shined, and even though broken, a smile etched onto her lips. I moved in slowly and kissed my girl. I kissed and kissed her, trying to erase the sadness in her soul.

As I pulled back, June said, "You hold my entire heart in your hands."

I smiled. "And you hold mine in yours." I lifted her hand and traced her palm with my fingertip. I met her eyes. "If anything happens to me—"

"Please, don't," she whispered. "I can't hear it right now."

But I needed to say this. Seeing Emma tonight was proof that anything could happen to us at any time. I didn't want anything unsaid. "Junebug, if anything happens to me, I want you to look at the palm of your hand, the one that holds my heart, and know that I loved you more than anyone has ever loved before."

"Jesse," June murmured.

"You have been the biggest blessing in my entire life, Junebug. Not football, not *anything*...but you. I just want you to know that. If all we ever get is a few more weeks at this ranch, then it will be a life well lived."

June began to cry again, and although the moment was heavy, I felt lighter telling her these things. "You have *become* my life," she said. "And for however long we have left, that will never change."

She flipped my hand over and traced a heart with her fingertip on my palm. I smiled at her. "My heart is in your hand too," she said.

Leaning over to her bedside table, I found June's pencil case and pulled out a permanent marker. Taking off the lid with my teeth, I lay back beside her and opened her hand, palm facing me. Then I began to draw. June didn't watch the pen. She watched my face, like she was committing every part of me to memory.

"There," I said when I was finished.

June took her intense focus off my face and looked at her hand. The peal of sweet laughter that fell from her mouth made my heart stutter. June flicked her gaze up to me and said, "You couldn't have just drawn a love heart, could you?"

I put my hand on my chest. "June, jocks can know biology too."

She laughed again, and then traced the heart I had drawn in permanent black ink—a perfectly sketched anatomical heart that now sat in the center of her palm.

My heart.

June opened my right hand and said, "You need a matching one."

I held up my hand and drew another anatomical heart on the center of my palm—exactly like June's.

"There," she said, and pressed our palms together. "Now we'll always take care of the other's heart." I kissed the heart on June's palm, and she kissed mine.

The room was silent. I ran my hand over June's smooth head. "Are you okay?" It was a ridiculous question, but I didn't know what else to say.

"No," she said. "Are you?"

I thought of Emma on the bed and felt my chest cave in. "No."

"I hate cancer," June said.

I agreed: Cancer sucked. "I do too."

June played with my fingers, and I dropped a kiss on her head. I had squeezed Emma's hand as we left her room, and I was startled by how cool it had felt so quickly. As June's body heat warmed me, I made sure to treasure it—it meant we were still alive.

"All I keep thinking is: What if we do survive? What if the antibodies work this time...only for one of us to relapse?" June's breathing was choppy, fearful. "All the fighting just to have it happen again."

The thought sent shivers down my spine. "If that does happen," I said, "I want it to happen to me."

"No, Jesse," June said, shaking her head.

"Yes. God, Junebug, I couldn't take it if it happened to you. I couldn't."

"I feel the same about you."

I knew she did. But my decision was made. If God wanted one of us to do this all over again, it had to be me.

"I miss her already," June said. The deep sorrow in her voice destroyed me.

I caught sight of June's notebook on her dresser. "In our other life, the one you are bringing to reality," I said, and tipped my chin at her notebook, "keep Emma alive."

June stilled.

"We may have lost her in this one, but we're living in the other one too." I smiled sadly. "In our parallel universe."

June tried to smile too, then nodded. "She's alive in our happily ever after. Thriving."

"Thriving," I repeated, and held June close as she cried until her breathing eventually evened out, and I listened to her inhales and exhales as she slept.

She loved me and I loved her. I lifted her hand and kissed the heart that now sat on it. This girl truly did have my heart in her hands.

And I was fine with never getting it back.

chapter twenty-two

June

Jesse and June's Happily Ever After

I squealed when I saw Emma step out of the rideshare. After months apart, I finally got to see my best friend at my college. Emma grabbed her overnight bag and rushed toward me. Tossing her bag on the ground, she wrapped her arms around me and squeezed tight.

"June!" she cried. "I'm so happy to see you!"

"You too," I said, and stepped back to look at her.

Emma's hair had grown to her ears. Straight, golden-blond hair. Clearly thinking the same as me, Emma touched the ends of my dark hair—my hair that was now free of extensions. In a bid to work on myself, I'd had them removed. I couldn't change what had happened to me, so I was embracing it. I'd survived cancer and I should be proud of it. It wasn't all I was, but it was a part of me that I shouldn't run from.

My hair was now a similar length to Emma's, though it was styled very differently. It was now a short, chic French bob, with bangs.

"I'm obsessed with this haircut. I loved the long extensions, but this is so stunning!" Emma said.

"You look incredible too," I said, and hugged her one more time. Every time I saw one of my friends from Harmony, I saw them as the living miracle they were—I didn't think it would ever change.

"Did you come here with Chris?" I asked.

Emma nodded. "He's with Jesse now, at his dorm." She tilted her head at me. "Jesse seemed quiet, sad, when I saw him."

My heart broke. I didn't want him to be sad or quiet. I missed him so much, loved him so much, I just wanted to run to his dorm and kiss him until I could no longer feel anything but his lips. But I was doing better since our break. In the time we had been apart, I had been talking to Michelle, our therapist from the ranch, to work through my insecurities. It was helping so much. When Jesse and I spoke again, I wanted to be stronger for him—for both of us.

But I had kept up with the Longhorns and was so unbelievably proud of him. He was breaking every freshman record, and there was even talk from the sportscasters that he may become the first-string QB even when the senior player returned.

I linked arms with Emma, and she picked up her overnight bag. Sydney was visiting her parents, so Emma had Sydney's bed, and I was ready for a full weekend with my best friend. It had been far too long.

As we walked into my dorm room, Emma placed her bag on the floor and sat on my bed. When I joined her, she bit her lip, and said, "You haven't broken up with Jesse, have you? Jesse didn't really say what was happening, but both Chris and I have felt some kind of distance between you." Emma reached for me. "Please say you haven't. I don't think I'd ever believe in love again if you and Jesse couldn't make it after all you've been through." Emma's voice grew quiet. "You're soulmates, June. Anyone can see it."

"I believe that too," I said, fiddling with a loose thread on my bedspread. "No, I know it." I took a deep breath. "I've just struggled to adjust. Michelle said it's very common. We've gone from being told we were going to die to miraculously being cured, then moving to college and my boyfriend finding celebrity overnight. She said just one of those things can really affect a person's mental state. All of them? Yeah, I didn't cope well."

Emma held my hand. "And now? How are you now?"

I really thought about it before I answered. "Better. I feel so much better."

Emma paused, and I could tell she wanted to say something. I waited until she said, "How would you feel about getting dinner tonight with Chris?"

My face lit up with a smile. I had been wondering when I would see him.

"And Jesse?"

I blinked at my friend.

Emma's expression seemed hopeful, but then it quickly turned to guilt. "Ignore me, June. I shouldn't have pushed you."

"No," I said, when it was clear she was going to continue apologizing. Emma stopped and, taking a breath, I said, "I'd...I'd like that." It was the truth. Lord, I had missed Jesse every minute of every single day. In some ways, it had felt like I couldn't breathe without him, but I was glad I'd taken the time to grow stronger.

"Really?" Emma said.

"Really."

She grabbed her phone and texted someone. Chris or Jesse, I assumed. "And are you going to the game tomorrow?" she asked. Jesse had gotten Emma and Chris tickets for the game. He always got one for me too, though I hadn't been to the past few.

"Um, yeah," I said, and some off-center part of me slotted back into place.

Emma put down her phone, and I quickly changed the subject. Just the thought of seeing Jesse tonight made butterflies swoop in circles in my stomach.

"Soooo, have you met anyone?" I asked.

Emma playfully pursed her lips.

"You have!" I said excitedly. She had omitted that information from our texts and phone calls.

"He's in my math class." Emma shrugged. "It's early days, so we'll see how it goes. His name is Damon. And he is hot!"

"I'm so happy for you," I said, hugging her. When I pulled back, I asked, "Has Chris met him?"

Emma laughed. "Yes, and of course he has been relentless about him being another math nerd."

I laughed, picturing the amount of teasing he must give her and Damon. "And Chris? Has he met anyone?"

Emma nodded. "My roommate, Nikki." I laughed, as Emma gave herself a facepalm. "So he's around all the time. It's like being back at Harmony, twenty-four seven. He's an annoying itch that just won't go away." She winked at me, and I knew she was joking. That was just her and Chris.

As my laughter trailed off, a burst of warmth filled my chest. *We are doing it.*

Emma must have shared my thought, as she said, "Chemo Club for life, remember?"

"Chemo Club for life," I said, then got to my feet. "How long until dinner?"

"An hour, okay?" Emma said and started making plans again on her phone.

I was seeing Jesse again for the first time tonight in four weeks. The nerves were back tenfold, but when I sat in front of my vanity to do my makeup, only happiness glowed on my face.

I was more than ready to see him again.

⸺

I wore high-waisted jeans and cream-colored, cropped sweater to the restaurant. I'd styled my hair just like my stylist had shown me, wearing a light layer of makeup and a red lip stain. Emma linked our arms, chatting away about a party she went to at A&M, but all I could think about was seeing Jesse again.

Minutes—it was mere minutes until we met up.

As we rounded the corner, the familiar sight of Chris and Jesse standing outside the restaurant made my heart flip.

Chris turned first, and seeing us approach, he broke away from Jesse and ran toward me. "June!" he greeted, picking me up and spinning me around.

I laughed, holding on to him tightly. Just like Jesse, Chris had filled out and looked great.

When he put me down, I looked up and felt lightheaded at the sight of Jesse standing across from me. He wore a long-sleeve, white Henley, his favorite faded jeans, and his old, orange Longhorns cap, worn backwards, of course. His hair had grown a little more, his curls peeking out beneath the rim.

My heart kicked into a sprint as his forest-green eyes met mine. I watched as his gaze roved over me, his focus mostly on my hair. Jesse's lips parted and a flush spread on his cheeks. I knew I blushed too, under his attention.

He stepped forward cautiously, and I smiled. That smile seemed to be all the assurance he needed to walk right up to me. "Junebug," he rasped out, so much feeling in that one term of endearment.

"Hey, Jesse," I said, reaching out and taking hold of his hand. The minute our fingers entwined, I felt reborn, like my body had been restarted by an electric jolt.

"Your hair," Jesse said, exhaling deeply. "It's so beautiful." I knew he meant it—Jesse always meant everything he said to me. "You are so beautiful." He reached out with his free hand and ran the back of his finger down my cheek. "I've missed you so much, Junebug." His voice shook at that confession.

I leaned into his touch. "I missed you too."

Jesse smiled. My heart soared. "I'm glad you came tonight." He appeared nervous. "I wasn't sure you would."

"I wanted to," I answered quickly, and tried to tell him with my eyes how much I missed him but how good it was that I'd found myself again and grown stronger. I stepped closer still, and just an inch from his chest. "I really wanted to see you again."

"Yeah?" he said, swallowing deeply.

"Always," I said, and his smile grew bigger.

"Um, guys?" Chris said. "Just gonna say it—this is kinda awkward for me and Ems." It was so like something Chris would have said at the ranch that it made me burst out laughing.

Jesse laughed too. Chris and Emma were giving us amused expressions.

"Fine," I said. "Let's go inside."

Chris and Emma led the way.

I moved to follow and realized that Jesse still hadn't released my hand.

"Is this okay?" he said.

"More than," I said in return.

chapter twenty-three

June

Jesse and June's Happily Ever After

"Holy shit!" Chris said as the team was called and they ran out into the stadium. It was something to see, one hundred thousand people screaming and dressed in orange.

"I get it now," Emma said, and looked at me. "Why it was overwhelming." When we had gotten back to my dorm last night, I had told her everything. It took all I had to not allow her to go and find the girls who said things about me and give them a beat down. But like the best friend she was, she understood why I needed a break from it all.

It was a lot.

"There's my boy!" Chris shouted as Jesse stepped onto the field.

By the time the second half started, Chris was hoarse from screaming, and my cheeks ached from smiling. Jesse was on fire once more. It was like he couldn't put a pass wrong; every move he made was perfection.

As a whistle blew, Emma took hold of my arm. "June," she said, like she'd forgotten to tell me something. "Your story," she said, and I saw tears quickly fill her eyes. "It's so beautiful. Brutal," she said with a watery laugh, "but beautiful."

"Oh, thank you," I said, embarrassed.

"You know you're going viral, don't you?"

I did. But I never really talked about it with anyone. Outside of my family, Jesse, Chris, and Emma, no one knew it was me who was writing the story that had become one of the most read publications on the platform.

My face blazed at Emma's mention of it. It was what I adored about writing. This thing I did, the worlds I created, the characters I gave life to felt so big and consuming, yet behind the scenes, I could live a normal little life—one of privacy and beauty and peace.

"Kind of," I eventually answered.

Emma playfully rolled her eyes at me. "Kind of? June, this could be huge for you. Like, life-changing big." That's something else that had happened within the past month—the story of me and Jesse at the ranch, about our treatments not working, had exploded. To be honest, I was trying not to think about it too much. It all felt a bit overwhelming when I did. And I didn't want it to take away my joy of writing. I wrote because I wanted to. I didn't think I could cope with the pressure of *having* to.

A roar from the crowd pulled our attention, and I watched a throw by Jesse sail into the air. He had thrown it so far, my mouth dropped open at the skill...then it landed right in the end zone, in Sheridan's hands.

The crowd around us lost their minds, and we jumped to our feet. Jesse's face flashed up on the Jumbotron. My hands were over my mouth, but then my eyes narrowed. Jesse's team was all jumping around him in celebration, but I was fixated on Jesse.

Every part of me froze. Something was wrong. My heart plummeted when, through the gaps in his helmet, I saw his eyes losing focus. I knew Emma and Chris had seen something too because Chris stopped jumping and Emma gripped my arm.

"Jesse," I whispered to myself, just as his eyes rolled back and he collapsed onto the field. A scream ripped from my throat, and I looked to Emma and Chris.

What was wrong? What was happening?

Terror, pure and strong, took me in its hold, and I watched the big screen as medics ran out onto the field and took off Jesse's helmet. He was unconscious, that much I could see. The crowd began to quiet, realizing that Jesse was down and wasn't getting back up.

"Get up," I said to him. "Get up! Jesse, get up!" My voice was shrill and in the silence of the stands, people began looking at me.

My cell rang, and I saw it was Jesse's mama calling. "Cynthia," I said by way of greeting.

"What's happening, June? Is he okay?" The game was televised today, which meant anyone watching this game was watching Jesse on their screens right now—not getting up.

"I don't know... I don't know." My bottom lip wobbled. "I'm scared."

Cynthia said, "I know you are, sweetie. So am I. But—" she went quiet, then: "June, someone is calling. I'll call back."

I nodded like she could see me.

A stretcher was brought out onto the field, and I watched helplessly as Jesse was placed on it, and the medics rushed off the field with the love of my life.

Someone nearby had a broadcast playing loudly on their phone beside us. "We're not sure what has happened, but we know that Jesse Taylor is a survivor of acute myeloid leukemia. In fact, he was diagnosed stage four last year, but he was chosen for a clinical trial that saved his life. He fought hard to keep his scholarship and his place on the Longhorns. I truly hope he's okay, and it has nothing to do with his past health issues."

Blood drained from my face. Was Jesse relapsing? Is that what was happening? Chris and Emma must have heard the broadcast too, as when I turned to them, they had paled.

Chris grabbed Emma's hand, and she took hold of mine. "Let's go. We'll find out where he is. He needs us."

We rushed through the stands, garnering curious stares. Then a whistle blew and the game was back on. I wanted to run onto the field and scream at them all for carrying on when Jesse, my Jesse, had just collapsed. But Chris was pulling us down the stairs, trying to find a way to the locker rooms.

The stadium was huge and packed with security, but just before we reached them, my phone rang again. "Cynthia," I said.

"They're taking him to the hospital," she said, and told me which one. "I'm trying to get cover at work so I can get out there."

"We're going now," I said, running for a nearby exit.

Chris and Emma followed. My head was full, and my nerves had engulfed me.

"I've got an Uber coming. Two minutes," Chris said, and pulled me along to where it was picking us up. I heard an ambulance in the distance and wondered if Jesse was in it.

"June, listen to me," Cynthia said. "I'll call ahead to the hospital and tell them you're coming. I won't be able to get there until tomorrow and he needs someone with him. I'll get you permission to be by his side." Her voice cracked, and it caused my numbness to break and fear to race through me. "You okay, sweetie?"

"Yes, ma'am," I said, just as a white SUV pulled up beside us. "We're leaving now."

"Call me as soon as you know anything," she said.

"I will," I whispered, hanging up as Emma pushed me into the car. We set off, and it only took me a few minutes to realize the radio was the commentary of the Longhorns game.

"We're waiting on any word from the Longhorns on the status of quarterback Jesse Taylor…"

Tears built in my eyes, and Chris leaned over to the driver and said, "Can you turn the channel, bro?" The driver did what he said, but I noticed his curious glances.

"He's gonna be okay," Chris said, reaching across Emma squeeze my hand.

"He is," Emma said, linking her arm with mine. "It was probably just tiredness or overexertion." They were trying to make me feel better, but none of us were saying what we were all thinking—that his cancer might be back.

Dr. Duncan had said 50 to 85 percent chance of relapse.

The traffic to the hospital made it take forever, and by the time we got there, all my darkest thoughts were filling my body with dread. I was terrified of walking in there and being told he hadn't made it.

"June?" Chris said, and I realized I was standing, unmoving, in the entryway.

I shook my head, and tears fell from my eyes. "What if he's not okay?" My feet were rooted to the spot. I couldn't move. "He's the love of my life, Chris. He's my everything." I looked at my two friends. "What if he's not okay?" My voice shook. "What if it's back, only this time it takes him from me?"

"We can't think like that," Emma said, but I heard the concern in her voice.

"We have to go in and see how he is," Chris said, holding out his hand. I felt like if I took his hand that would make all this real. And if I didn't, this would just be a bad dream that I would wake up from. "June," he said again, only ripping me from my fear when he said, "he needs you. Jesse needs you."

My feet began to move then, and the sound of the hospital engulfed us. Chris spoke to a receptionist, and I briefly heard him mention my name, but I just held onto Emma, trying to keep it together.

"We need to have a seat while they find out what's happening," Chris said, and led us to a nearby couch. "I'll get us coffee," he said, and walked away to a vending machine.

"Are you okay?" Emma said. When I shook my head, she put her arm around me and just stared at the doors that seemed to lead deeper into the hospital.

Chris came back with coffee, but I let mine go cold in my hand. It felt like we waited forever before a man in a white coat came toward us. My eyes widened when I saw it was Dr. Duncan.

He headed straight for us. "Chris, Emma, June," he greeted.

"Is he okay?" I whispered.

Dr. Duncan regarded me silently, then said, "Please come this way." My heart beat so fast, I felt like I couldn't breathe. Then it hit me: Dr. Duncan was here—it had come back. Jesse's cancer had come back.

I didn't realize I had stopped until Dr. Duncan turned around and said, "Please, come this way, Miss Scott."

My palms were sweaty as I followed him down a hallway. It took so long it felt like a marathon until we arrived at a door. Dr. Duncan walked inside, and a sob tore from my throat when I found Jesse in a bed, eyes fixed on the ceiling. He was no longer in his football uniform; instead, he had on a hospital gown and an IV of fluids in his arm.

At my cry, Jesse's gaze snapped to me, his eyes filled with sorrow. "Junebug," he rasped, and I ran to him, throwing myself over where he lay. I looped my arms around his neck and vowed to never let go. He wrapped me up in his strong arms and held me back. I felt wetness on my neck and pulled back to see he was crying too.

"Jesse?" I said, a question in my tone.

Jesse nodded, and I collapsed against on his chest, holding him again.

It was back. The cancer was back.

I couldn't breathe. I couldn't lose him. We were just getting started. And, oh God, I had forced us into a break; I had wasted precious time not being by his side.

"June," Jesse said, and rubbed my back. I lifted off him, and Jesse motioned with his head to the foot of the bed.

Dr. Duncan stood there with a file.

Jesse clasped my hand and squeezed. He was nervous. Of course he was.

"Miss. Scott," Dr. Duncan said. My heart was in my throat as I waited for what he would say next. "Jesse and I have already discussed this, but unfortunately, his blood work and scans have shown that his acute myeloid leukemia has returned."

Dr. Duncan's words circled my head, playing on a constant loop, breaking my heart into tiny fragments. I turned to Jesse. His back was straight, and he nodded. He was so strong. So perfect and brave.

I kissed Jesse's hand, as Dr. Duncan said, "The good news is, we believe we have caught it early."

"What happens now, Doc?" Jesse asked.

Dr. Duncan continued to study the file. "The same treatment as before. It worked the first time, so the chances of it working again are very high."

I dropped my head to lean it on Jesse's arm. Chemo—aggressive chemo and immunotherapy again. For the next several months.

Football…he won't be able to play anymore this year…

"Okay," Jesse said, his voice calm and unwavering. I looked at him then and he met my eyes. "Then I'll just have to beat it again. Easy." He tried for humor, but this time, it didn't land. My lip wobbled and Jesse grew serious. "I'm not leaving you, Junebug. We have too much life to live together."

I nodded, but sadness had captured my voice.

"I love you," he said.

Finding my voice, I said, "I love you too, more than you'll ever know."

Jesse lifted his fist, and a wide smile took up his face. "Group two for the win...again."

A strained laugh did slip from my mouth this time. But I held out my fist and bumped it against his. "Group two for the win again."

And he had to win. I would entertain no other outcome.

Jesse Taylor had to live.

chapter twenty-four

Jesse

I took a deep breath and sat down in Doc Duncan's office. My mom answered the video call and gave me a strained smile. Today was the day. Another long, enduring phase of immunotherapy had passed, and today, we found out my fate.

Doc Duncan turned to me, and I held my breath as he said, "I'm so sorry to have to tell you this, Jesse. But the treatment has failed, and we are now at the stage where we must switch to palliative care."

My mom's agonized cry filled the room from the phone, but I didn't cry. I had known this was coming. I had felt it. It wasn't pessimism or giving up—my body had told me.

Over the past several weeks, I had become more exhausted than ever before. My bones ached nonstop, and I was so breathless some days that I found it difficult to walk.

It wasn't the side effects of the monoclonal antibodies. I had known, deep down in my soul, that the treatment hadn't worked. And worse, as I looked at June every day, seeing her fading before my eyes, I knew it hadn't worked for her either. We hadn't spoken it aloud to one another, we didn't want to out those words out into the universe while there was still a chance, but we'd known.

"How long?" I said, feeling like I was having an out-of-body experience. Discussing your mortality—limited to now a mere set of days—was the most surreal thing on earth.

Mom reined in her cries, and Doc Duncan said, "From your most recent results, I would estimate between four and six weeks."

It was funny—as a kid, four to six weeks would have felt like a lifetime. Summer vacation seemed to last forever, long lazy days and nights. Now, four to six weeks felt like no time at all.

Sand in an hourglass.

"Jesse, I'm coming to the ranch. I'll find a way," Mom said, and there was no argument from me this time. Because this was it. This time, there was no miracle cure for me. There was no place to go but onto the next of life's adventures.

Susan was in the room with me, and when I looked at her, there were tears in her eyes. "I'll walk you back to your room," she said.

I shook my head and turned to my mom on the phone. "I...I'll speak to you later, Mom. I..." I knew she could see in my face that I needed...well, I didn't know what I needed. Time? Space? A new damn body?

No...I just needed June. But she hadn't yet had her appointment with Dr. Duncan. I prayed that I was wrong and that her treatment *had* worked, but one look at us both, it was clear that our time here was limited. Chris, Silas, Cherry, Toby, and Kate—they were stronger.

They'd been put through the ringer, but there was a light in their eyes that had dulled for me and June.

Susan put her hand on my back as I left the room. It felt nice. We'd become a little team of sorts these past couple of months. Susan had filled in the role of parent for me as best she could. Nurses were superheroes.

I wandered aimlessly, just walking the hallways numbly until I found myself at the chapel. I'd never been here before. I knew Mrs. Scott came here a lot, but I had never been big on religion. I believed in something bigger that could have been God. But now that I was close to death, I suppose my soul needed some guidance, some answers.

Soft, soothing piano music played as I entered—worship songs, I realized—and I sat down in the back pew and just stared at the altar. A cross was in the middle, along with depictions of Jesus in various stages of the crucifixion, and finally, the resurrection.

"Jesse?" Pastor Noel said, as he came into the chapel behind me. "I'm sorry, I didn't know you were coming in today."

I smirked. "Neither did I."

Pastor Noel clearly noted something was up, and he sat down beside me. He didn't say anything, just let the silence dance around us.

"I'm dying, Pastor," I said, and for the first time since I'd been told, I felt a crack of fear spread through my chest. My voice was weak, and it shook.

"I'm so sorry," Pastor Noel said, and just let that sit with me too. He wasn't pushing me to talk, and I appreciated that.

I studied the cross, and then the detailed painting of the resurrection. "What do you think happens after death?"

Pastor Noel relaxed beside me. "Me, I believe in heaven. But many people believe other things."

I nodded.

"I believe that what happens next is beautiful and serene and filled with peace and happiness. No pain, and all ailments will be cured," Pastor Noel said.

A lump built in my throat. "That sounds nice," I whispered. I rubbed my hands together. "Do you think it's painful? Dying?" I turned to the pastor and looked him dead in the eye. I needed his complete honesty. "I can face death, I know I can," I said. "I just don't want it to hurt for..." Pastor Noel tipped his head to the side, waiting for me to finish. "For June. I don't want her to feel any pain. I couldn't bear it."

Deep sorrow shone in the pastor's brown eyes. He didn't look much older than mid-thirties. And he seemed like a good man. Silas, Kate, and Cherry talked to him often, attended services every Sunday. I kind of wished I'd maybe talked to him more before this.

"I've been a pastor for ten years now, Jesse. And for five of them, I've worked with people in hospices or hospitals. In essence, I mostly sit with people as they pass."

"So you've seen a lot of people die?" I asked.

"Hundreds," he said.

I smiled at that. "You're like a regular Texan Grim Reaper, huh?"

Pastor Noel laughed. "Believe me, I've been called worse."

I laughed again, and even that small movement hurt my chest. It was strange thing to feel your body begin to fail you day by day, getting defeated by a too-strong opponent. "It must be a weird-ass job, watching people die, Pastor. No offense."

"None taken," he said. "But it's actually really beautiful." I raised a doubtful eyebrow at him, and he smiled. "I find the most curious things occur when people die. Magical, even."

"Like what?" I asked.

"I've seen many things. The way some people, the second the pass, go with a smile upon their face. Peaceful. Happy. Like they are being bathed in healing light."

My nose tickled, as I fought back the tears that brought to my eyes.

"The *most* curious to me is just as the person dies, they seem to see something in the room with them—or some*one*." Pastor Noel held out his hand in reassurance. "Nothing bad. More like a familiar face. Like someone they loved is coming to meet them as they cross over. Or it could be an angel, guiding their soul to the next chapter." He looked me in the eye. "Or maybe they are simply welcoming them home."

A tear fell down my cheek and splashed onto my hand. I wiped it and caught sight of the drawing of June's heart in my palm. Whenever they faded, I drew them back on. If I had been able to, I would have gotten it tattooed. But I didn't think Neenee would allow us to hitch a ride to downtown Austin and get tattooed underage.

"I'm here for you, Jesse. For whatever you need," Pastor Noel said.

"Thank you," I said, truly meaning it, and stayed still and silent for a few moments more. I eventually got to my feet.

June would have had her meeting by now. Giving the pastor a farewell wave, I made my way back through the maze of hallways, only to find June standing at my door, waiting silently with her parents.

She heard my approach, met my eyes, and I instantly knew—just like me, she now had only weeks left to live.

Feeling every inch of my heart break, I opened my arms for her and allowed silent tears to pour down my cheeks. June wrapped her arms around me too, and I held her to my body, letting her warmth and her love seep into me while I still had it. June's parents were holding each other up while simultaneously falling apart across from us. June's dad gave me a sad smile, and I closed my eyes and just held my girl.

The first day I saw her, I knew June would change my life. I never dreamed that it would end this way between us, but I vowed to myself that, for as long as I breathed, it would be with the sole purpose of loving her.

And to die madly in love with my soulmate? In the end, I couldn't think of a better way to go.

chapter twenty-five

Jesse

June's head lay against my arm as I swung us on the egg chair. We were bundled up in a blanket, the night a little cold. I stared out at the millions of stars above us.

"What are you thinking?" June asked and glanced up at me. There was a spark missing from her deep brown gaze. Her parents had sat with us for hours. They clearly hadn't wanted to leave, but seeing that June wanted some time alone with me, her mom called it a night.

All of us were emotionally battered. My mom was arriving tomorrow, and she wasn't leaving until…well, until there was no more reason for her to stay. She was bringing the rugrats too, and even just knowing they'd be with me made me feel a little stronger.

"The stars," I said, answering June's question, my voice raspy. I'd shed too many tears to count. Not for myself but over the fact that my girl, my Junebug, was fading too. I'd prayed so hard for her to be saved.

Those prayers hadn't been answered.

"They look so pretty out here," she said. Both June and I had been offered the chance to return to our hometowns when the time to pass was close. Both of us had declined. We would pass here at the ranch, with the others, where we had met.

"See that star there?" I pointed at one in the sky.

"Mmm?" June said, running her hand up and down my stomach. We could barely let each other go, clinging to the other with palpable desperation.

"Silas was telling me about it a few weeks ago," I said. "He was outside his suite with a telescope. When I asked him what he was doing, he showed me that star."

"What did he say about it?" she asked, staring up at the sky. She looked so beautiful, head tilted up and eyes filled with wonder.

"That it was four thousand light years away." June flicked her focus to me and shivers ran up my arms—I had the love of this girl. This brave and perfect girl. She held my heart in my hand, and I held hers in mine. I was dying, had just a handful of weeks left. My life was a miniscule grain of sand in the universe's hourglass. So was June's. Yet sitting here beside her, it felt like *everything*. I was born to meet her. To walk this rocky path hand in hand and be there, together, at the end. I'd come to the realization weeks ago that UT and football weren't in my future. Any remaining weight on my shoulders had fallen away, and though my body was failing, my soul was at more peace than ever.

A lump built in my throat. I cleared it and said, "Silas said it has taken four thousand years to reach our eyes from its home." A small smile etched on June's lips. I took hold of her hand and kissed my heart in her palm. "He said that star would have long burned out, yet its shine remains to us all the way across the universe. Beautiful and lighting up our skies."

"Jesse," June rasped, understanding what I was saying.

I kissed her fingers, and the back of her hand. "We might not have a long life ahead of us, but maybe our love story will last like that star and be a comfort to somebody out there who needs to hear it, long after we're gone." Tears trickled down her face. "I love you, Junebug."

June sat up. "I love you too, Jesse," she said, and then kissed me. She kissed me deeply. Sliding her hand to my face, she pulled back and met my eyes. "I'm getting weaker," she said, and a wave of intense fear crashed through me.

I nodded, unable to speak.

"I know you are too." June inhaled. She closed her eyes and placed my hand on her face. A smile broke out onto her lips. When she opened her eyes again, she said, "I want to be with you, while we still can."

My heart kicked into a sprint. "Junebug…"

"You love me, and I love you. And in no time at all, we'll lose the strength to show each other how much." I placed my hand over hers that was still on my cheek. I dropped my forehead to hers and nodded.

I wanted this girl in every way possible.

Getting up off the chair, I helped June get to her feet, led her inside my room, and moved to the door to turn the lock. "Just in case," I said, smirking, and June laughed. My heart swelled. I would never tire of hearing that sound.

She pulled the drapes over the porch's doors, and in the low light of the lamp, began to undo the buttons of her pajama top. June was free of her headscarf, her skin was pale, yet I couldn't remember when I had ever seen anyone or anything so beautiful. And there wasn't an ounce of insecurity within her, which was the most stunning thing of all.

I held out my hand for her, then guided her to the bed. We lay down, and I kissed her. I kissed her and kissed her, telling her how much I loved her until we became one.

Afterward, June lay in my arms, and I had never felt so peaceful in my life. June was tracing the heart on my palm. I kissed her head and wished on that four-thousand-year-old star that we could go just like this. In one another's arms, no pain, just happiness and light until we drifted away.

"We'll never go gray," June murmured, and I stilled. June lifted her head, and I met her watery gaze. "We'll never get wrinkles."

"People spend a lot of money to avoid them." I chuckled.

"I wouldn't," she said, then crushed my heart when she added, "I would want nothing more than to see a wrinkle form on my forehead, evidence that I was getting older and living my life. I would smile with pure joy seeing a gray hair on my hairline because it would mean that we were being given *time*."

June sighed, and it took all that I had to not break down in tears.

"And laughter lines," she said, smiling. "I would watch those laughter lines grow deeper each year, rejoicing that I had the energy to laugh." June moved up to my chest and rested her chin on her hand. "Because that's my favorite thing to do with you: laugh. Through all the pain and the sadness, you have helped me keep joy in my heart this entire time, Jesse." June's eyes shimmered. "I don't think you know what a gift that has been to me."

"I know, June. Because you have been a gift to me too."

June lay back down on my chest and, with a hitch in her breathing, said, "I know this is our fate and that death is hovering close to us, but I would have really loved to have a life with you, Jesse. Not even a big life—I'd have been content with a little one. I would have loved to have been your wife and had children with you. And year by year, we would watch them grow from our home in the country, until they were old enough to move on, then we'd watch the grandchildren grow too."

June smiled up at me. "And we'd sit on our porch swing, eighty years old and still holding one another's hearts in our hands, with a map of wrinkles on our faces and gray hair on our heads. And our laugh lines would be deep and speak of a life lived with so much laughter, gratefulness, and love." June cupped my cheek. "Because we would have *lived*, Jesse. We would have lived such a beautiful life."

"That sounds real nice, Junebug," I whispered, because I could hardly speak. That life sounded perfect.

June took her hand off my face and laid it over my heart. She laid her head down there too, and I listened to her breathe as she listened to my heartbeat. Her breathing was sweetest sound to me these days because it meant I still had her beside me.

Eventually, her breathing evened out, and I reached for my sketchpad and pencil and began to plan. I couldn't make all June's dreams come true; we would never be those people sitting on the porch watching our grandchildren play. But I could do one thing—one huge, extra-special thing.

We had the time. Just a little more time to make it come true.

But it would be just enough.

chapter twenty-six

June

Jesse and June's Happily Ever After

I walked into the hospital room where Jesse was watching last week's Longhorns' game on the TV from his bed. Although he could no longer play this season, he was determined to be back for the next. Knowing Jesse Taylor, he would be. His hair was gone, and I smiled at the familiar faded, Longhorns hat on his head. He looked just how he had when I met him.

For weeks now, Jesse had been enduring the intense treatment. It felt strange not to do it alongside him. And it terrified me too. But he was taking every day as it came, and I'd never felt more useful to someone than I did sitting beside him and just being there with him.

When I came in, he turned, smiling, and immediately held out his hand. I walked straight over to him and kissed him on his lips. Every time we kissed, my heart sang with relief.

It was working again. Thank the Lord, it was working.

During the first month of Jesse's treatment, I hadn't been able to function. I couldn't eat or sleep, worrying that it wouldn't work this time—like in the book I was nearly done writing, the one where Jesse and I had not responded to the clinical trial and we were losing our lives at seventeen.

But the treatment was working, and although the road he'd traveled had been another filled with rough terrain, he was doing well. Every time I saw the level of his strength and courage, it just made me love him that much more. Jesse Taylor was determined to walk this life beside me, was fighting to stay with me. There was no greater expression of love in the world than that.

We'd talked in depth about what we wanted in life. We had agreed that it was to grow old, have a family, and watch them grow from our porch swing. And that's what we were holding on to. That was our dream that we were determined to make come true.

A knock sounded, and Chris popped his head through. Emma followed behind. "Chemo Club assemble!" Chris shouted, and Jesse got to his feet, laughing. We all hugged as we said our hellos.

"How long are you here for?" Jesse asked, and Emma and Chris sat down on the chairs around the bed. Jesse sat on the bed and pulled me down beside him. He put his arm around me, and I sank into his embrace. When I wasn't at school, I was here, with my love.

"All weekend," Chris said.

"I'm going to the game tomorrow," Jesse said, smiling. "You coming?"

Chris held out his arms. "Why do you think we're here, bro? I'm not missing the hero's welcome you're gonna get as you step onto the field." The Longhorns were making it to the playoffs, and a huge part of that was due to the start Jesse had given them this season.

"At last!" Jesse declared. "I'm finally getting the recognition I deserve!" The playful cockiness was back in his voice. He had been so tired, emotionally and physically, and had more still to endure, but just knowing the cancer was being defeated was enough to get him through the bad days.

We all laughed, and Emma turned to me. "And you, June? Have you said yes to the bookstore?"

My eyes widened, and I snapped my gaze up to Jesse.

Emma smirked, knowing damn well I hadn't told Jesse of the invite.

"Junebug?" Jesse said, confusion in his voice. "What bookstore?"

I scowled at my friend, who just shrugged nonchalantly. I sat up and faced Jesse. "Our alternate love story, the one that's been doing well online—"

"More than doing well, Junebug," Jesse interrupted. "It's a sensation." He supported my writing 100 percent. When he relapsed, I'd paused in writing for a while. In the story, Jesse and June had just been told the treatment didn't work and that there was nothing more that could be done. I had stopped writing the next chapters because I didn't want to even entertain Jesse not making it through. I couldn't write of him dying in my book when we didn't know the outcome of his treatment in this life.

But Jesse being Jesse had made me promise to keep going, telling me that the story made him even more determined to heal. And he echoed what the story version of June had said—he wanted the wrinkles, the gray hair, the laughter lines.

He told me the story made him want to live.

But I hadn't entertained any of it yet. It seemed too crass a thing to do when Jesse was in this hospital, fighting to live.

"Junebug?" Jesse pushed. "The invite?"

I sighed in defeat. "The bookstore wants me to do a meet and greet with the readers of our book." Jesse's eyes lit with excitement. "There's a literary agent who wants to meet with me there too. To talk about my future in publishing."

"Are you joking? That's epic, baby." I smiled at his excitement, but he tilted his head to the side, studying me. "Why didn't you tell me?"

"I wanted you to focus on getting better."

Jesse put his hand on my cheek. "Watching the love of my life get the acclaim she deserves will help me get better. June..." He shook his head. "The story is of us. Of all we've been through—are still going through—to get our happily ever after." He nodded determinedly. "We're going to that meet and greet."

Tears built in my eyes. "We?"

Jesse kissed me and pressed his forehead to mine. "We. You think I'd miss my Junebug being told what I already know—that you're perfect and deserve all the praise that's coming your way?"

A retching sound came from beside us. We turned to see Chris pretending to puke. "Guys, please," he said. "I've just gone through a breakup. Can we cut it with the lovey-dovey shit?"

I laughed and Emma pushed him on his arm. "He's just jealous that no one on the planet thinks he's perfect." She rolled her eyes, then looked at me again. "So that's a yes to the bookstore?"

"What," Chris said to Emma, "are you her manager now or something?"

"Maybe one day," Emma said, shrugging. We'd joked about it, but in all seriousness, I would trust no one more than my best friend to do this with me.

I turned back to Jesse. "You'll be strong enough to come?" I worried my lip. "Your immunity is low, and I don't want you getting sick. I…" Fear rushed through me. "I would never forgive myself if that happened."

"Then make it so the meet and greet happens when Jesse is done with treatment and is stronger. There's no rush. The bookstore wants you when you can make it," Emma said. When I'd told Emma about the invite and the interested agent, she had taken over all the correspondence. She was a business manager in the making.

"There," Jesse said and wrapped his arms around me. "That's settled. You'll do it." Nerves accosted me, but they eased when he said, "I'm so proud of you, Junebug. So proud."

"Thank you," I whispered, a blush creeped up my face. But the truth was, without Jesse, there wouldn't be a story. It was falling for Jesse at Harmony Ranch that showed me what love really was. His love gave me the ability to transfer us onto the page.

From the day we met, it was Jesse and June against the world. It still was. His achievements had been mine and mine were his.

"Right," Chris said, and whipped out his cell. "Pizza all around?"

"Pizza all around," Jesse said, dropping another kiss to my head.

Jesse

Jesse and June's Happily Ever After

My hand was clutched tightly in June's as we entered the stadium. I fixed the baseball hat on my head. The team had been to see me often in the hospital, but this felt strange. I hadn't stepped foot in the stadium since I'd relapsed a few months ago. The last time my feet had touched the soil was when I'd collapsed in front of a one-hundred-thousand-strong crowd.

That was one way to make them remember my name.

"You okay, baby?" June asked as we made our way down the hallway that led to the field.

I nodded and kissed the back of her hand.

"Bro, all you had to do was relapse to get me a backstage tour?" Chris joked, and I couldn't have appreciated it more. He threw his arm around my neck. "I appreciate your commitment to our friendship."

"A one-time offer only," I said, and looked at June. "This is the last time I do this chemo and antibody crap. Only smooth sailing from now on."

"Amen," June said from beside me, making me laugh more.

"I recognize that laugh," Coach said, appearing from the locker rooms. "Jesse," he greeted, and I released June to give him a hug. "You're looking good, kid." He turned to June. "June, good to see you again."

"Hello, sir," June said, her impeccable southern manners. They had met in my hospital room when the team had come to visit. Coach clearly adored her.

I introduced Chris and Emma, and Coach tilted his head the direction of the locker room. "Your team is eager to see you." A flash of nerves hit my stomach. June must have felt my apprehension, as she took my hand in her own.

"They love you," she said, and kissed my cheek. I knew they did. But it felt strange going back inside that locker room. My life had done another 180 from the beginning of college to now, just like it had in high school.

I took a deep breath and stepped into the locker room. It was loud, and my teammates were everywhere. I took a moment to just take it all in. It felt like home—a feeling that was only intensified by June holding my hand.

Sheridan was the first to notice me. "Taylor!" he shouted, his smile wide. He rushed over and lifted me off the floor. I grunted at the contact, and he jumped back, letting me go.

"Shit!" he said when the room got silent. Horrified faces looked at me like I might break.

"Ease up, bro. If the cancer doesn't kill me, your eager greeting might." Awkward laughs trickled filled the locker room, my teammates unsure whether to laugh or not.

I grinned, and Sheridan playfully punched me in the stomach. "Don't do to that to me, man! We need you back. I thought we were winning against the big C?"

"I'll be back," I said, believing every word. "We will win, and I'll be back for next season."

"That's what I want to hear!" Sheridan said and stopped himself from lifting me up again. He shook his head, disappointed at himself. "I don't know what's wrong with me."

Each one of my teammates came up to say hello. Most had already met June, but I introduced them to Chris and Emma as my best friends from A&M, which earned them some boos. As we left to let the team get ready, Coach followed us into the hall.

"You okay walking onto the field before we start? The fans have been real worried about you. It'll be nice for them to show their love to you and see you're doing well."

"Sure," I said, but my heart beat a million miles an hour. My collapsing on the field, on live TV, had been quite the viral moment. It would be nice to show them I was alive and doing well. Coach had already had to release two different statements when people had posted I had died. People could be unreasonable.

Coach went back in with the team, and June's hand in mine, we followed Chris out near the team tunnel. The cheerleaders and band were already out there doing their thing, riling everyone up. The screams of the fans were deafening, and I felt a shot of nerves run through my veins.

"Are you ready for this?" June asked.

"Sure," I said, smiling, but June gave me side-eye.

I laughed.

She smiled back, then, just for me, said, "I'm so proud of you. I know I say it all the time, but if I had been the one to relapse..." Her eyes shined. "I don't know if I would have been so brave a second time."

"You would," I said, meaning every word. "Because you want our porch dream, Junebug—the one we'll move heaven and earth to get."

"How are y'all eighteen and already act like an old married

couple?" Chris joked. June rolled her eyes again, this time at Chris, but I couldn't hear anything but the roar of the crowd.

Married. As soon as Chris had said those words, something inside of me shifted and it just felt…right.

June looked to me, eyes bright and happiness glowing on her face. Her dark bob showed off her beautiful face to perfection, and I saw it—I saw our entire future playing out ahead of us. Need burned through me, the need to make her mine. Fully and legally mine.

A hand on my shoulder broke my trance, and I turned to see Coach. "You ready, son?"

I nodded just as the announcer said, "Please, welcome back to the field, number nine, Jesse Taylor!"

The people in the stands went wild. June squeezed my hand twice and started to let go, but that wasn't happening. She had told me that the book she was writing, our alternate story, couldn't have happened without me. Well, I felt the exact same way about my football.

Pain sliced through my heart at those girls who had made my girl feel less than, insecure. What they didn't know was that June was my strength, she was my heart, she was the reason I was still alive—twice over.

It was time to show the world that, without her, there was no me.

I took a step forward and brought June with me. "Jesse! What are you doing?" June hissed, but I looked to her and smiled.

"Group two for the win." I raised my fist, and June's startled stare softened. She ducked her head to look at everyone in the one-hundred-thousand-seat stadium on their feet through the entrance of the tunnel. Then, she took in a deep breath and held up her fist.

"Group two for the win," she whispered, and hand in hand, like we always should be, we headed onto the field.

The stadium erupted when they saw us, and I could hear Chris and Emma shouting from behind us. I glanced to June as we stepped onto the grass and her eyes were huge. I lifted my hand and waved to the stadium in thanks.

We were in full view on the Jumbotron. If I'd thought June would have appreciated it, I would have dropped to my knee right then and asked her to be my wife. But that wasn't her. She wanted a simpler life, a quieter one. She didn't want the fanfare. But with her hand in mine, here on the field, it was telling the world that June Scott was my life, my heart and forever, and whoever thought she didn't deserve a place by my side could, frankly, fuck off.

"Jesse…" June whispered as she released my hand and held on to my arm. I dropped a kiss on her head and waved again. I had dreamed of this as a kid, standing in the middle of a football field to rapturous applause. Now, it paled in significance to the love of my life holding my arm like I was then reason she breathed.

With one last wave to the crowd, we headed back into the tunnel as my team ran out, clapping my hand as they passed.

"Okay, that was movie-level epic," Chris said, slapping me on the back.

"You okay, June?" Emma laughed.

June shook her head, shell-shocked, and looked to me. "I have no idea how you do that week in and week out. It was terrifying!"

I kissed her on her head, and we moved to our seats to watch. But the game wasn't what held my attention. I kept looking at June, my phone burning a hole in my pocket. I had a call to make; I had someone's permission to get.

Then I'd ask my girl the most important question I'd ever ask anyone in my life.

chapter twenty-seven

Jesse

"She's still at the stables?" I asked Mrs. Scott as she hung the lights up in the rec room.

Mrs. Scott laughed. "Yes, for the thousandth time. We've got this covered, Jesse."

I nodded, then blew out a long breath, hands on my hips. "I haven't seen you this nervous in…" my mom said, trying to think. "Never."

"It's a big day, Mom," I said, and her eyes shiny with unshed tears.

"I know it is, sweetheart." She kissed me and went to help Mrs. Scott finish hanging the lights before she broke down again.

I ran my hand over my neck, then looked up to see Mr. Scott walking through the doors with Chris. They were carrying more decorations. Chris tapped me on the back as he passed. My stomach fell as I looked to my best friend.

When June and I had told him our palliative status, he was

devastated,. I hated seeing him this way, so defeated, so broke the tension by saying, *"Hell, you chose the wrong team, Chris. Out of the four of us, you're the only one who's making it out alive. Chemo Club for one!"* Chris couldn't help but laugh and it had been the lightness we'd needed to break through the heavy sadness.

Mr. Scott stood in front of me. "You ready, son?"

"Yes, sir," I said, with 100 percent conviction. Mr. Scott put his hand on my shoulder, and I remembered when I'd crossed the yard from the ranch to the parent's quarters a few days ago.

"Jesse?" Mr. Scott said as he found me at his door. "Is June okay?" His face had gone ashen.

"Yes, sir," I said, fighting back my nerves. "I've come to ask you something."

I knew I caught him off guard, as he blinked at me in surprise. I'd gotten to know Mr. Scott well through watching football together. He was a good man and a good dad to June. He'd turned into someone I could lean on too and, not having a father around, that meant everything to me. I was pretty sure this visit would go okay, but now that I was standing here, it didn't matter that I only had weeks to live—I was the same as any man asking for their daughter's hand.

I walked into their suite and sat down. My legs ached just from the walk over from the ranch house. I was breathless and had broken out into a pretty good sweat. Mr. Scott placed a glass of water before me.

"Take your time, son," he said, and sat beside me.

I took several sips of water, then, looking Mr. Scott straight in the eye, said, "Can I please have your permission to marry June?"

Mr. Scott's eyebrows rose in shock, then he glanced away. My heart slammed against my ribs. I couldn't get a read on what he was going to say.

Then he faced me again, his eyes glassy. "I never thought I'd get a chance to walk my daughter down the aisle."

His answer made my heart ache.

He leaned toward me. "Jesse, you have my permission. Of course you do, son. You have made my daughter happier than I ever thought she could be."

I fought to swallow the lump in my throat.

"I wish this were happening differently for y'all. I wish you were asking me and you'd go on to have your forever."

"We will," I said, recalling my talk with Pastor Noel. "Our forever is there; it just looks a little different to most people's."

Mr. Scott turned away as he choked on a sob, then took a few deep breaths. Facing me again, he said, "It would be my honor to have you as a son-in-law, Jesse. And thank you for the gift you're given me of walking my baby down the aisle. I've dreamed of that moment since the day she was born."

I gave a nervous laugh. "She has to say yes first, sir."

"It's gonna be a yes, son. My baby loves you more than I've ever seen her love anyone before."

"You look smart," Mr. Scott said just as my mom and Mrs. Scott turned on the twinkle lights. It was sunset, and the orange glow of the Texas sun was shining its beams through the rec room's windows. With the strings lights everywhere inside, it looked incredible.

"June is on her way back," Neenee said, coming into the room.

I took a deep breath. Mr. Scott gave me a hug. Mrs. Scott followed suit. Then, my mom was last. "I'm so happy for you, baby. You both deserve this and more." Mom had been given time off work to come here for my final weeks. And in the typical fashion of coming from a small town, the close-knit community had raised enough money for her to be here, so she wouldn't struggle financially being here and so she could take time away from work...afterwards.

I'd never loved my hometown more. People often couldn't wait to leave their rural hometowns for the bright lights of a big city. But June and I agreed that, if we'd gotten to live our happily ever after, we would have eventually settled in a town full of people who knew our names, who greeted us each day with happy faces.

I moved into the center of the room. I wore a linen button-down and cargo shorts. I'd lost so much weight now that they hung off my frame, but June wouldn't mind. She just loved me, not how I looked. And of course, I had to wear my baseball cap. It was my lucky charm.

The clicking of the door to outside sounded, and I heard my little sisters running. We'd distracted June by asking her to show my sisters Ginger and the other horses. Bailey had joined her, now that it was a bit far for her to travel on her own and she needed support.

Then, June walked through the door and instantly took my breath away. She was dressed in her sage-green dress, the one that I adored. Her matching headscarf brought out her deep-brown eyes and her face was flushed from being outside in the fresh air.

"Jesse?" she said, looking around the room in confusion. It no longer looked like the rec room; it looked like something from a movie, with lights glittering in every corner and a carpet of rose petals on the ground.

June froze, eyes wide. "Jesse?" she said again, but I saw her swallow a nervously.

Walking to her, I took hold of her hands and said, "Junebug." Her breathing hitched as I squeezed them. Looking her straight in the eyes, I said, "June Scott, I love you more than I ever knew I could love someone." I'd hoped my voice would stay strong, but the minute June's hands were in mine and her attention was all on me, it broke. "Meeting you has been the most amazing thing that has ever happened to me." Tears began to fall down her face. "I hoped that we would have had more time. I prayed to anyone who would listen for us to be able to continue this love story out in the big, wide world." I cleared my throat, so I could keep going. "But in the end, all we have is now. And I couldn't wait one more minute to ask you a very important question."

June held her breath as I got down on one knee. My joints screamed as I did, and it wasn't a pretty descent—the aches and pains were almost too much to bear. But when I looked up at June and her hand was over her mouth in happiness, all the pain washed away.

"June Scott, my Junebug, would you please do me the honor of a lifetime and become my wife?"

A sob tore from June's mouth. "Yes," she whispered. "It will *always* be yes, Jesse."

I pulled the ring from my pocket. Mr. Scott had given it to me; it had belonged to June's grandma. It was a simple gold band with a small diamond in the center. It was understated but beautiful, exactly like the girl who would wear it from now on.

I slid the ring on her finger. It was a little big, but June looked down at it like I'd gifted her a star from the sky. I made a move to get up, but my leg screamed in agony.

June stared at me adoringly, and I said, "I should be kissing you right now, Junebug, but I might need some help in getting up."

Her lips twitched and then she filled the room with her beautiful laughter, only making the twinkling setting more magical.

Mr. Scott appeared and helped me to my feet. I rolled my eyes at him, knowing he—and most of our families—had been listening just outside the room. After I was standing, he left us alone, and June was staring up at me like I was her everything.

"There," I said, heart melting at her beaming face. "I made it off the floor." I placed my hands on either side of her face, then moved in to kiss her. June's lips were soft, and I tasted her tears as they cascaded down her cheeks. They mixed with mine, but none of them were from sadness. I was so full of happiness that I thought I'd burst.

When we broke apart, I pressed my forehead to hers. "You're going to be my wife." *Wife.* Never had a word sounded so perfect.

"I love you," June said, and I studied every part of her face.

"How does a wedding in three days sound?" June watched me, questions in her gaze. "Pastor Noel has agreed to marry us."

"In three days?" she asked, eyes wide.

"I thought we'd better move fast, seeing as how we don't have the luxury of time," I joked, and June fought a smile. "Or else our wedding might just turn into a funeral."

"Jesse!" June said, shaking her head in admonishment. But the glint in her eyes showed me she was enjoying my dark humor, despite it perhaps hitting too close to home.

"Three days sounds perfect," she said.

I wanted to walk to the chapel now and make it happen. But I also knew that June had dreamed of her wedding her whole life, and if there was one thing I wasn't selfish about, it was June's happiness.

"Can we come in now?" Chris shouted from the doorway. "Your parents are about to barge in you if you don't say yes!" We turned and laughed at our family and friends waiting in the doorway.

"Yes!" June said, holding her left hand up to her mom and dad. "I'm getting married!" Mr. Scott scooped June up in his arms. "You get to walk me down the aisle, Daddy," June said, and Mr. Scott's eyes closed.

"I know, baby. I cannot wait," he whispered, opening them again and staring adoringly at his daughter.

Mom hugged me, and Lucy and Emily ran straight to June, forgetting about me entirely. "Can we be your bridesmaids?" Lucy asked my fiancée.

My fiancée.

Emily hit Lucy on the arm. "You have to ask nicely! We talked about this!"

I laughed, and as June's eyes met mine, there was no more fear, no more pain, just happiness reflecting back at all of us.

"Of course you can," June said to the little monsters. "Who else would I have? You're going to be my sisters." Those words were an arrow to the chest. Lucy and Emily jumped on June, screaming in excitement.

For the first time since I'd been told I was on palliative care, I wished time to go faster. I couldn't wait for three days from now to get here.

I couldn't wait to be able to call my Junebug my wife.

chapter twenty-eight

June

"June..." my mama said as she finished buttoning me up and stepping away.

I stared in the mirror at my reflection. I wore a white dress that clung to my frame. It was fully lace, with a high neck and long sleeves. Patterns of feathers were woven into the lace. It was perfect. The bridal store had even made me a headscarf made of the same material, with crystals sewed in it to give me a little sparkle.

It was my vintage dream.

A makeup artist had heard about our wedding from Neenee and had come to the ranch to do my makeup, giving me soft smoky eyes and a natural pink lip.

I'd never thought of myself as pretty, but looking at my refection now...I finally did. I couldn't wait for Jesse to see me. I lifted my left hand and ran my fingers over my ring—Mamaw's ring.

The wedding had been pulled together in just three short days. Neenee had handled almost everything, telling the local community near the ranch about our nuptials and many reaching out to help. The bridal store had donated the dress, and a catering company was currently setting up in the formal dining room, where we would eat afterwards. A party-planning company was making a dance floor in the grand hall. I liked to think Mr. Owens would have approved of our marriage too. He never got to see his daughter marry; she died too young.

A throat cleared behind me. I turned, and my daddy stood there in a tux. My lips wobbled as his eyes softened seeing me in my dress.

"Do you like it?" I asked, smoothing my hand down the delicate lace.

"June," Daddy whispered, and he had to wipe at his freshly shaven face.

He walked up and took hold of my hand. His breathing was shaky, as he said, "I've never seen anyone more beautiful in my life."

"You look real handsome, Daddy," I said, and fixed a yellow rose on his lapel. "Have you seen Jesse?" A flutter of nerves gathered within me. I wasn't nervous in a bad way. If I could have, I would've run down the aisle and become Jesse's wife that very second. I wanted this so badly.

"He's good," Daddy said. "He's already at the chapel." Daddy playfully rolled his eyes. "I'm pretty sure he got ready there last night and has been waiting for you by the altar ever since."

I smiled so wide my jaw ached as I raised a brow at him. "Is he wearing his Longhorns cap?"

My daddy laughed. "Darlin', if he'd have been wearing that

too-worn cap, I would have pulled it from his head and burned the damned thing to ashes." Daddy still hadn't gotten over how Jesse had worn it to propose to me.

I laughed, and Daddy sobered. "He looks great, darlin'. He's just waiting on his beautiful bride to arrive."

"Then let's go," I said, and I linked my arm in my daddy's.

Mama kissed my cheek. "You're the most stunning bride I have ever seen," she said, then straightened her shoulders. "I'll get to the chapel and see you both in there." Mama kissed Daddy, then left us alone.

"Shall we?" I said to my daddy.

I went to move, but Daddy stepped in front of me. He met my eyes, and a lump lodged in my throat at the mixed emotions I saw there. "June. I've never been prouder of anyone in my life," he said, his voice breaking on the last word.

"Don't make me cry, Daddy," I said weakly.

He flicked away a tear on my cheek with his thumb. "Let me say this, baby, please."

I nodded. I had to give him this moment.

"Me and your mama, we waited so long to have you. Kids, they just weren't in God's plans for us, or so we thought. So when we found out your mama was pregnant with you, you were all our wishes come true."

I breathed deeply and slowly, trying to keep myself from falling apart. "We were never able to give you a sibling, so instead we tried to give you the world. We loved you as best we could, darlin'. You are the bravest, sweetest human on earth, and it has been an absolute privilege to be your father."

"Daddy..." I said and couldn't stop the tears.

"Today, walking you down the aisle to the boy I'm pretty sure God designed perfectly for you...well, baby, it's the greatest honor of my life. And for as long as I live, I will cherish it. I will always cherish you for showing me what unconditional love is and making all my dreams come true."

I threw my arms around his neck and held him close. I couldn't imagine how hard this moment was for him and my mama.

Pulling back, I laughed weakly at us both. "We're a mess."

Daddy shook his head. "You're perfect, darlin."

I took a deep breath and checked my face in the mirror. It was okay. The makeup artist had done a good job of making it waterproof. Turning back to my daddy, I said, "In case I never get to tell you, you and Mama have been the most precious people in my life. I have loved every second of growing up with y'all. And..." My breathing hitched, but I managed to say, "And even from heaven, I will miss you. So very much."

My daddy held me then, and I soaked in every moment. Eventually he pulled back. "We had better get you married, baby," he said, voice hoarse.

I linked my arm with my daddy's, and we walked down the hall to the chapel. Neenee was waiting at the entrance, and she gasped when she saw me. From behind her, Lucy and Emily came barreling toward me, and I melted at the sight of them in their little white dresses. Both had baskets full to the brim of yellow rose petals. Susan was watching them, so Cynthia could be with Jesse inside the chapel.

Emily and Lucy stood before me. "Y'all look so adorable," I said, and was met with two very proud faces. My heart skipped when, in their eyes, I saw Jesse looking back at me. Their blond hair was curled and clipped up with flowery barrettes.

"You look real pretty, Junebug," Lucy said, and warmed my heart.

"Thank you," I said, and Susan came and took their hands.

"You do, darlin'," she said and kissed my cheek. "That boy in there is gonna be so overawed when he sees you."

Neenee gave a nod to the pianist at the front of the chapel, and my favorite piece of classical music, "River Flows in You" by Yiruma, began to play. Susan guided the girls down the aisle, and Neenee took my hand.

"You look beautiful, June." She gave me a kiss on my cheek and said, "Count to twenty, then come on through."

Neenee went inside the chapel, and I began my countdown. When my daddy looked at me and mouthed *twenty*, we stepped forward and rounded the corner. The intimate chapel was full of our friends from the trial and their families who were staying at the residence.

Yellow roses were gathered at the end of each aisle. A white carpet led the way to the altar, and at the very end, I knew Jesse stood with Chris by his side. I hadn't looked up yet though, not wanting to see Jesse until I'd made it to the end.

I passed Silas, Toby, Kate, and Cherry. All of them were watching with smiles on their faces. Their mamas and daddies and siblings were there too. The nursing staff were there, out of their scrubs and dressed in their finest. Even Dr. Duncan gave me a nod as I passed.

My eyes landed on Cynthia in the front pew, and I fought back my own tears when I saw her cheeks were wet, but her smile was adoring and wide. I hadn't known her long, but I loved Jesse's mama so much. She had raised Jesse to be the man he was today. Even if I'd never met her, I would have known she was a good person to have made such a beautiful soul. I would have loved her for giving me the gift of my soulmate.

My mama took my hand as I passed and squeezed it. Suddenly, I stopped walking—on a chair all to herself, Emma's pretty face smiled up at me from a large photograph. A single yellow rose was laid before her.

Leaning down, I kissed the tips of my fingers and touched her cheek, my chest aching with how much I missed her. I just knew it had been Chris who had placed my best friend front and center at my wedding. Emma would have loved this. She would have been my bridesmaid too. I hoped that, wherever she was, she was looking down and cheering us on.

I stood and gathered myself. Then, I reached the end of the aisle. I closed my eyes and, on the count of five, opened them and looked up.

My heart skipped a beat as I saw that standing before me was the most handsome boy in existence. My daddy turned me around and pressed a kiss on my cheek. Reaching out to Jesse, he shook his hand and then went to stand beside my mama.

Pastor Noel stood before the altar, patiently waiting. Jesse held out his hand, and the moment I slipped my hand into his, one heart meeting the other, total peace drifted over me, a sense of rightness. I didn't understand why my life was being cut short, I would never understand how someone with Jesse's spirit was being deprived of a long life. But in that moment, I knew we were meant to be husband and wife.

I let my gaze rove over every part of him. He wore a black tux that fit him to perfection—I giggled when I saw his head was free of his cap.

Jesse must have seen my amusement, as he leaned in and whispered, "I thought your daddy would kill me if I wore it, so I didn't dare. I didn't want to forfeit the few weeks I have left."

I squeezed his hand, his joke for my ears only. But then Jesse's humor faded as he stepped to me and said, "Wow…you're beautiful." I threw back my head and laughed until I felt giddy with joy.

That was the first thing Jesse had ever said to me. It seemed apt that, as we stepped into our new life as husband and wife, it would start the same way.

"You look real handsome too, baby," I said, and Jesse leaned in for a kiss.

A throat cleared and we broke apart.

"That doesn't happen until the end, son. But I'll let it slide this one time," Pastor Noel said, and our friends and family chuckled.

"I couldn't help it," Jesse said, then cupped my cheek. "Have you seen my girl?" I felt my face blaze, and when Jesse gave me a playful wink.

When the laughter died down, Jesse took both of my hands in his and Pastor Noel began the ceremony. It was a sermon full of joy and hope and about soulmates finding each other.

When the time came for vows, Jesse and I had written our own.

Jesse went first. "Junebug," he said, and I caught the telling rasp in his voice. "If someone had told me months ago that I would be here right now, marrying the girl of my dreams, I would never have believed them." He gave me a lopsided smile, and said, "But from the very first day I bumped into you in the hallway, you've had my heart."

I replayed that day so clearly in my head. Because I had felt the same way. One meeting, and butterflies had invaded my chest.

"We didn't know the outcome of the trial; we didn't know if we would even have a chance at life." The room was silent, the topic heavy. "And although it hasn't gone the way we had hoped, today, you are the fulfillment of a dream I didn't know I had. And I wouldn't change our story for anything in the world. If all we have are the next few weeks as husband and wife, then I will call our marriage a triumphant success."

I held back my emotion as best as I could, but my hands shook and my lips trembled.

"You are the love of my life, and I'll stand by your side for whatever time we have left on this earth and wherever we go next." I nodded in agreement. "I love you, Junebug." Then Jesse lifted his hand and formed it into a fist. I laughed a watery laugh, as he said, "Group two for the win."

I tapped his fist and then Pastor Noel turned to me. "June, please say your vows."

Pushing away my nerves, I focused entirely on Jesse until the rest of the room fell away and it was just us two. He brought my hands to his mouth and gave them each a kiss, his forest-green eyes locked on mine. "Jesse," I said, making sure I spoke clearly and strongly. "My dream was always to be a writer. I wanted to write a love story—the greatest love story ever known." I smiled and looked to my mama and daddy. "My parents have the best marriage I've ever seen. They have loved each other since their teens, and I wondered if I'd get a love like that." I swallowed. "When I was told I had terminal cancer and that the treatment wasn't working, I was sure I never would."

"June," Jesse said, whispering my name as he felt my pain.

I stepped closer and put my hand on his cheek. Jesse leaned into the touch. "Then I came here to get a second chance at life. I came here to heal and get better, so I could go into the world and find that love." I shook my head. "I didn't know I would find my great love on a ranch just outside Austin. I didn't know my soulmate would be the cheeky football player who was staying next door."

Jesse smiled wide at that.

"The truth is that I wanted a great love and I wanted to write about it. And I have. But what I didn't realize was that the greatest love story I could ever know is the one that I was going to live. Through the ups and downs, through the rough and the…well, rougher."

Everyone chuckled at that.

"Jesse Taylor, you have swept me off my feet. And although we won't have long together, like the burned-out star four thousand light years away, our love will shine bright long after we're gone. Because you and I were meant to be. Jesse and his June. Forever."

A tear fell down Jesse's cheek. It fell onto the petal of the yellow rose on his lapel.

"You hold my heart in your hand, and I hold yours in mine. For eternity." Taking his example, I held up my fist. "Group two for the win."

Jesse laughed, then bumped his fist with my own.

"We'll now exchange the rings." Pastor Noel said, and then we slid our rings on the other's finger never breaking our gaze.

"It is my absolute pleasure to pronounce you husband and wife," Pastor Noel said. "You may kiss."

Jesse moved forward like he couldn't wait one more minute to seal our marriage with a kiss, only he paused at the last second and turned to my daddy to say, "You might want to look away, sir."

Chris whooped in encouragement as the crowd broke into applause. And then, I was consumed by Jesse's lips on mine, making us one in front of family, friends, and God.

We were married.
He had officially tied his soul with my own.
I was Mrs. June Taylor.
Nothing had ever felt so good.

chapter twenty-nine

Jesse

WE WALKED OUT OF THE CHAPEL TO CHEERS AND APPLAUSE. THERE wasn't any room for sadness today. Today was about celebration and love. Because, hell, I had just married my Junebug.

She was my *wife*.

The guests made their way to the dining room. I could smell the delicious food all the way from down here, but June and I were at the back of the line, and I pulled her into the alcove in the hallway for a moment alone. I guided her back against the wall. June smiled up at me like I was her entire world.

She was mine, so I understood the sentiment.

I stepped back and just took my fill of her. I shook my head. "Junebug," I said. "You look incredible." Every inch of her lace dress clung to her petite frame. And her head scarf was perfect—everything was perfection. She was beauty personified. Her cheeks were still flushed and her pink lips just begged to be kissed.

So I did. I kissed and kissed her until we were breathless—which these days, wasn't a difficulty.

I broke away and June took hold of my left hand and studied the plain gold band on my ring finger. She looked up at me with nothing but love in her brown eyes. "You're my husband," she whispered in awe, and those words sounded like paradise.

I took her left hand and ran my thumb over the matching gold band and her mamaw's ring. "Mrs. Taylor," I said. "Why do I love the sound of that so much?"

"We're married, baby," June said, and just from the glow on her face, I felt ten feet tall. This was one of June's dreams. I couldn't give her more time. I couldn't give her wrinkles or gray hair. I couldn't give her deep laughter lines or children. But I could make her mine in every way that counted, and in the end, that would be more than enough for us both.

I kissed her one last time, deeply and with all of my heart, then said, "Shall we go to our reception?" I held out my hand and June took hold of it and held it tightly.

As we walked down the hallway, I ignored how my muscles ached and my joints rang with pain. I ignored the way we were both breathless and June's limp was more pronounced. Death wasn't invited to our nuptials today.

As we rounded the corner and walked into the dining hall, Mr. Scott held up a glass of champagne and said, "Introducing, Mr. and Mrs. Jesse Taylor!"

Our guests all cheered.

We sat down for dinner and the atmosphere was relaxed and happy. Even the few speeches made were light and positive. We had asked for tonight to just simply one of celebration, and our family and friends helped make it come true.

By the time we moved to the part of the night in the grand hall, exhaustion had taken us in its hold. June and I sat hand in hand, June's head leaning on my shoulder, watching our guests dance. June laughed as Emily and Lucy ran circles around Chris, who was wiped by the time they were done.

I smiled as my mom danced with Pastor Noel, her sadness momentarily forgotten. June's parents rarely left the floor, cheeks pressed together, and I understood how June had grown up a believer in true love with them as an example. We drank it all in.

The day had been perfect, but the truth was, we were tired. Clearly seeing that was the case, Neenee came over and said, "First dance, then we can say good night?"

"Yes please," June said, and turned to me. "What song did you pick for our first dance?"

"You'll see," I said, and June groaned in trepidation.

"That doesn't fill me with confidence, Jesse."

"Mrs. Taylor!" I said and watched June beam at her new name. "Don't you trust me? Your husband?"

June sighed, and I took her hand. I helped her to her feet, and it took us longer than I'd hoped to get to the center of the dance floor. I nodded at Neenee and the opening bars of Alphaville's "Forever Young" began to play.

With June's hand in mine and her arm around my back, she dropped her head onto my chest and said, "A bit on the nose, isn't it, Jesse?"

I shrugged but knew she had found it as funny as I did by the shaking of her shoulders. "It felt appropriate." I kissed June's head. "Eternally seventeen," I said, and dropped my cheek to lay on her head. "Eternally yours," I added and could tell June liked that better by the squeeze of her hand on mine.

We swayed, unable to do much more. I wanted to soak in every minute of this night. I didn't know what would happen for us after this, didn't know how much time we had together. But we would always have this night. We would always be joined as one.

As the song ended, Mom and Mr. and Mrs. Scott came over. Emily and Lucy were asleep on the benches at the side of the room. Mom kissed my cheek and hugged June. "I am so unbelievably happy for y'all. I'll see you both tomorrow. I'd better get those two to bed." She motioned to my sisters.

Mr. and Mrs. Scott gestured for us to follow them out into the hallway. I placed my arm around June's back and helped her walk. My heart fell a little at how much of a struggle it seemed to be for her. It wouldn't be long until she needed a wheelchair to get around. But I knew how determined she'd been to get through today unaided.

A flare of panic ran through me. Selfishly, I didn't want to live a single day without her. Even if it took me only a few days to follow behind, every single minute without her would feel like a lifetime of loneliness.

"Jesse?" June said, moving her hand to my face. She was exhausted. I looked to Mr. Scott, and he must have seen it too by the worry lines on his face.

"I'm good, baby. Let's just get to bed." I didn't want her to know I was worrying about her.

"Speaking of," Mrs. Scott said, stopping at a bigger suite a few doors down from where we had previously been staying. June and I both looked at her in confusion.

Mrs. Scott opened the door, and we saw all of our things were there. A king-sized bed sat in the center, with June's notebook full of our nearly finished happily ever after story on one bedside table and my sketchpad and pencils on the other.

"Mama?" June whispered, seeing the wall of my drawings that June had previously had in her room.

"Y'all are married now," Mr. Scott said. "This is your new home. Together."

I itched my nose to chase away the tickle of emotion that ran up it. "Thank you, sir," I said, and shook his hand.

"Let's get you both inside." He could clearly tell we were exhausted. We had pushed ourselves too hard today, but it was all worth it.

"We'll see y'all tomorrow," June's parents said, and shut the door behind us.

I helped June sit on the bed, and she drank it all in. It was beautiful. "Do you need help with your dress?" I asked, and June nodded.

She turned and I unbuttoned the long row of buttons that ran to the bottom of her spine. She slid the dress off until all that remained was a silk slip underneath.

Her cheeks blazed under my heavy attention. I peeled off my suit until I was down to my boxer briefs. We had already made love and slept in each other's arms most nights. But this felt more intimate. It felt bigger somehow.

June yawned and I laughed. "That wasn't at you," she teased.

Pulling the covers back from the bed, I said, "Into bed, Junebug."

"Are you trying to seduce me?" She attempted a terrible wink.

"Junebug," I said, "we're both on so much medication right now, we couldn't do anything if we tried." Her light peal of laughter rang around the room. I climbed in beside her, sliding her headscarf off and turning off the main light switch. Only the dull light of the beside lamp remained.

We faced each other and joined hands, content to just stare at one another.

Mr. and Mrs. Taylor—I could barely believe it.

"I love you," June whispered, and even those three words sounded more important somehow.

"I love you too," I said and kissed her lips. I ran my hand down her side, over her silk slip, and said, "Just so you know, if I were at full health, I would be devouring you right now."

"Oh, I believe it," she said and giggled. I laughed too. "I adore your dimples." She ran her fingertips along them, then yawned again. "I don't want this night to end, but I don't think I can stay awake much longer."

"Before you sleep," I said, and reached for my bedside drawer. I just hoped June's parents had put my wedding gift in the same place I'd had it in my old room.

Luckily, they had. I pulled out the picture that I'd had framed. It was wrapped in white. June struggled to sit up, but when she finally did, I handed her the picture.

"I didn't get you anything," she said, worrying her lip.

"You gave me you, Junebug. That's more than enough." I tapped the frame. "Open it."

June carefully opened the package of the picture I'd drawn for her. She gasped when it came into view and her eyes filled with tears. "Jesse..." she said and ran her fingertips over the glass front. She turned to me with a sad smile. "Our dream."

I swallowed the lump in my throat. "I couldn't give you it in this life. Maybe it's in our happily ever after, I don't know. But I wanted you to have it some way, even if it was just in picture form from my imagination."

June held the frame to her chest and closed her eyes. When she opened them again, she looked at me and said, "It's exactly how I see it too."

My heart was full to bursting as she leaned down and kissed me, holding the sketch to her chest.

June took hold of my hand. "We'll have this in some way, baby. In heaven, this dream awaits."

"I know," I rasped out, and kissed June's fingers as she fell asleep. When she was deeply asleep, I took the frame from her hands, so it wouldn't break. Looking down at the picture, I closed my eyes and saw it in my mind's eye—us, sitting on our porch swing, the view from our home's back door. Our heads were close together, and we were older. Before us were our children and grandchildren, playing in the back yard as we watched on.

It was June's biggest dream.

I'd had to give her this too. I'd had to give her one more dream, even if it was just etched in pencil.

I would have given her the world if I could.

But I'd had to settle for giving her my last name, and that was a dream come true in itself.

chapter thirty

June

Jesse and June's Happily Ever After

"How are you feeling?" I asked, as June looked out of the car window. The bookstore had sent a car for us—how fancy. The weather was bright and warm, and the sun was blazing in the blue sky.

June wore a floor-length, fitted, sleeveless green dress which made her eyes look like dark chocolate swirls. I was still staying in the hospital, but as of last week, my latest test results had returned as "no evidence of disease." I had only a few weeks left of my treatment, and soon, I would be out and fully considered in remission.

I couldn't believe it. After months and months of chemo and immunotherapy, sickness and June never leaving my side, we'd gotten through it.

I was exhausted, a little weak and sore, but I wasn't going to miss this event for anything in the world. June turned to me and took a deep breath. She still wore her dark hair in a bob, and she looked beautiful. But then, she always was to me.

"I'm beginning to regret my choice," she said, lips twitching in nerves. I kissed the back of her hand. Her skin had paled a little with anxiety. "What if no one turns up? What if the event is a bust?" she said, panicked.

"Junebug," I said, shifting closer to her on the back seat. "Look at me." She did, and I cupped her cheek. She closed her eyes and breathed deeply at my touch. "Our story has millions of reads online. I'm pretty sure you have no idea what you'll be walking into."

Her eyes opened wide.

"Not in a bad way, baby. But in a good." I kissed her forehead, her short bangs tickling my nose. "I've read the comments on every chapter you post."

"You have?" June asked. She had stopped reading them long ago, when the sheer number of people reading her words made her more terrified than not. This was our story she was writing. The story of us had we not made it out of Harmony Ranch. It was special to us, and it made June feel vulnerable. She was determined to protect that Jesse and June with everything she was. She adored them. We adored them—we *were* them. We held them tightly in our hearts. She didn't want anyone's comments to hurt them in any way.

I nodded. "They are loved," I said. "Your words have helped so many people, Junebug. You have no idea. You've given terminally ill Jesse and June a chance to live in millions of peoples' hearts. You've done them justice."

"We're nearly there," the driver announced, interrupting us.

I looked out of the window, and I had to rub my eyes to be sure I was seeing what I thought I was. "June," I whispered, dumbfounded. Pride, thick and strong, flooded my veins, and with my arm around her shoulders, I pulled her to the window to look.

"Oh my gosh," June said in utter disbelief. The line to the bookstore stretched around the block. It was so long that we couldn't see its end. "They're not…" she trailed off. "They're here for me?"

As we got closer, we saw the excited faces of hundreds of people—mainly teens—waiting patiently in line.

They were here for my Junebug. They were here because of our story.

The car came to a stop where Emma and Chris were waiting, at the back entrance. Like they had at my Longhorns games, they wanted to support June too—Chemo Club for life! Plus, Emma had worked with June to make all this happen, and she wasn't going to miss it for the world.

We had traveled to A&M a few times to see our friends. And we intended to watch Chris play baseball there later in the year. Emma had stepped back from band life she'd participated in, in high school to concentrate on math. These were our best friends for life. And because of what we'd been through, we were never going to take one another for granted. Any one of us might not have made it, just like in June's story. I couldn't imagine a world where that happened. We four had a bond that nothing could break.

I ducked out of the car first and gave Chris and Emma hugs. When I turned back around, June was still sat in the back seat, unmoving, staring straight ahead, lost in her panic.

"Junebug?" I said softly.

"I'm nervous," she said, and my heart melted.

"They love you, baby. Just like we love you. There's nothing to fear." I pointed to myself, Emma and Chris. "It's understandable to be nervous, but they just want to meet you and thank you for your words." I held out my hand.

June quickly put hers in mine and held on like she wouldn't ever let go. "Stay with me," she said, and I kissed the back of her hand.

"Always."

I guided June from the car and Emma threw her arms around her. "You're gonna kill it," she said excitedly, just as the door opened to the bookstore behind us.

"Hello. You must be J. Taylor?" the bookstore manager said, and my heart skipped a beat. It always did whenever June's pen name was used. It played in my head on repeat, and I prayed that, soon enough, it would no longer be just a pen name but her legal name too.

"Yes, ma'am," June said, and in that moment, she seemed so young. We were so young for so much of what had happened to us. But June's success...she was eighteen and more successful than some people twice her age were.

Keeping her hand in mine, we entered the bookstore. "We'll do the Q&A first," the manager said. "Is that okay?"

"Yes, ma'am," June said again. We were led to a room behind where the meet and greet would be.

"Okay, this is epic," Chris said. "Do y'all think they'll ask about me too? Being one of the main characters in the story and all."

We all laughed, and I rolled my eyes at my friend, but then wrapped my arms around June when I saw how nervous she still was. "Just be you," I said to her. "They'll adore you."

June nodded, then the manager came back through. "Are you ready, Ms. Taylor?" That name flipped my stomach again. When she'd decided on her pen name, she had wanted to incorporate us both, being that it was our joint story. So June had used Taylor. It was the greatest honor of my life so far. I could only think of one more that would top it.

June nodded, then followed her out into the store. The minute June came into view, the people—who were now seated and waiting patiently—began to cheer. June's step faltered, but I helped her onto the stage.

She met my eyes, disbelief shining in hers, and I kissed the back of her hand, flipping it over to kiss the anatomical heart that was drawn on it. "I'll be in the front row," I said, and pointed to the seats Emma had reserved for us.

June inhaled deeply, then stood and faced the crowd. There wasn't a free space in the store, some readers even having to stand.

June waved, a blush coloring her cheeks. As I sat down, I was breathless—not from the treatment, but from seeing my girl up there, all the attention she deserved (and feared) being showered upon her. From the moment I had met her, I knew she was special. Seeing her up there now only confirmed it.

June took a seat, and the crowd settled. The audience was completely silent as she answered each question—about her writing process, about her love of books, and about why she wanted to be a writer.

When the crowd was asked for questions, a girl stood up. "I love the story of Jesse and June. It's so beautiful but so tragic at the same time. There are rumors that it's based on a true story. Can you tell us if it is?"

June's brown eyes found mine. I could feel people following her gaze, and murmurs broke out. I knew what they were seeing. Me in my Longhorn's cap, bald head underneath.

"In parts," June said, and then asked me a question with her gaze. Could she mention us? Our journey? Could she make it public? I gave her firm nod. Our story—in both worlds—was beautiful. I wanted her to scream it from the rooftops.

Then, June held out her hand for me. I got to my feet and heard several gasps and excited murmurs. I got up on the stage with her and knew that the crowd was seeing their favorite characters come to life.

A bookstore worker put a chair beside June for me. I sat beside her and held her hand. "This is Jesse," June said, and the crowd's reaction got louder. "And I'm June," she said. Her eyes shined as she looked at me and said, "We met at Harmony Ranch, during a clinical trial for teenagers with stage four acute myeloid leukemia. And that's where we fell in love." June explained our story, and by the time she was done, there wasn't a dry eye in the house.

Another reader stood up. "It feels like you're approaching the end of *Write Me for You*. I..." The reader's voice hitched. "I'm not sure I'm ready for it to end."

June nodded—I knew she felt the same way.

"In *Write Me for You*, June is writing *Jesse and June's Happily Ever After*; in real life, you are writing *Write Me for You*." The reader tilted her head. "Which story feels more real to you?"

June thought about the question, then said, "Both." She looked at me. "Long ago, Jesse talked to me about parallel universes, that maybe stories that we write in this life are happening in another. That's why I decided to write the book, to explore what would have happened had our cancers not been receptive to the trial's treatment."

"Jesse?" the reader asked, addressing me too. "What do you think?"

"I think that, as the reader, you can decide which version of our story is true. Jesse and June's love in *Write Me for You* is powerful and perhaps more beautiful because they don't have time. Everything is bigger and brighter as their time together is more condensed, finite, limited." I inched closer to June, pain in my chest just talking about us not having the time we do now. "In *Jesse and June's Happily Ever After*, their love is sweeter because they have time to live and share more experiences." I smiled and fought the heavy emotions that were rising up my throat. "They will get the wrinkles, the gray hair, and get to be the older, aged couple on the porch." I leaned over and kissed June's cheek. June met my eyes, and I spoke directly to her. "I see us as living both lives simultaneously." I winked at the audience. "What happens in the end, well, that's up to you."

The applause was loud, and June dropped her forehead to mine. "I am obsessed with you," she said, and I laughed.

"Ditto."

June stood for hours and signed her name and spoke to her much-loved readers. When she finished, the agent she had been emailing with for a few months spoke to her for an hour more, discussing her future in the publishing industry. I sat and watched it all, feeling like the luckiest guy on the planet.

When the store began to prepare for closing, I stood up and walked up to June. Her eyes were bright from all the excitement, but I could see my girl was tired.

"We'll leave you both for tonight, but we'll see y'all tomorrow?" Emma said.

"Sounds like a plan," June said.

Emma hugged my girl, then said, "I am so, so proud of you, June."

"Thank you for all your help," June said.

With one last wave, we got in the car that was waiting for us outside. In the back seat, I cupped June's cheek and kissed her. I tried to show her just how proud I was with my touch. I was so proud of how powerful her words were and just how much she was changing people's lives.

"Never lose this," I said when I pulled back. "Never lose this happiness I can see on your face right now. Your purpose, the reason you write, the reason you survived—it makes the world a better place, Junebug."

"I'm happy because of you," June said. "You told me at the ranch to write you for me, and I did, and you have changed my life—in every single way that matters." June wrapped her arms around my neck. "I love you, Jesse Taylor. So very much."

"I love you too."

Those words just didn't seem adequate enough, so I planned to show her instead.

I lay in the hospital bed; June lay beside me. I stroked her hair, and I felt the nerves build within me. Finally, on a deep breath, I reached into my bedside table and pulled out my sketchpad.

June lifted her head from my chest, clearly wondering what I was doing. "You want to draw?" she asked, and I shook my head.

June frowned.

I placed the sketchpad in front of her. "I want you to look through it."

She was confused, but when she opened the first page, her confusion morphed into love. "Jesse," she said, and ran her fingers down the picture of us at the ranch, sitting in our egg chair.

"Keep going," I said, and June turned the page. It was us smiling and holding our diplomas at the ranch's graduation. Next was June beside me after my first Longhorns game.

June choked on a sob when she turned to the next picture, which depicted us in this room, me on chemo and June holding my hand, looking up at me like I hung the moon.

"Jesse, what is this?" she asked in awe.

"Us," I said. "My own version of the story of us. You have your words; I have my sketches."

"I love it," she said.

"There's one more," I said, my chest squeezing tightly.

June froze when she turned the page. She glanced back up, tears in her eyes, and I'd retrieved the ring from my pocket—her mamaw's ring, the same one from our love story. Her father had given it to me when I'd asked for his daughter's hand in marriage.

"Jesse," June whispered, speechless.

"Marry me, Junebug?" I took her hand in mine, drawing her gaze away from the picture of her left hand wearing this ring too. "Marry me. Tonight, tomorrow, next week, next year, I don't care. Just say you'll be mine forever?"

June

Jesse and June's Happily Ever After

Hopeful, passionate, forest-green eyes waited for me to respond. My heart was fit to burst, to overflow with love. I glanced down at the picture Jesse had drawn. It was of my hand, and on the left ring finger was the ring that was now being offered to me. And I recognized the ring—it had belonged to my mamaw. Which meant Jesse had asked my daddy for permission.

My heart exploded all over again.

"Yes," I said—there was no other answer to give. I looked at Jesse. "Yes. Yes, I will marry you. In any lifetime, in any love story, I will always choose you."

Jesse's responding smile was euphoric. With shaking hands, he lifted the ring from the box and slid it on my finger.

It was a perfect fit.

Jesse kissed me, and I kissed him back with all that I held in my soul. Total adoration. When I pulled back, I laughed and said, "We're getting married!"

"We're getting married," Jesse said, and as I looked at him on the bed, a few weeks away from reclaiming his life…again, I realized I didn't want to wait.

"Now," I said to Jesse, and his lips twitched. "I want to marry you as soon as we can." Jesse stroked my hair back from my face. "I love you and you love me and you're walking into remission, and I just want our life to begin. If I've learned anything over the past year, it's that we can't waste time." Calmness washed over me. "You asked me to marry you tonight or tomorrow or whenever I liked."

Jesse held his breath.

"I pick as soon as we can," I said, then held my breath as I waited for him to reply.

But this boy, this playful, rule-breaking country boy only returned my smile and said, "We'll need a license." I nodded, trying to quickly work through the semantics in my head. "But then there's a chapel on the hospital's ground floor." He let that idea burst into the air above us and it sounded like fireworks. Jesse ran his lips over the ring that now lived happily on my finger. "You're going to be my wife, Junebug. My *wife*."

I kissed his lips and said, "My husband." I let that settle between us, then added, "I cannot wait."

chapter thirty-one

June

THE WARM BREEZE WASHED OVER US AS I TRIED TO KEEP ON writing. Even writing a sentence now took me so long. But I was close to the end of the story, and I was determined to finish.

Our oxygen tanks gave us both much-needed air, and tiredness began to drag my eyelids down.

Jesse was already asleep beside me on the egg chair. I ran my finger down his face. Three weeks had passed since we'd been married. Three weeks of talking and loving and being safe in one another's arms.

And three weeks of falling fast into the afterlife's awaiting arms as well. We could no longer walk, and some days we slept all day, the pain meds making it too difficult to stay awake. But we were still here, loving and laughing and cherishing every numbered breath.

I kissed Jesse's bare arm. "Baby," I said, deciding it was time for us to go back to inside. Night was drawing in and the orange sunset we loved was trailing across the sky. Ginger grazed on the grass, close by. He had kept close to our spot for the past couple of weeks now, as we both knew that, one night, we would stop coming out here all together.

"Jesse," I said again, but he didn't stir. Panic came quickly as I tried to shake him awake. When his arm fell limply at his side, my heart began to tear. "Jesse!" I said, louder now. I pressed the emergency button I wore around my neck and Susan and Bailey came running from our room and out onto the porch.

"I can't wake him up!" I said, urgency in my weak voice. "I can't wake him up!"

Susan lifted me and placed me in my wheelchair. Bailey didn't even bother with Jesse's chair. Instead, he lifted him and rushed him into our bedroom, laying him on the bed. As he did, Jesse's Longhorns cap fell to the ground.

Bailey began working on him, paging the team, but I couldn't stop looking at the baseball cap. Jesse never took it off. He needed it on his head. In seconds, the door burst open, and Dr. Duncan and his staff filled the room.

"Help him," I said helplessly, wishing my legs would work so I could run to him. I caught Jesse's arm falling to the side of the bed. It was a beacon to me—I wanted to hold his hand. I *needed* to.

"Susan, take me in there," I said, as we were still in the doorway.

"June, they need to—"

"Please!" I begged, tears streaming down my cheeks. "He can't go like this. I need to see him. He needs his hat. I need to be with him. Please, Susan. That's my husband. I want to be with my husband."

She pushed me inside, stopping to retrieve Jesse's hat, which I clutched tightly. I brought it to my nose. It smelled of him—woodsy and smoky.

Once inside, I tried to reach for Jesse's hand. I managed to grip his fingertips just as my parents entered the room, followed by Jesse's mama.

"No!" his mama screamed, and they all looked my way for explanation.

"He wouldn't wake up," I said, voice shaking, as the staff kept on working on him. "I couldn't wake him up." I couldn't see Jesse's face. I wanted to see his face. I wanted to see his eyes open, and I wanted to see him smile at me and tell me all this had just been a mistake, that he was fine.

"Please..." I begged everyone and no one at the same time.

My plea was lost in the void.

Dr. Duncan began hooking Jesse up to machines. Eventually, he turned to the room calmly and said, "His body is tired, and his organs are shutting down. I've given him medication to make him comfortable. But I'm afraid it won't be long now."

I broke down, racking sobs coming from my chest.

"Will he wake up? Will we get to say goodbye?" Jesse's mama asked.

"Possibly. He may drift in and out of consciousness," Dr. Duncan said. "Hopefully long enough for you all to say your goodbyes."

"Good nights," I said empathically, shaking my head. "We don't say goodbyes, only good nights."

Bailey arranged Jesse on our bed, so he was comfortable. When he had finished, my daddy lifted me onto our bed beside him. I shifted until I could lay my head against Jesse's chest. Cynthia was on his other side, holding his hand.

I had known this moment was coming—for both of us. But now that it was here, I...I couldn't do it. I couldn't lose him. My mama and daddy sat beside me, each putting a supportive hand on my leg.

There was so much love in this room, it was palpable. There was so much strength, and I wanted Jesse to wake up to see it, to feel it.

I lay there for I didn't know how long when Jesse's body moved under my cheek. I sat up, breath held, waiting... Then Jesse's eyes flickered open, and his confused gaze looked around the room.

Cynthia glanced up at her son.

Confused eyes then looked at me and the haze in Jesse's green eyes cleared.

"Junebug," he said, wincing like his throat hurt. "What...?" His breathing was labored, and he must have seen in my terrified eyes what was happening. His eyes filled with tears. "Don't...cry...Junebug," he rasped and lifted his weak hand to brush away my tears.

I leaned over and kissed him. I kissed every part of his face. I kissed his lips and then his hand. "I love you," I said, and realization sparked on Jesse's face. "I love you, I love you."

"How long?" he asked.

"I don't know," I said, and I broke. I lowered my head to his chest, and he ran his hand over my scalp.

"My...sisters," Jesse said, and I knew he must have been speaking to his mama.

"I'll get them, son," my daddy said.

I couldn't let go of Jesse. I wanted to die with him. I didn't want to be here in this life without him. We were meant to do this together. I didn't want to be left behind.

"It's…okay…Junebug," he said, his voice becoming a little clearer the more he was using it.

I lifted my head, and he wiped my tears. "Don't leave me," I begged, and pain flashed in Jesse's gaze.

The door to our room opened, and Chris stepped through. He was doing so well. He was walking stronger, and he had color back in his face. He was doing it. He was surviving; he was going to walk out of this place cured.

"Hey, bro," Chris said, the only giveaway about how he was feeling was his hand at his side, balled into a fist. "How's it hanging?"

Jesse forced a smirk, and my heart shattered. "Oh…ya know… thriving."

Chris laughed, but that laughter was cut off by a strangled cry. He leaned down and threw his arm around Jesse. "I'll miss you, man."

When a tear leaked from the corner Jesse's eye, I didn't think I could take anymore sadness.

When Chris pulled back, he said, "Say hi to Emma for me."

Jesse nodded, then said, "Live a good life… for us all."

"I will," Chris rasped, leaning over and kissing my cheek. "Love you guys. So much."

And I knew in that moment, he was saying bye to me too.

Chris left the room, glancing over his shoulder at us one more time, expression racked with pain and grief. I brushed the tear off Jesse's cheek just as Lucy and Emily walked in, quiet and scared.

Cynthia hugged them with her free arm. Like me, she couldn't let go of her son, not even for a second, because seconds were all we had left. "Lucy, Emily, y'all need to say your goodnights to Jesse," she said, and I felt a shred of flesh rip from my slow-beating heart. How

Cynthia managed to keep her voice strong was unclear to me. She was an incredible woman with incomparable strength.

My daddy lifted Lucy and Emily onto the bed.

"Hey, gremlins," Jesse said, and I caught another tear trickling down his face.

"Where are you going?" Lucy asked, brazen as always. But there was a tremor to her voice, like she could tell this wasn't merely a trip away to a ranch to heal.

"Heaven," Jesse said plainly.

"I don't want you to go," Emily said, and I had to turn my head away for just a moment. My mama's face was what I saw as I did. Racking pain was etched in her expression.

"Remember what I told y'all before?" Jesse said.

"That you'll be our guardian angel," Emily said, repeating how Jesse explained what was happening to his little sisters a few weeks ago.

He nodded. "I'll always watch over you both. I promise."

Emily looked down at her hands, then threw herself over Jesse's chest. Jesse hugged her and kissed her, only for Lucy to then do the same. "I'll miss you," Emily said, being so good for someone so young.

"I'll miss you more," Jesse said, and his voice broke.

"I'll take them to Susan," my daddy said when the girls had said their farewells.

As Jesse watched them leave, his resolved completely cracked. I wrapped him in my arms, and his mama did too. The two women who loved him most, comforting him with so much love as he passed.

I inched back, still holding his hand as his mama sat beside him. She smoothed her hand over his head. "I love you so much, Sunshine," she said. "Thank you for being there with me through the thick and thin. Thank you for teaching me how to be a mom. It's been the best thing I've ever done, and it was all down to you."

"I love you, Mom," Jesse said, then embraced Cynthia so tightly it broke me.

Jesse rolled his head to me as his mom sat back on her chair. "Junebug," he said and opened his arms.

I fell into his embrace and held him with all the strength as I had left. "I can't do this without you," I said, sobs tearing from my throat.

Jesse pulled back and put his finger under my chin. "You have a book to finish, baby. You need to complete our happily ever after." I shook my head, but then Jesse said, "Remember what Pastor Noel said."

I did. Jesse had told me all about his and Pastor Noel's conversation in the chapel, about how people see something or someone when they pass. That people can come and get them—loved ones, to help them cross over.

"Don't leave for heaven without me," I said. "Stay by my side until I go too."

Jesse nodded.

I meant his soul. I'd told him that if he went first, he had to wait for me until I followed.

"We go together," Jesse said. It was our pact.

"Promise it'll be you who comes and gets me," I said. I squeezed his hand twice. "Just like this. So I know it's you." Jesse squeezed my hand back, twice, showing me exactly what he would do.

Jesse and I just stared at one another, soaking in these final moments. I studied his face, his dimples, his smooth skin. I committed every fleck in his green eyes to memory. And the longer we lay there, the weaker his grip on my hand became.

Hearing Jesse's breathing grow heavy, I leaned closer and said, "You have made me happier than I've ever dreamed, baby. And I have loved every second of being your wife. *Thank you.*"

I lifted my hand and turned it into a fist. Jesse tried to laugh, but his chest barely moved. "Team two for the win," I said weakly.

Jesse stared at my fist. His fingers curled around it, and he rasped, "We won…Junebug. We…didn't beat…cancer, but we…won each other…in the…end."

"We did," I said, and Jesse's eyes began to droop.

I looked to Cynthia with urgency, and she jumped up and kissed his cheek. "Sleep, my baby boy. I'll see you again someday soon."

Jesse managed to open his eyes and, looking at me, whispered, "Good…night, June…bug."

I kissed each of his eyes and rasped out, "Sleep tight."

Then Jesse fell into a deep sleep. He slept for just over an hour before his chest began to slow. I laid my head over his heart, holding tightly to his hand as his inhales and exhales grew into stillness.

Dr. Duncan checked him over, then said, "I'm so sorry for your loss."

Torrents of tears sailed from my cheeks, and I cried and cried until I had nothing left. Jesse lay unmoving beneath me, and I prayed that he would open his eyes and crack an inappropriate joke.

But when I ran my fingers over his brow, his cheeks, only stillness met me. "I love you, I love you, I love you, I love you," I whispered over and over again until my throat was raw.

A hand on my back made me jump. I turned to see my daddy.

"They need to take him away, darlin'," he said, sadness in his gaze.

Susan and Bailey were standing in the doorway to the room. I shook my head. "No," I said. "No, you can't. He needs to stay with me. He promised me he would stay."

"Sweetie," Cynthia said, and put her hand on my cheek. "He's gone. We have to let him go."

I held him tighter. Jesse couldn't leave me. We didn't go anywhere that wasn't together. "He sleeps beside me," I said, imploring them to understand. "He's my husband. He's…" I hiccupped. "He's my husband and this is our bed. He sleeps beside me."

I heard my mama begin to cry, but my daddy sat beside me and put his hand on my back. "It's time to let him go," he said.

It was pitch-black outside. And I felt so cold. Everyone was looking at me holding onto my husband with pain in their eyes.

"We were meant to live," I whispered, and Daddy dropped his head onto my back. "We were meant to live, Daddy. We were meant to have our dream on our porch."

I tucked my head into Jesse's chest again. I stayed that way until I finally lifted my head and saw in Jesse's face that he had truly gone. The light that lived in his eyes was no longer there. The twitch to his lips had stilled, and the love that I felt from his heart lived within *me* now.

I stared at his beautiful face one more time. I kissed his lips and said, "Keep your promise. Come for me soon." Then I released him and watched as Bailey and Susan put him on a gurney and took him away.

I sat in the middle of our bed not knowing what to do. I looked down and realized that I still held his cap in my hand. I hugged it to my chest as though I were holding Jesse himself.

"I'm so sorry, baby," my mama said, and I nodded numbly. As I looked around the room, *our* room, I didn't want to be here anymore. My happiness had left with my husband. Then a picture on my wall—the picture of our dream, our porch—called out to me.

You have a book to finish, baby. You need to complete our happily ever after...

Jesse was right. I had to complete it. I had to complete our happily ever after, so that somewhere, in another life and universe, we didn't have to have this moment. I reached for my pen and opened my notebook. And I began to write. I would finish this book, then I would say my farewells.

And I would wait for my husband to come and get me.

chapter thirty-two

Jesse

Jesse and June's Happily Ever After

I walked into the familiar locker room and made my way to my cubby. I put my hand on my number and surname on my jersey. I closed my eyes and exhaled deeply.

I was back.

After months of training and building back up my strength, I was here...again. I glanced down at the tattoo on my wedding finger and smiled. June and I had been married now for months. Just like we'd wanted, we had been married four days after I proposed, in the hospital chapel. Chris and Emma were our witnesses. We would have done it sooner, but for law making us wait three days before we could.

Then this summer, we'd had a bigger ceremony in the backyard of June's childhood home. Mr. Scott wanted to walk June down the aisle, and we wanted to give him that dream too. She'd worn a vintage lace wedding dress patterned with feathers. Chris was my best man, and Emma was June's maid of honor. It couldn't have been more perfect.

When we had returned to campus, we got a place in the married couple housing. To come home to my Junebug, my wife, every night was everything I had ever wished for.

Now I was back with my team and fully in remission. And I was determined, after two battles with AML, that I was done once and for all with cancer and would live my life with my Junebug. A little life, as she said. Although, with her bestselling book now published in bookstores and more deals on the way, my wife fought hard to keep our circle small and our life as calm as she could.

And most importantly, we were happy. Happier than I'd thought ever we could be.

"Right, suit up!" Coach called, and I snapped myself out of my thoughts.

"He's back, baby!" Sheridan said and jumped on my back—I was less breakable these days.

I shrugged him off, laughing, and began to dress for the game. I could hear the crowd stamping their feet above. The place was bouncing. The first game of the season was in full effect. I looked up at the ceiling and felt calmer knowing that June was up there. My wife was in the stands, waiting for me to run onto the field.

And tonight, I was starting. A hard preseason had seen me winning back my position as first-string QB. No cancer, no fear—I was only looking up and forward from here on out.

After we'd changed into our uniforms, we lined up in the tunnel.

I kept a tight hold on my helmet and bounced on my feet. Then the announcer called us onto the field, and I ran out first.

With my helmet in the air, I waved to the crowd, then looked up at the only person I wanted to see. Even among the thousands of fans, I found June easily—she was standing with her hand in the air, pointing at my heart on her palm. I did the same, then kissed the tattooed ring on my left hand.

June grinned and blew me a kiss. I caught that kiss and threw her a wink. Then, turning back to my team, I put on my helmet and began to live out our perfect, little piece of forever.

chapter thirty-three

June

My hand shook as I wrote the two words that I wasn't sure I would ever get to—*The End*.

My hand fell to the bed, and I sucked in a much-needed breath from my oxygen mask. Turning, I ran my hand over the place where Jesse used to sleep. Two days—he had been gone for two days and I didn't think it was possible to miss someone so much. I barely slept, I couldn't eat, and my body had begun to fail. His cap rested on his pillow, the scent awarding me with a miniscule amount of comfort.

But I had worked hard to get our happily ever after finished. I smoothed my hand over the notebook, and a sense of accomplishment washed over me. "I've done it, baby," I whispered into the empty room. "I've given us the happily ever after that I promised us." I closed my eyes and could see his wide smile. I could feel him lean in and kiss me.

I'm so proud of you, Junebug.

My parents had just gone out to get a drink, and as I felt myself begin to sink into the mattress, I hoped they'd come back soon. My breaths were coming slower, but I smiled as I saw Ginger move to the fence near our porch.

The stars were shining in the sky, and the night was still. A perfect Texan night. My bedroom door opened, and my mama and daddy walked in. I didn't know what they saw when they looked at me, but they rushed to my bedside.

Mama sat on mattress beside me. Tears filled her eyes.

"I've finished," I said, voice barely audible.

Mama nodded, placing her hand on my notebook and leaning down to kiss my head. "I love you," she whispered.

Daddy sat down too. "Is there anything you want, darlin'?" he asked.

I looked at the beautiful horse outside again. "Can you take me to see Ginger?"

Daddy stared at me a touch too long. He knew what I was saying—that I wanted to say my goodbyes.

"Of course," he said, voice gravelly. Daddy scooped me up in his arms and placed me in my wheelchair. Mama opened the doors, and I let the warm Texas breeze wash over me. It felt like silk being brushed over my cheeks. Daddy pushed me out to the porch, and I glanced at the egg chair that held so many memories. If I closed my eyes, I could feel the back-and-forth sway of Jesse and I wrapped in one another's arms, sharing our dreams. Sharing our words and drawings...

Sharing our hearts.

Ginger whinnied at the fence, and my daddy pushed me toward

him. As I reached the fence, Ginger bent his head over, and I lifted my hands and ran them down his face. "Thank you for being here for me," I said, and kissed him on the head. "I'll miss you."

I patted Ginger until my arm ached and I had no more strength. With a final kiss to the beloved horse, my daddy helped me back into my chair.

"Wait," I said, and held up my hand. I pointed up at the star that I now felt belonged to me and Jesse.

My parents were quiet for a spell as we watched it sparkle, until my daddy said, "We'll always look at that star and know it belongs to you and Jesse, darlin'. We'll search for it every night for the rest of our lives to keep you close to our hearts."

Imagining my parents doing that, from our beloved home, filled me with happiness. But then, "I'm tired, Daddy," I said, and heard his quick inhale.

My mama took my hand, and we walked silently back to my bedroom. Daddy lifted me from my chair, and as he placed me down on the bed and tucked me under the covers, I took hold of his hands. "I love you," I whispered. "Thank you for being my daddy."

He lowered his head and his shoulders shook.

I turned to my mama, who was lying on the edge of the bed beside me. I pushed a strand of hair from her face. "You're the best mama I could have wished for. Thank you for loving me so much."

Mama shook her head. "You have been a dream." She kissed my head. "Rest easy, sweetheart. You deserve some peace."

I smiled and let sweet numbness wash through me. My eyes grew heavy, and I began to feel the tempting pull of sleep. But just as my eyes closed, I caught sight of the picture of Jesse and I on the porch, our dream etched out in charcoal. My heart swelled, knowing that I'd given that dream to the Jesse and June in our Happily Ever After.

Out there, in that universe, we were living that dream.

My breathing got slower and my eyes drifted closed. I held out my hand as I sank further and further into painlessness, only to feel a familiar hand wrap around mine.

He squeezed it twice.

And my heart swelled with happiness.

He had kept his promise.

epilogue
June

Jesse and June's Happily Ever After

The rush of at least ten pairs of feet padded through the house, and the smell of barbeque sailed into the kitchen from the backyard.

Laughs and screams could be heard as the sun blazed brightly in the sky. I dusted my hands off on my apron and took two glasses of sweet tea out onto the porch.

Jesse was already there, waiting for me. "You beat me to it," I said, and sat down beside him on our old, cherished porch swing.

As soon as I handed him his drink, he set it beside him and held my hand. He raised our joined hands to his mouth and pressed a kiss to mine. I cuddled in beside him as he used his foot to push us back and forth.

I laughed as our youngest grandson sprayed his daddy, our son, with a water gun. Jesse chuckled, then pressed a kiss to my head. And as I looked out onto the garden, our home full of love and happiness, I then glanced up to my husband.

Our faces were heavily lined with wrinkles, our hair was thinning and gray, and our laughter lines...they were my favorite. They were deep and long and boasted of a life filled with fun and joy.

"You're still beautiful," I told Jesse.

He turned to me with a cheeky smirk. "Junebug, are you flirting with me?"

"Always," I said, and my husband kissed me on my lips.

I laid my head on his shoulder and basked in the peace that was this life. We had lived a full and happy life, Jesse as a football coach and artist, and me as a writer. After his two battles with cancer, Jesse's body wasn't as strong as it once had been. The NFL had no longer been in his future. But he loved coaching more than he'd ever loved playing. We had moved to my hometown, where he became a high school football coach—an amazing one at that. And with his local gallery showings of his art alongside his coaching career, Jesse never wanted for anything else.

I still wrote, the passion within me never wavering. And every love story I put to paper was somehow inspired by my own. We got our little life. But our greatest achievement played out before us now. One boy and one girl of our own, and a whole load of grandkids.

"I've loved our life," I said to Jesse, a smile in my voice.

"I've loved our life too," he said, and placed his finger under my chin. Then he kissed me again—he kissed me like he had in all our many years together. He kissed me like we were still seventeen and we had just met our soul's other half.

Jesse squeezed my hand that was still in his. With his free hand he raised his fist and said, "Group two has won, Junebug."

I raised my fist and bumped it to his. "Group two has won."

Because we had. We had lived, we had thrived, we had loved, and we absolutely, positively had won.

THE END

Bonus Chapter Exclusive to Tickled Pink

JESSE AND JUNE'S HAPPILY EVER AFTER

June
Age 22

I clutched onto Jesse's hand as we drove up the familiar driveway. It had been years since we'd been here. We had lived the most exciting and fulfilling life since we'd left, yet I was thrust back into my seventeen-year-old body and mind as the trees blew in the summer breeze around us. The sun was high in the sky and as the ranch appeared, it appeared as magical as it always was.

"So crazy," Chris remarked from the backseat. "Being back here." I turned my head to look at Chris whose gaze was affixed to the window. Emma was here too, and she gave me a warm smile that echoed Chris's sentiment.

When Jesse and I were invited to be here at the ranch today, it was a given that Chris and Emma would be coming too. We were a team, the four of us. In this ranch we had forged a bond that nothing could break. We had faced death together and had come out of it bursting with life. That was something only those who had experienced life here could relate too.

My stomach rolled as we approached the main building. I was so honored and excited to be here today, but the ranch was still a hospital for teens with cancer, and it broke my heart to know I'd be meeting kids who were in the middle of that fight.

And those at the end.

As if feeling my aching heart, Jesse pulling my hand to his mouth and kissed my fingers that were wrapped around his. I met his eyes, and his lips tilted into an empathetic smile. "You doin' good there, Junebug?"

Just seeing Jesse here now, driving us to the ranch in his truck, healthy, hair grown back and curling over his ears and forehead made me fill with gratitude so potent I was sure it would never wane.

I had almost lost him again a few years back when he had relapsed. But my husband had fought hard once again to stay in this life beside me. A miracle I had never taken for granted.

"I'm good," I said, and took a deep breath. This was a joyful day. This was a special day. Today, the new wing I had sponsored was opening. Another twenty rooms for younger children fighting cancer. Rooms that could accommodate parents too, so they would never have to be left alone or separated.

The past few years had seen my novel, *Write Me For You*, soar.

Just when I felt the train would slow in terms of sales and popularity, it never did. Our tragic love story had burrowed into the hearts of millions of readers, until it was no longer only mine and Jesse's story, but the world's. Our heartbreaking alternate love story had now inspired people to *live.* To never give up, and to have not one single regret.

And in an even crazier turn, now it was going to be a feature film. I could scarcely wrap my mind around it. A quiet story written about a couple of sick Texas teens when we were on the brink of death, has turned into a dream come true.

The money I was given for the film, in my mind, could only go to one place—the ranch that saved us. Neenee was still the ranch director and had invited us here today to open the new wing—the Jesse and June Taylor Center for Pediatric Oncology.

We pulled to a stop, got out of the truck, and the doors to the ranch flew open. Neenee came rushing through and my face split at seeing her kind face. Neenee threw her arms wide, and I met her halfway only to be wrapped up into a tight hug. "My girl," she whispered, voice thick with emotion. My throat clogged within her embrace.

"Thank you for having us here today, Neenee," I said, and she drew back to meet my gaze.

"No, thank you, June. The gift you have given us . . ." she shook her head. "It will save so many lives." My heart swelled. I stepped back and Neenee embraced Jesse, Emma and Chris. When they had caught up, she led us into the ranch and Jesse immediately took hold of my hand.

He tugged me back and let Emma and Chris through first. I looked to my husband in confusion, but he placed the palm of his hand on my cheek and said, "Before we go in there, I just want to say how proud I am of you."

"Jesse . . ." I said, shyness taking me over.

"No, June. What you have done here," Jesse pressed his forehead to mine. "It's incredible. *You* are incredible." My lip began to tremble with emotion because I could hear in Jesse's voice just how much he meant that. "I love you, and I adore you. And I am so damn lucky to be your husband."

I wrapped my arms around Jesse's waist. "I couldn't have done any of this without you, baby." Jesse winked playfully and made me laugh. "And of course I love you too."

"Oh, I know *that*," he said dryly, "So much you had to immortalize me with your words." I rolled my eyes at him and went to walk away, when he pulled me back and crushed his lips to mine. I melted into him, more in love with him than ever.

"Can you let go of each other for just one second!" Chris said from behind us. "I don't know if you know, but there's a whole load of people waiting for June to cut a ribbon and make a speech. And here I find you sucking face like y'all have all the time in the world."

My cheeks heated and a flash of nerves zipped through me. I stepped back from Jesse and brushed my hands down the skirt of my pink dress. "You look beautiful, as always," Jesse said, and I took in his navy-blue suit with a silver tie. He was stunning.

"You too," I said, and Jesse held out his arm for me.

"Shall we?" he said, and I let him guide me through the foyer. The antiseptic smell of the ranch sent a barrage of memories hurtling through me. But Neenee was quickly before us, taking us to the new wing.

As we rounded the corner, I stopped dead, seeing the new addition . . . and all the people out front. Emma and Chris came to stand at my side. Emma worked with me now as my business manager. And Chris . . . he was our fourth musketeer and had to see this, too.

"Incredible," Jesse murmured.

"June?" Neenee said, cutting through the white noise that had filled my ears. "Would you like to say a few words before you cut the ribbon?"

I was still terrible with attention, but the past few years of book signings and appearances had given me a bit more confidence. But this . . . this was huge.

I nodded my head, and felt Jesse squeeze my hand. I turned to my husband. He kissed my cheek and whispered, "You deserve this, June-bug. You can do this."

I suddenly looked around me, and my chest tightened seeing the patients all waiting for me to speak—and some of them clutching my book for me to sign. As I stood in the center of the ribbon, the room fell silent.

"Hello," I said, trying to keep my voice from shaking. "I'm June Taylor, and I was once a patient here." I gestured to Jesse, Chris and Emma, "Along with my husband and our best friends." I suddenly saw Bailey—our old nurse—in the crowd and Susan—who cared for Jesse—smiling proudly as she moved to his side. Jesse affectionately threw his arm over her shoulder. They had always kept in touch.

"Nobody here expected to have to fight for their lives at such a young age. I know I didn't. But this ranch, the staff and the other patients became my family." I pressed my hand over my heart. "This ranch became a home from home, filled with warmth and love and *belonging*. It truly was a lifeline." A tear slipped from the corner of my eye. But I didn't chase it away. Everyone in this room understood why this place meant so much to me.

"As I fought to stay alive, this ranch was a protective cocoon, holding me close as I healed. And I did." I smiled at Jesse and our friends. "We all did." Emma wiped away a tear from her cheek. I faced the crowd again. "And I want nothing more than for children—of all ages—fighting cancer, to be able to enter through this ranch's doors and feel the love that I did, only to walk out free and healed, knowing there is always a part of their soul they shall leave upon this ranch's grounds." I smiled. "And a sentence of their life's story that will always be written on these walls."

I took a deep breath. "It is my absolute honor to declare the Jesse and June Taylor Center for Pedatric Oncology, officially open!" Neenee handed me the large scissors, and I cut through the ribbon.

My friends ran at me and immediately wrapped me up in a hug. "Chemo Club for life!" Chris said, voice hoarse with emotion.

"Chemo Club for life," we all echoed, and I felt someone tugging at my elbow. When I released my friends and turned, it was to see a girl of about fourteen holding my book. She was wearing a headscarf and was clearly in the depth of her treatment here.

"Hello," I said, and she timidly held out her copy of *Write Me For You*.

"Can you sign this for me please?" she asked.

"Of course," I said, and took it from her. Emma passed me a pen (she was always armed with several). As I signed the book, I asked. "What's your name, lovely?"

"Isabel," she replied shyly.

"Isabel," I said, and wrote her name. Giving the book back to her, I asked, "How long have you been here?"

"Four months," she said. In that moment, I prayed with everything I was that she was responding to treatment. The odds of success were high, but there would always be some that the treatment didn't work for. I hoped she wasn't one of them. Then a wide smile took up her face. "The treatment is working for me." I exhaled a quiet, but relieved, breath.

"I am so happy for you," I said, and wrapped her in her hug.

Isabel hugged me back, then whispered, "Thank you for writing *Write Me For You*. I know it's sad, and, in my situation, could have been scary for me to read. But instead it gave me hope." Isabel squeezed me harder. "It gave me peace with whatever would happen to me here."

Tears pricked at my eyes, and I whispered, "Thank you." It was all I had ever wanted from my stories.

After that, everything was a whirlwind. I signed books, had photos taken for patients and the press, and then Neenee gave us a tour of the new wing. We spoke to the patients as friends and people who had walked their path. Spoke to the parents and staff. But then the patients began to grow tired, and night began to fall, bringing an end to the most amazing and special day.

I was utterly exhausted, but I was happy.

As we were readying to leave, I found Emma and Chris sat with Bailey, Susan and Neenee, but Jesse was nowhere to be seen. Emma must have caught me looking, as she tipped her head back and said, "He said to tell you he would be outside, waiting for you."

"Okay," I said, and headed down the familiar maze-like hallways running my hand over the name plates of two familiar suite doors. Pushing open the door to outside, the balmy breeze immediately kissed my cheeks. I heard the sound of creaking and knew before I even rounded the corner what I would find. When I found Jesse, he was on our egg chair, swinging back and forth looking out over the paddocks. My heart lurched, as in the distance, I saw a familiar chestnut gelding grazing in the field.

When I turned back to Jesse, he was waiting for me, hand held out for me to take. I walked toward him, and taking his hand, sat beside him on the chair. Like the journey up the ranch's driveway, I suddenly felt seventeen again. Getting to know this handsome boy who had called me beautiful.

The sound of crickets and the chair creaking made a soothing soundtrack to the summer's night. Jesse wrapped his arm around my shoulders and said, "I can't believe this is our life, Junebug. That we're here again, but happy and healthy and living out our dreams."

I looked up into Jesse's forest-green eyes and knew that I would always fall in love with this boy, in every given lifetime. "Ditto," I said, and Jesse threw his head back and laughed.

"Junebug," he said with incredulity, "you stole my line."

I laughed too but then snuggled further into Jesse's side, bathing in the peace that had always found us here, on this chair, on this ranch. Jesse kissed my hair, then held out his fist. "Group two for the win," he said, and I held up my fist.

I bumped my fist against his, "Group two for the win."

The sound of hooves padding on hard ground suddenly grew closer, and when I lifted my head, I smiled wide. I got up from the egg chair, feeling Jesse watching my every move as I made my way to my favorite horse.

Ginger lowered his head over the fence, looking exactly the same, and I pressed my forehead to his, breathing in his calming horsey scent. "Hello, my beautiful boy, I've missed you so much." I wrapped my arms around his neck and closed my eyes. "But I'm so happy to see you again," I said, and thanked God that we were all okay, that the ranch was seeing more and more success, and with the new wing, more children could be healed. "I'm happier than you'll ever know."

The End

Acknowledgments

Write Me for You came to me mid-flight on my way to Book Bonanza in 2023. Relaxing in my chair, June and Jesse popped into my head and made themselves known. By the time I landed a few hours later, I had the skeleton story of *Write Me for You*.

I have always been a dreamer, a romantic. And as hard as real life can be, I always try to see some good in any situation. Even when it seems hopeless.

If you are a long-time reader of mine, you know that my family has been plagued by cancer and loss. The past few books of mine have allowed me to share my grief in the only way I know how—writing. *A Thousand Boy Kisses*, *A Thousand Broken Pieces*, and now *Write Me for You* have allowed me to say everything I wish I had said to those who I've lost. These books have been my therapy. My biggest wish is that you, the reader, have taken something from my stories too.

Write Me for You has given me two of my favorite protagonists ever. Jesse and June, I adore you. You have been an absolute pleasure to write. I left bits of myself scattered between you both, and it was a true honor to write both of your love stories, the sad and the HEA. I think of my lost ones every single day and love to picture them doing what they love most. Jesse and June's story allowed me to lean onto those wishes, to accept the reality of their situation, but also imagine what life would be like if it had played out differently. This book has given me another slice of personal healing.

Isn't that truly magical? I love the power of stories and words.

To get *Write Me for You* out in the world, it would not have happened without my amazing team (Team Tils for the win!).

Firstly, I want to thank my husband. You always support me no matter how gutting or crazy my ideas are (and some are rather obscure!). You support me when I'm deep in my grief and need to write to help climb out of it. I love you to pieces.

My children. You're my world. I love you both so much. You're my reason for everything.

Mam. Another book to push you. As I'm writing this, you still haven't read *A Thousand Broken Pieces*. It's just too personal for you. And I understand. You may never read this one either. And that's okay. You have lived the past several years with me, and reliving it is difficult. But you are the strongest person I know. You have fought cancer and won. You're my forever hero.

Samantha. You have encouraged me in my darkest times and when I felt like I was on the ropes. Love you so much.

To my best friends, you are my solace. Chris and Emma are reflections of you all. The T-T-Teessiders, the Coven, my mams group who have become a treasured piece of my life, thank you all for being there for me.

Liz, my superstar agent. Ten years and we are still going strong. You have had my back from day one, and I cannot wait for the next ten years and all the things we have planned. What a journey. I am so lucky to have you in my corner, through the good and bad.

To Christa Heschke, Danielle and Alecia and everyone at McIntosh and Otis, thank you for working tirelessly on my behalf.

Christa Désir, the editor who changed my life. Thank you for everything you have done for me. Once again, you have championed this new story. You held me up through the writing of Jesse and June and helped make the book infinitely better edit by edit. We have cried together; we have laughed and you have held me up in the darkest of times. I adore you.

Dom, and all the others who work at Bloom Books, thank you for everything. I am so excited to keep writing books and working with you. You're an incredible team.

A huge thank-you to Rebecca Hilsdon, my editor from Penguin UK. Like Christa, you were so supportive of this book and of Jesse and June. Thank you for your endless support and guidance in making this book the best it could be.

Thank you to all my foreign publishing teams for always believing in me—Italy, Brazil, Germany, Poland, Spanish speaking territories and all the other many publishing houses around the world who have taken my works and given them a home. I am truly grateful for you all.

Nina and the team at Valentine PR, thank you for being the most amazing team to work with. I value you more than you know.

My readers. Once again, I have put you through the wringer with this book. Thank you for always standing beside me. Thank you for understanding me and thank you for always believing in me. You have no idea how much you all mean to me.

Shout out to my Tillsters. My ride or die's. I love you.

To all of the bookstagrammers, booktokers and reviewers who help tell the world about my books. You have changed my life. Thank you.

And to the author community. What an uplifting and supportive place to be. Thank you for always cheering me on. I want nothing but the best for you all too.

If I have missed anyone, just know that I am thankful to you too!

Finally, to Dad. It'll be three years this year that you have been gone. I can't believe that much time has passed since I've seen you, given you a hug and told you all about the stories that are circling my head over a three-hour coffee chat. Not a day goes by that I don't think of you, miss you and wish you were still here. But I think of you with every word I write and can hear you (Scottish accent as thick as ever) telling me I can do it. I'm sure I could write about grief and loss forever, as your loss hit me so deeply. I don't think I'll ever get over it. But I wanted happiness in this novel too, because life is a balance, isn't it? Highest of highs and the lowest of lows. You taught me that.

Dad, you were loving, so inspiring and utterly weird in the best possible way (a trait you passed down to me!). I will forever keep writing in your honor.

I love you and will miss you forever.

Like Jesse says, no goodbyes, only goodnights…so, goodnight, Dad. Sweet dreams.

On a station platform, with nothing to read,
and a four-hour train journey stretching ahead of him...

That's where the story began for Penguin founder Allen Lane.
With only 'shabby reprints of shoddy novels' on offer,
he resolved to make better books for readers everywhere.

By the time his train pulled into London, the idea was formed.
He would bring the best writing, in stylish and affordable
formats, to everyone. His books would be sold in bookstores,
stationers and tobacconists, for no more than the price
of a ten-pack of cigarettes.

And on every book would be a Penguin, a bird with a certain
'dignified flippancy', and a friendly invitation to anyone who
wished to spend their time reading.

In 1935, the first ten Penguin paperbacks were published.
Just a year later, three million Penguins had made their
way onto our shelves.

Reading was changed forever.

—

A lot has changed since 1935, including Penguin, but in the
most important ways we're still the same. We still believe that
books and reading are for everyone. And we still believe that
whether you're seeking an afternoon's escape, a vigorous debate
or a soothing bedtime story, all possibilities open with a book.

Whoever you are, whatever you're looking for,
you can find it with Penguin.